AF422130

Realm of Shadows

ALSO BY REKTOK ROSS

Writing as Rektok Ross:

HEIR OF HADES SERIES

Realm of Shadows

DARK SEASONS THRILLER SERIES

Ski Weekend

Summer Rental

Spring Harvest

Salem's Fall

STANDALONE TITLES

The Pop Star and the Devil

*

Writing as L.G. Ross:

Prodigal

NEVER MISS A RELEASE.

Get exclusive giveaways, review copies, and enter to win free gifts and more. Subscribe to my newsletter:

www.RektokRoss.com

Realm of Shadows

REKTOK ROSS

Ic13 Books

Published by Ic13 Books
Wilmington, Delaware, USA, 19808
www.Ic13Books.com
Ic13 Books name and the Ic13 Books logo are trademarks of Ic13 Books or its affiliates.

Published 2026
Printed in the United States of America

Print ISBN: 979-8-9937897-2-9
E-ISBN: 979-8-9937897-3-6
Library of Congress Control Number: 2026906830

Cover design by Artscandare Book Cover Design
Printed edges by Painted Wings Publishing
Various artwork by @Mageonduty and Rektok Ross

For those who were told they didn't belong… and found their magic in the shadows.

Abandon all hope, ye who enter here.

—Dante Alighieri, *Inferno*

The king of shadows saw her, loved her, and carried her away.

—Ovid, *Metamorphoses, Book V* (modernized paraphrase)

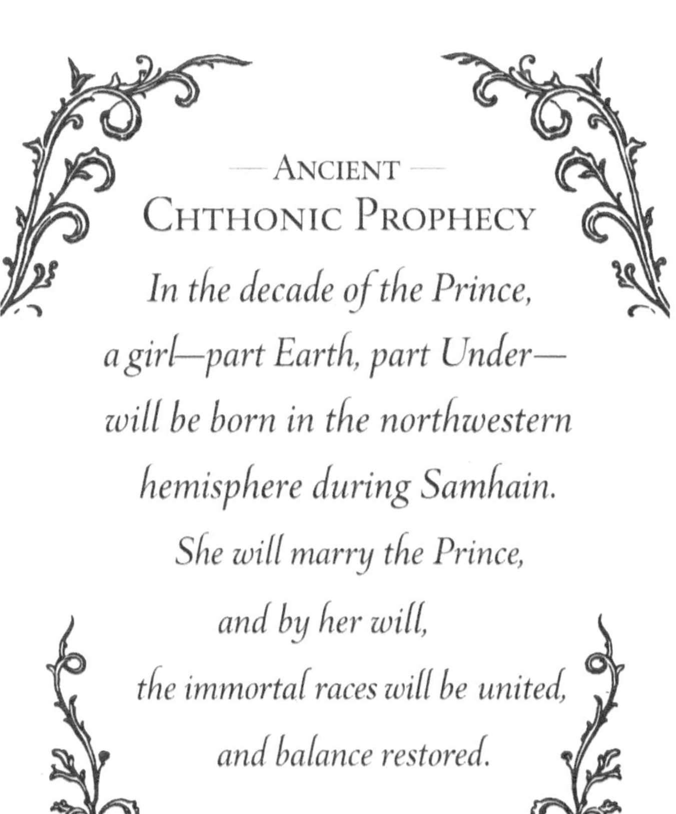

— ANCIENT —
CHTHONIC PROPHECY

In the decade of the Prince,
a girl—part Earth, part Under—
will be born in the northwestern
hemisphere during Samhain.
She will marry the Prince,
and by her will,
the immortal races will be united,
and balance restored.

EARTH
THE UNDERWORLD

OLYMPUS
N
W
E
S
The Three Realms

CHAPTER 1

I pull into Laguna Hills University at exactly 7:30 a.m. on a sweltering Monday morning, even though freshman classes don't start for another week. I'm still in pajama bottoms, an oversized sweatshirt hanging off one shoulder, long dark hair twisted into a half-dead bun. I barely slept last night. The Laguna Coast Players are posting the cast list for *Hercules* this morning, and I've never wanted anything more in my life than the role of Megara.

Well... maybe one thing.

But *he's* never wanted me back.

The lead in the local town play, at least, feels plausible. Not some impossible, pie-in-the-sky fantasy love story but something real. Attainable. The kind of thing you can actually earn with talent and a lot of hard work.

That's why I spent my entire summer vacation holed up in my bedroom, memorizing lines, studying Greek mythology for character work, and watching *Hercules* on repeat until I could sing every word of "I Won't Say I'm in Love" backward in my sleep. Then I learned "The Gospel Truth," "Zero to Hero," and "A Star is Born" for good measure—even though Megara doesn't even sing those songs.

Megara isn't just another character in *Hercules*. She's the heart of it. Not some simpering, insipid princess, but fierce. Witty. Jaded, but not broken. She has a sharp tongue and a soft heart buried beneath all that armor, with a backstory soaked in heartbreak. The kind of part that sinks its teeth into you. That feels like me.

I don't just want the role. I was made for it.

And I'm going to get it.

My heart thunders as I reach the doors of LHU's Performing Arts Center, where the Players share space with the local college. I spot the cast list right away, pinned to the lobby bulletin board, and make a beeline for it. The first thing I notice is my little sister's loopy, overly girly handwriting. The lined paper even smells like her too-sweet, vanilla-scented body lotion.

That little snake.

Amber must've come early to help the director post the list. I'd overheard her bragging to Mom last night about how tight she and Mr. DeWitt had gotten over summer after she'd spent the break volunteering and helping out with auditions.

I scan the paper eagerly, my eyes darting straight to Megara. I expect to see my name there—need to see it. It *should* be there.

Except… it isn't.

I read through the list again.

Then again.

My name isn't next to Megara. It isn't next to anyone. I'm not even listed as a damn understudy. It's like I was never even considered for any role. Like I didn't exist at all.

I clench a fist behind my back, resisting the urge

to rip the paper off the board and stomp it under my black combat boots.

There must be some mistake. I crushed that audition. I know I did. So what the hell happened?

College students I don't recognize start trickling in, along with a few seniors from my old school, Laguna Hills High. They push past me, elbowing in without so much as a glance in my direction.

One by one, I hear their delighted squeals and giddy laughter as they find out they got the roles they wanted. Blood pounds in my ears as my eyes keep coming back to the name listed next to Megara, instead of mine. I want to scream. Or cry.

Maybe both.

How can *her* name be there instead of mine?

"How the hell did Amber get the lead?" I snap at the board, too furious to care who hears me. "She's tone-deaf!"

"Oh, don't be such a sore loser. I won Megara fair and square."

I turn around to find my sister standing there with a smug little smile tugging at the corners of her mouth. With her pale blonde hair and mermaid-blue eyes the color of sunlit water, Amber looks like some kind of fairy-tale Disney princess. Which is ironic, considering the fact she's usually playing the villain in my life.

Today, she's all soft curls and bronzed skin, dressed in a frilly, bubblegum-pink dress that looks like it came with a tiara. Flanking her sides are her two best friends, Brooke Bancroft and Tiffany Voss, nodding along in synchronized approval.

"How could you do this to me?" I whisper, low and sharp. "That part was mine."

Amber just shrugs. "Guess you should've gone for the Cyclops. That role had your name all over it, *Alysander*."

She says it with that fake-innocent tone she's perfected, like my name itself is the punchline. Her friends chuckle—not because it's actually funny, but because it's Amber. She always knows how to get a laugh at someone else's expense. And she knows exactly how much I hate my name. It's supposed to be a modern twist on the great Greek hero Lysander, but all it's ever done is confuse people. No one can ever pronounce it or spell it right.

"You don't get it. I really needed this." Heat crawls up my neck as I dig my nails into my palms.

"God, no need to be so dramatic." She groans. "I already asked DeWitt to stick you in the chorus. He's basically obsessed with me, so I'm sure he'll find you a spot."

"Chorus? Are you serious?" I gape at her. "You can shove chorus up your ass, *Ambrosia*!"

I feel a small flicker of satisfaction as her face flushes red. She can't stand her own weird name any more than I can stand mine.

"My name is *Amber*," she hisses, jaw tight.

I flip her off and stalk toward the campus parking lot. Sadly, whatever petty thrill I get from the jab doesn't even come close to the sting of losing Megara.

I yank open the rust-flecked door of my beat-up Toyota Camry and collapse inside. I won't give anyone at school—or this damn town—the satisfaction of watching me break. Certainly not my stupid sister and her friends. It's just… I really did need this.

Megara was supposed to be the thing that saved me.

Last year, I got rejected from my dream school, NYU. I'd spent my whole life wanting out of this too-bright, shallow little beach town, with its perfect façade and pastel everything. I'd never fit in here. But New York? That city breathed people like me. NYU's elite performing arts program, Tisch, had the best theater training in the country, and Broadway was right around the corner. NYU wasn't just a school to me. It was a way out.

I'd been gutted when the rejection came.

My high school guidance counselor said I could try applying again as a transfer after my freshman year of college. My grades weren't the problem. I'd graduated with a 4.0 unweighted GPA and an almost perfect SAT score, but everyone applying to Tisch had numbers like that. What I lacked was real "performance arts experience." I'd taken Advanced Performance Choir in high school last year, but apparently, that wasn't enough.

I'd pinned all my hopes and dreams on community theater this fall and landing the lead in *Hercules*. I figured this way I could pad my résumé enough to earn a shot at a live audition. I just knew once I got in front of the actual decision-makers at NYU and they heard me sing, they'd have to let me in.

Now what was I supposed to do?

I start the car's engine and Thom Yorke's haunting voice fills the space as the radio syncs with my phone's playlist. The aching melody of "Let Down" wraps around me like a second skin, and I close my eyes, letting the lyrics settle in. The song's about the kind of helplessness that makes you want to scream and, right now, I feel every single word.

A wave of failure crashes over me, and I tear off the tourmaline quartz necklace my mom made me wear for good luck, tossing it into the glove box. I know my eccentric, hippie-dippie mother means well, but no amount of "magical" crystals is going to fix the mess that is my life.

Fucking Amber.

It's just like her to ruin this for me. My sister and I have been butting heads since birth.

Less than a year apart—both October babies—we've always been locked in some twisted sibling rivalry, fighting over everything: clothes, toys, Mom's attention, even who got the biggest slice of cake at our shared birthday parties. Separate celebrations were a luxury we couldn't afford. Mom did her best, but there was never quite enough to go around.

Our father walked out right after Amber was born, and Mom's been scrambling to raise us ever since. She calls herself a "mystic artist," which is basically code for painting people's auras and peddling healing crystals to bored housewives.

I've never believed in that stuff, but it pays the bills. The women in town flock to her readings with the same manic energy they bring to their overpriced hot yoga classes and bulk-buy kombucha hauls at Erewhon.

I should've known Megara was a lost cause the second Amber got involved with the Players. It doesn't matter that I can sing circles around my sister. People just love Amber for some reason. Always have. She's got that thing, that effortless, impossible-to-name *It* girl factor.

One time, we were walking through Sephora when a casting director from LA stopped her mid-aisle and offered her a national cereal commercial on the spot. It aired during the freaking Super Bowl, too. That's just how Amber's charmed life works—opportunity finds her.

The most obnoxious part? She doesn't even like musical theater. This whole play is just practice for her. A stepping stone.

What she really wants is to be some glossy, vapid Hollywood starlet or maybe the next reality-star Kardashian, as long as it means paparazzi and a designer wardrobe. Fame is the goal and looking good while getting it.

Unlike my sister, I've never been the girl everyone likes.

I mean, yes—technically—I know I'm attractive, in my own emo-Elvira-meets-Wednesday-Addams kind of way. Pale, icy-blue eyes. Jet-black hair down to my waist, thick and shiny enough to land a shampoo deal. Mom's begged me to cut it for years, but I'd rather stick needles in my eyes than lose even one inch.

Even Hayes—my best friend and lifelong source of brutal honesty—once admitted the guys on the LHU football team think I'm hot. Like goth Megan Fox hot. But apparently, I also give off "major demon succubus vibes," like I might devour their souls in the quad between classes. So they're all too freaked out to actually ask me on a date.

Still, good hair and some locker-room talk doesn't change the fact that I've never fit in. Not in Laguna Hills, at least.

I wasn't the cool girl in high school. The only parties I went to were the ones Hayes dragged me to, and even then, I always knew I was only there because of him. I was the plus-one no one actually invited. The tag-along.

That's why, even if this play was mostly about NYU, part of me hoped it could mean something more. I thought maybe my freshman year at LHU could be a fresh start. That maybe *Hercules* would give me an actual in—a way to be seen. To finally be accepted. To belong, even just a little.

It's stupid, I know, but it's the truth.

If only I could be more like Hayes.

My best friend isn't anything like the typical preppy Ken-doll guys around here, with their sun-streaked hair, Abercrombie jeans, and popped collars. But somehow, it works for him. People here absolutely worship Hayes. He's practically royalty. Sometimes I wish—

"Yo, Alligator!"

I look up, and as if my thoughts alone conjured him, there he is.

Hayden Basileus Vassilios.

LHU's golden-boy campus legend strolls through the parking lot like he owns the place. Which, I guess he sort of does, as the school's new star quarterback.

My breath catches for a moment at the spectacular view. Carved cheekbones. Dimpled chin. Proud, aristocratic nose. Blue eyes so dark they read almost violet, like a stormy night sky lit by lightning. He's like some brooding, devastatingly gorgeous Greek god come to life.

Judging by the gym bag slung over his shoulder and the damp, inky-black hair pushed haphazardly off his forehead, he must've just come from morning practice. He's in a black LHU hoodie and leather jacket, somehow managing to look both effortlessly cool and vaguely dangerous.

"Do you really have to call me that in public?" I scowl at him through my rolled-down window.

Even if he thinks it's cute, it annoys me to no end that the best-looking guy in town has nicknamed me after a scaly, smelly, prehistoric swamp creature.

"Oh, my bad. You prefer Alysander now?" He grins, mischief dancing in his eyes. Hayes only ever uses my full name when he's trying to get under my skin—or remind me he knows me better than anyone.

"Good point."

Amber and her clones linger near the Performing Arts Center entrance, her gaze locked possessively on Hayes, like he's still hers, even though they've been broken up all summer.

They've been on-again, off-again for years, and while I'd love to believe it's over for good this time, I know better. They always seem to find their way back to each other, eventually.

"So what's the word?" he asks, voice bright with anticipation. "You got the part, right?"

I don't feel like smiling, but whenever Hayes looks at me like this—dimples and dazzling white teeth on display—I can't help but grin back.

Unfortunately, he misreads my smile and yanks open the car door, pulling me out of the driver's seat in one big swoop and wrapping me up in his arms.

"Hell yes! I knew it!" he yells, spinning me around so wildly my feet leave the pavement. "How's it feel to be Laguna Hills' newest star?"

I stiffen in his arms, the sting of embarrassment creeping under my skin.

"I wouldn't know. I didn't get Megara—Amber did."

His face falls instantly.

"Shit. Are you serious?"

I shrug, scuffing the toe of my boot against the pavement. "It's fine."

"I'm so sorry, Al. I really thought you had it in the bag." He sets me gently back on the ground, eyes wide with sympathy. "But if those fools can't see it, screw 'em." Then he smirks. "Well… except Amber. We've got a date tomorrow."

"Since when?" I lift a brow. "I thought she wanted to be single senior year. Explore her options, whatever that means."

"It's not that deep." He shrugs. "She won't stop texting me, so I figured—why not? We're going to Souvlaki's for dinner and then catching the new Blumhouse flick."

"Wait—what? You can't see that without me." I fold my arms across my chest, fighting the stupid twist in my gut. "And Amber hates scary movies."

I probably sound like a jealous girlfriend, but horror movies are *our* thing, and he damn well knows it. It's tradition: every new release is just the two of us, followed by way too much Souvlaki's takeout and an hours-long postmortem discussing the movie.

"Relax, dude. Obviously, I'm watching it with you first," he says with a wink. "Come over tonight, okay? Around six?"

"Yeah, sure. That's cool."

I try to sound indifferent, but I'm sure the small smile tugging at my lips gives me away. I can't help it —I love when I come first.

"Besides," he adds, lowering his voice, "I'm not really going to watch the movie with Ambs anyway, if you know what I mean." He gives my shoulder a playful bump like I'm one of his over-sexed football teammates.

"Okay, gross. Enough about my sister," I say, swatting at him.

He catches my hand mid-air, and something in his expression softens. "I really am sorry about the play," he says, pulling me into a big hug. "I wish I could fix this for you. I hate seeing you unhappy."

A little thrill of electricity runs through my body at his touch, but I ignore it.

I have to.

I'm only human—no more immune to his good looks and charm than any other mere mortal—but it's pointless to give in to the feelings. Hayes has never seen me that way. I'm his best friend. Safe. Familiar. Like a favorite pair of cozy socks. Or raggedy old pajamas.

And then there's Amber.

He's still into her, no matter how much he pretends otherwise. I don't know why. He deserves so much better, but she's always had a hold on him I can't understand.

That's why, instead of getting lost in the warmth of his delicious embrace, I fixate on the new tattoo curling along the side of his neck.

It's stupid hot.

A bold circle with three spirals and three dots, the Greek symbol for strength. I know there's another one, even bigger, etched along the inside of his arm. A coiled serpent, ready to strike. He got them both right after his eighteenth birthday.

"They're going to regret passing you over," he says, so close I feel his cool breath on my cheek. "One day, they'll all see how special you are, just like I do. I promise."

I push him away.

"Oh, please. Get real. That's never going to happen." I sigh, my gaze dropping to the cracked asphalt. "Not here, anyway."

"Don't say that." His voice cuts through the air, sharp and angry. "You're amazing and anyone who doesn't see that is either blind or just stupid."

My breath catches. The way he's looking at me, I can tell he means every word.

"Careful," I say, forcing a crooked smile to cover the sweet ache blooming in my chest. "Keep talking like that, and I might start thinking you're secretly in love with me."

His jaw ticks. "You don't have to turn everything into a joke, you know. It's okay to be hurt," he says. "You don't have to hide that from me."

"I'm not," I lie, stepping back. "It's just a stupid play."

His gaze doesn't waver, too steady, too sincere, as if reading every crack I try to hide. I know he cares. I know he sees me. But he'll never really understand what it's like to be me. To have something you want so badly snatched away from you. Over and over.

Not when he's Hayden Vassilios—the guy who always wins.

He gets whatever he wants. Perfect life. Perfect family. A mother that adores him, and even though his father is gone on business most of the time, he still makes it clear how much he loves Hayes. How proud he is, always showering his only son with gifts and attention.

Me?

I don't even know my father's last name.

He left before I was old enough to remember his face, and Mom barely mentions him. Even if I wanted to find him—and I don't—I wouldn't know where to start. For all I know, he's some meth-addicted crackhead who abandoned his two daughters to go snort drugs and rob banks.

"Al—"

"I said I'm fine!" I snap, my eyes stinging. "In a few months, I'll be at NYU where I belong, and I'll never have to see any of these assholes ever again."

I turn away, cheeks flushed with embarrassment. I don't—won't—allow myself to cry, even in front of Hayes. Crying is for silly girls like Amber, the kind who weaponize emotion to get what they want.

Not me.

I take my hurt and bury it so deep, sometimes even I forget it's there.

Blinking hard, I force the burn behind my eyes to disappear.

Well, this is just great.

Freshman year hasn't even started yet, and everything's already falling apart. And somehow… I know this is just the beginning.

CHAPTER 2

Later that day, I drive to Hayes's house for dinner and our horror movie night.

Since classes haven't started yet, he's still crashing at his parents' place. He has a brand-new posh apartment near the university—of course he does, he's loaded—but nothing compares to the Vassilios family estate in Laguna Hills.

It's a literal mansion, complete with its own orchard, vineyard, sprawling pool, hot tub, tennis courts, horse stables, a personal chef, and a full-time housekeeper. If I were him, I wouldn't be in a rush to trade all that for paper-thin walls and flickering fluorescent lights either.

Wind cuts through the open windows of my car, whipping hair into my eyes as I race through the fancy, secluded hills where Hayes lives. I've always had a thing for speed. I figure adrenaline is probably cheaper than therapy, even if my last two speeding tickets say otherwise.

My tires shriek dramatically as I take the corner a little too fast and turn into his gated community. Jerome, the guard who's manned the entrance at Laguna Hills Bluffs since I was a kid, waves me through with a smile, and I keep cruising until I reach Hayes's private drive.

I punch in the code at the electric gate and head down the long, tree-lined path, watching as the full splendor of the Vassilios estate unfurls around me. No matter how many times I've been here, I still never get used to its beauty.

On either side of me, the manicured gardens blur past—blood-red roses, inky clusters of dark hellebores, and near-black calla lilies tossing in the breeze. Rows of silver-green olive and pomegranate trees stretch toward the hills, their branches heavy with ripening fruit, before giving way to terraced vineyards that have quietly produced award-winning wine for decades.

Then come the meadows and—my favorite part of all—the stables. That's where Hayes's father keeps his prized racing horses.

Normally, I'd look for them grazing lazily in the late afternoon sun. Dozens of sleek, pedigreed racers with long, fancy names and plenty of attitude. I love all the horses, but two especially have my whole heart.

There's Steopethe, my first love, the coppery old gelding I first learned to ride on. Patient, kind, always nosing around for sugar cubes tucked in my hoodie.

And my latest obsession, Phaethon, the striking dapple-gray stallion Hayes's father brought home last spring. He's all restless energy and untamed beauty with a past full of first-place trophies and photo finishes. I only recently started working with him in the ring but fell for him instantly.

But today, the paddock is empty. All the horses are gone. Hayes's father flies them to Greece every summer when the family retreats to their ancestral estate in Athens.

The Vassilios family owns one of the largest shipping empires in Europe, and every year they return to manage business interests and reconnect with family and friends overseas.

This year, for the first time, Hayes came back a few weeks early ahead of his parents to start football training. I know he misses them, even if he doesn't talk much about it. I do too—especially his mom. And I really miss the horses. It's been a long, quiet summer without them.

After the stables, I drive by the archery fields, where Hayes and his father often spend afternoons sinking bullseyes, perfecting their aim one ten-ring at a time. Both Vassilios men are top-ranked competitive archers. Some of my favorite memories are of lounging in a lawn chair under the warm California sun, watching them land shot after shot with their custom-fitted bows while Hayes's father spun Greek mythology stories like epic campfire tales.

Aidan Vassilios is not a warm man—busy, curt, rarely smiling—but when he talks about his Greek heritage, something shifts. His voice softens. His eyes glow with pride. From him, I've learned more about ancient Greece and its great legends than I ever did in AP World History.

He's told us tales of champion archers, the gods Artemis and Apollo, yes, but also of ancient beings like the Fates, who wove destinies both glorious and cruel, and the Sirens, whose deadly songs lured sailors to their deaths. The Siren stories always felt like they were especially for me. He knows how much I love to sing.

And then, of course, there was Heracles, also known as Hercules, the golden hero of Olympus. Hayes's father could talk about Hercules for hours, detailing each of the Twelve Labors with the reverence of a priest retelling scripture.

I wince.

Shit.

Now I'm thinking about that damn play again and my disastrous morning.

My fingers tighten around the steering wheel as I blow past the tennis and basketball courts until I finally arrive at the Vassilios family's mega-mansion.

From the outside, it looks like an old-world European castle that lost its way and somehow ended up in Southern California. Hayes's mother hired the most famous architect in all of Greece to design it. Grand Doric columns line the façade, and gorgeous terracotta tiles—imported from the family's favorite island, Santorini—crown the roof in warm, sunburnt hues. It probably cost more than my mom makes all year just to ship those tiles halfway around the world.

I pull into the circular driveway and park directly across from the sweeping courtyard fountain, grabbing my purse and the snacks I brought for movie night. Two king-size chocolate bars and an extra-large box of sugar cookies for me, plus a little container of boring dried mangoes for Hayes. He claims everything I like is 'too sweet for human consumption.'

He's a weird eater, as far as I'm concerned, but I try to accommodate.

Just as I head for the front door, a low, guttural bark cuts through the warm afternoon air. I whirl around—and freeze.

Standing a few feet away, as if appearing out of thin air, is the most majestic creature I've ever seen. Enormous, almost otherworldly, like some mythical wolf-dog hybrid. The animal's coat is obsidian-dark, shimmering with an unnatural sheen like moonlight rippling across still water.

And his eyes—*God, his eyes.*

They burn with an eerie, golden light, so piercing and radiant, they don't just reflect the sun. They seem to contain it.

"Hey, pretty boy," I whisper, inching forward with one hand outstretched. "Are you lost?"

Maybe a smarter person would be wary of a strange dog the size of a small pony just randomly showing up in the middle of a driveway, but not me. I fucking love dogs. All animals, really, but dogs especially. I've been begging my mom for one ever since I was old enough to say the word *puppy*. She's never caved, always blaming it on some imaginary allergy we both know is complete bullshit.

I can barely contain the impulse to throw myself at the dog and smother him in kisses, but I do my best to seem nonthreatening and friendly as I approach. My movements are slow and deliberate, careful not to go too fast and scare him off.

"Stop—don't move!"

I jolt, stumbling, as Hayes's hand clamps around my wrist, firm and protective, yanking me backward.

"Jesus, Hay!" I gasp, breathless, knees wobbling. "You scared the shit out of me!"

He's changed out of his practice gear from earlier, now clad in black athletic sweats and a matching hoodie, a backwards LHU baseball cap pulled low over his forehead. He must've come from inside the house, though I never heard the door open. Or his footsteps.

His face is filled with worry.

No, not worry—*fear*. And not just like he's scared we might get nipped by someone's runaway husky mix, but like some monstrous demon is sitting there in front of us, waiting to tear us both into little pieces.

"Get back," he orders. "Stay behind me."

"Relax. It's just a dog."

Hayes's eyes flick to the animal and then back to me, calculating, tight with tension. He shifts, like he's ready to bolt or fight, and I feel a slight tremble in his hand.

The dog, however, doesn't bark or growl. It doesn't even move. It just stares at Hayes, like they're locked in some silent exchange I'm not part of.

I try to sidestep Hayes to get to the dog, but he doesn't budge.

"Careful," he says, holding me back. "He could be dangerous."

I blink, surprised, when Hayes plants himself between me and the dog like a human shield. The gesture is totally unnecessary but also kind of adorable, in a ridiculous, over-the-top way.

Classic Hayes. Always ready to play the hero.

"Oh, quit being such a baby." I laugh, batting Hayes away and taking a few steps forward. I crouch low, my voice soft and soothing to the dog. "You're just a big teddy bear, aren't you, boy? Big, mean Hayes scared you with his big, mean voice, huh?"

The dog drops to all fours and lets out a soft, almost pitiful whine as he inches toward me, belly to the ground, his massive frame gliding along the pavement. There's something ancient in his gaze. Watchful. Knowing. That sleek, regal muzzle quirks upward, and I swear it almost looks like he's smiling at me.

"I don't get it. How'd he get in here?" I ask Hayes.

"Probably followed you."

"Hmm. You think so?" I shrug noncommittally. It seems unlikely. The gate was only open for a few seconds, but I suppose it's possible…

I reach out to pet the dog.

"Al, don't!" Hayes shouts, horrified, his voice sharp with warning.

Too late.

The dog presses forward—calm, silent—and curls into my lap. His massive body is warm and solid against my legs. He lets out a delighted, huffing yelp as I scratch behind one ear.

"Oh, he's adorable!" I squeal, checking under his neck for some sort of identification. "Weird. No collar or tags. How're we supposed to know who the owner is?"

"Probably a stray."

He doesn't look like a stray to me.

No, this is an animal that is healthy and well cared for. For one thing, he's got a full, filled-out face—not at all gaunt. His coat is glossy, and his body is packed with meat and muscle. Teeth white and straight.

"I'll take him to the shelter. They'll sort it out," Hayes says, voice tight.

I leap to my feet, aghast.

"You can't be serious. Don't you know what they do to dogs at the shelter? They *kill* them!"

"Al—"

"Over my dead body." I flash the dog a grin, rubbing his thick, muscular neck. "Don't worry. You're coming home with me, handsome."

The dog's tail thumps once against the ground, loud as a drumbeat, as if in agreement.

It feels like fate.

If I come home with a lost dog I just stumbled upon, what can my mother say? She'll have to allow him to stay with us while we search for his owners.

Naturally, I'll do the right thing. Check online for lost dog postings. Put up some flyers—not too many, though. I don't really want someone to come and take him away. With any luck, no one will claim him, and I'll finally have a dog just like I've always wanted.

"You're joking, right? He's enormous." Hayes arches a brow. "Where would you even put him? You barely have room as it is in that tiny-ass apartment. Where's he gonna sleep, the kitchen sink?"

I level him with a look. "Just because we aren't

gajillionaires—like some people—doesn't mean we can't have a dog."

"You know that's not what I meant." He shifts awkwardly, rubbing the back of his neck. "I just… Al, c'mon. You can't find some random dog on the street and just take him home with you."

"Sure I can." I cross my arms, chin lifting. "I think I'm in love."

"You just met the damn thing!"

I grin. "What, never heard of love at first sight?"

He doesn't return my smile. His eyes flick toward the dog again, then back to me, as if calculating something.

"You're not going to let this go, are you?"

"Nope," I say. "He needs a home, and I'm going to give him one."

"Okay, fine." He sighs, long and low. "What if I do it?"

I blink, confused.

"Do what?"

"I'll keep him," he says, voice suddenly all casual. He crouches down, slowly extending a hand to give the dog a tentative pat. To my surprise, the dog leans into it—pressing against Hayes's leg like they've known each other for years. "My parents love dogs. We used to have some back in Greece."

"Uh, what happened to 'he's dangerous'?"

"Can't a guy change his mind?"

He shrugs, still stroking the dog, calm and easy, like he's done it a hundred times before. Which, frankly, is weirder than anything else. It's a complete

180 from how he was just seconds ago, yelling at me to stay away.

I narrow my eyes. "A dog is a lifetime commitment. You can't even commit to the same girl for more than a month."

Even Amber—his longest relationship to date—barely made it a few weeks last spring before they broke up for the hundredth time.

"You really want to go there?" He smirks. "Remind me—when's the last time you went on a date?"

"Ouch. Cheap shot."

But he's not wrong.

I haven't gone on a real date since junior year, when I swapped numbers with a cute guy in the book aisle at Target because he was wearing a Ghostface T-shirt and said he liked girls who "don't scare easy." We went out once. He screamed during a silly jump scare in the new *Jurassic Park* movie, and I laughed at him.

I never saw him again.

It's not that no one ever asks me out. I just haven't met many guys I actually want to say yes to.

Unbidden, my gaze shifts to Hayes's gorgeous face.

Well… anyone *available*.

"Besides," he adds, teasing now, "everyone knows dogs are man's best friend—not woman's."

"Wow. That's deeply sexist." I place a hand over my heart, mock-offended. "I don't know if I can stay best friends with a rampantly misogynistic man."

I squint at him, pretending to think it over.

"I mean, maybe it's time I start looking for replacements. Someone who actually respects women. Someone who's an ally. Someone who—"

"Alright, just relax, Gloria Steinem." He lifts both hands in surrender. "Truth is, it's been kind of lonely with my parents gone. My apartment's nice, but weirdly quiet without a roommate." His tone shifts, the edges softening just enough to catch me off guard. "I was thinking… a dog might be good company."

A pang of sympathy pulls at my chest. I knew he missed his parents, but hearing him actually admit it out loud hits different, like maybe it's even harder for him than I realized.

"You can come over for dinner anytime," I say. "You know my mom loves you. You're basically the son she wishes she had."

"Thanks," he murmurs, eyes quickly flicking away. "It's okay. I'm sure my folks will be back soon."

I nod, glancing back down at the dog, his tail thumping lazily against the stone driveway. His big, blocky head tilts, tongue lolling out the side of his mouth as he blinks up at me with trusting eyes.

"I'm sorry about your parents, but you know how much I've always wanted a dog—this might be my only shot." A smile tugs at my lips. "Besides, I'm not exactly sure you're puppy-parent material."

"Hey, what's that supposed to mean?"

"Oh, please," I say. "Don't you remember what happened to Mr. Scramble?"

Back in Home Ec class freshman year, we had to co-parent a raw egg like it was a real baby. It'd seemed like an easy enough project until Hayes dropped our egg and broke it while he'd been busy flirting with Holly Clark, the captain of the dance team. It was the first—and only—C grade I ever got in high school.

"You're kidding, right?" He groans loudly. "I was fourteen! Will you ever let that die?"

"Oh, like you let Mr. Scramble die?" I ask, feigning outrage. "He was our egg-baby, Hayes! Our precious little egg-son. And you *murdered* him!"

Hayes's mouth opens like he's going to argue, but nothing comes out. For a second, he just studies me. And I can see it—the exact moment the wheels start turning. He exhales, then flashes a smile that's a little too smooth.

"Okay, fair enough," he says. "I've got an idea. Why don't we let the dog decide? Twenty bucks says he picks me."

I grin savagely. "You're on."

We both take a few steps back until we're spread out across the courtyard.

"Come here, sweet boy," I call gently to the dog while Hayes shouts from the other end of the drive.

The dog freezes, gaze flicking between us like he's torn. Then, slowly, he starts toward me. Victory stirs in my chest, and I can tell the dog is as good as mine.

But then, just before he reaches me, Hayes mutters something unintelligible under his breath and claps his hands together, loud as a thunderbolt.

The dog stops. Then pivots.

Hayes lets out an unfiltered, triumphant laugh as

the dog lopes straight toward him, tail wagging like crazy.

"Guess he made his choice," he says, dropping to his knees with a cocky grin. The dog plops down in front of him and starts licking his hands affectionately like they're old friends.

"You've gotta be kidding me," I mutter in disbelief. I'd been so sure the dog was going to pick me. I could *feel* it in my bones.

And then… I hear it.

A sharp crunching sound. Almost like wet chewing.

"Hey, wait a second—"

I run over and lunge for Hayes's hand. He tries to pull away, but I flip his palm over to find it coated in golden crumbs and dog slobber.

"You lousy cheater!"

Something hot and restless coils in my gut. Maybe it's the sting of this morning's humiliation and loss. Maybe it's just that I'm so goddamn tired of losing— roles, people, control.

Even if it's just a dog. Even if it's to my best friend. I don't want to lose again.

A sudden rush of power surges through me, a burst of energy rising from somewhere I didn't even know existed. I square my shoulders and shout, my voice bursting forth like a lightning strike.

"Come here. *NOW!*"

The dog jerks away from Hayes like a string's been yanked. In a blink, he's racing back to me. Then he's pressed into my legs, head bowed and tail sweeping side to side. His nose finds my palm and stays there. Solid. Certain.

"Holy shit," Hayes breathes, looking stunned.

I grin, slow and victorious.

"Guess he's mine now."

"This really isn't a good idea—"

But I'm already coaxing the dog into the backseat of my car and slamming the door behind him.

"Al, wait. Come on," he says, more urgent now, a panicked look on his face. "You don't know anything about him. What if he—"

"Later!" I shout through the window. "Gotta go convince my mom about a dog."

I slide into the driver's seat and reach back, my fingers brushing soft fur. The dog lets out a low, contented huff and melts into my touch. I can't stop the grin spreading across my face—wide, real, unstoppable.

But as I drive away, I catch one last glimpse of Hayes in the rearview mirror, still watching, still worried.

I hesitate, just for a second. The look on his face tugs at something deep in my gut… and I can't help but wonder if I'm making a huge mistake.

CHAPTER 3

A few days later, I pull out of the LHU Rec Center parking lot, blasting Sleep Token from my car speakers. My face is flushed, sweat dripping down my neck, my messy hair in tangled strands. The gym shorts and sports bra I've got on cling to me, drenched from the brutal workout I just finished. I probably look like I've just crawled out of a sewer drain, but I don't care. I feel invincible.

Boxing gives me life.

I get a thrill from every punch, every dodge. Blood pounding in my ears as I spar. Imagining my sister's face on every opponent.

I suppose today's instructor didn't hurt either—a seriously cute LHU junior with abs of steel and exceptional taste in music. He blasted old bangers like The Darkness and Mötley Crüe while I fantasized about landing a right hook straight at Amber's perfect little button nose.

Total win-win.

A happy sigh escapes me as I roll down the windows and crank the AC, letting the cool air wash over my skin. If only dealing with my sister in real life were that easy.

I've been dodging Amber all week.

Of course, she's been spinning her side of the story to anyone with ears—Mom, Hayes, the neighbors, probably even the mailman. Just the other night, my mother cornered me in my bedroom after dinner to try and explain how "devastated" Amber was that I didn't make the cast.

Mom hates when we fight. She's been begging me to make up with Amber and move on—like that's ever worked.

According to my mom, Amber had tried her best. She'd really pulled for me, but the director just didn't think I had "what it takes" for a lead role in the play. Perhaps most offensive of all, Amber claimed that *she* was the one hurting and felt betrayed because I didn't tell her about my applying to NYU in the first place.

It was all bullshit, but my mother has always been a sucker for Amber's lies. She lets Amber get away with murder just because she's the baby.

Honestly, I'd probably respect my sister more if she'd just own up to her lying, conniving ways instead of pretending to be such a goody-goody, always trying to make me look like the bad guy. I've learned the hard way: when Amber's in damage-control mode, full-scale avoidance is the only way to keep my sanity. That's why, instead of heading home after my work-out, I steer the car straight toward Hayes's house.

Unfortunately, Hayes was right about my mom and the dog.

She flat-out refused to let me keep him. Just one more splash of salt in the wound, I guess. As if it wasn't already depressing enough being stuck at home my freshman year because we couldn't afford campus housing—now I didn't even get the dog.

Hayes was a good sport about it. He offered to

keep the dog at his place, handed me the key to his new apartment, and reminded me of the code to his parents' house—not that I needed it. I've had that memorized since junior high. He said I could come by whenever I wanted.

Not exactly the setup I'd hoped for, but I guess part-time dog custody is better than nothing.

I catch my reflection in the rearview mirror as I turn into Hayes's driveway. My face is flushed, dark baby hairs clinging to sweaty cheeks. I'm in desperate need of a shower. If I were like Amber, I'd never show up to his house without a full face of makeup and perfect hair.

But I'm not, thank God.

And I'm way too excited to see my new dog to waste time with things like blotting powder or mascara touch-ups. Or a fresh blowout.

I slip into the house through the garage doors, punching the code into the keypad. As I head inside, I can't help but notice that Hayes's father's brand-new Lamborghini Aventador—the one that costs more than some people's houses—is missing from its car bay. Guess that means Hayes is already out.

Alpha Delta Omega is throwing their big "Welcome Back" party tonight. Hayes is pledging the frat and invited me to go with him, but I said no. I just wasn't up for it. Not after the week I've had. I'd rather stay in with the dog, a book, maybe a scary movie. Something chill.

Now, I can't help but wonder if I made the right call.

Did Hayes bring someone else tonight? Someone prettier. Cooler. Someone not weighed down by everything like I am.

I bite my lip, eyeing the empty garage spot again. Hayes has his own fancy Mercedes G-Wagon, so why take his father's new sports car and risk the man's wrath unless he's trying to impress someone?

Did he take my sister?

The idea makes my stomach curl. I know I'm not supposed to care who Hayes dates, but no matter how hard I try, I can't help it sometimes.

Hayes and I have been best friends ever since we were little, back when his family moved from Greece to our beachside neighborhood in elementary school. Those days, he was small and awkward and strange. He had ghost-white skin like he'd never been outdoors and a thick Greek accent that made everything sound funny. He didn't fit in, but neither did I. So we found each other.

We bonded over gory slasher flicks and traded dog-eared horror comics like *Tales from the Crypt* and *The Walking Dead*. Our friendship was easy. Safe. Everything was perfect.

But then the summer before high school, everything changed. Hayes filled out, got a tan, and somehow turned into a real-life Adonis. He tried out for football and basketball and made both varsity teams freshman year. Hayes leveled up overnight: taller, stronger, and with this insane, supernatural confidence that made everyone completely forget the weird little kid he used to be. Now he's the starting quarterback at LHU and pledging the best frat on campus. It's only a matter of time before the gap between us becomes too wide to ignore.

Eventually, he's going to wake up and realize he doesn't need some moody, emotionally twisted misfit from his past life. He'll outgrow me the way children outgrow beat-up old toys—kept for a while out of nostalgia, then tossed in a box and forgotten. It hasn't happened yet, but I know it will someday.

And when that day comes, I don't know what I'll do without him.

I'm still chewing on my depressing thoughts and my inevitable lonely future as I open the door to a shrill beep from the alarm, a flash of fur—and boom. The dog slams into me like a wrecking ball of joy and muscle and drool, looking up at me like I'm his whole world. The sudden impact of one-hundred-plus pounds crashing into me distracts me from going down another negative thought spiral.

Honestly, thinking back to Hayes's freakout over me taking the dog home feels almost laughable now. It's been nearly a week, and I'm already hopelessly, disgustingly in love with him. The dog—not Hayes.

At least, that's what I keep telling myself.

I laugh and kiss the dog's warm wet nose before grabbing his leash off the coat hanger in the mudroom. It matches his new studded collar, both courtesy of Hayes's limitless American Express, which we used with wild abandonment at the pet store yesterday.

Gourmet dog food. All kinds of toys. Treats. Even

an adorable black bandana with skulls and crossbones I picked out. It all went on Hayes's credit card without him ever batting an eye. He may be a privileged brat who gets whatever he wants, but it's hard to hold it against him when he's always spoiling me.

"Ready for a walk, Dog?" I ask, clipping the leash to his collar as he barks eagerly at me.

Hayes and I still haven't settled on a proper name for him, so for now he's just Dog. I've been too scared to name him, worried someone might come crawling out of the woodwork and claim him.

We hung signs, checked online listings, posted on Facebook, even drove around looking for flyers, but so far no one's come forward. At this point, I'm really starting to hope he might be ours.

As I lead the dog out through the garage, a sharp breeze makes me shiver. It's unusually cool for early September. Luckily, I keep a faded Pink Floyd sweatshirt in the trunk of my car for emergencies. I grab it as we pass the car and zip it all the way up, pulling the hood over my head. People always think Southern California is hot and sunny year-round, but it can get seriously chilly, especially this close to the ocean.

Or maybe it's just me.

My mother always says my blood wasn't made for cold climates. I'm constantly begging to turn up the heater or layering sweaters, even in summer. She claims I'll never survive a Northeast winter, that I'll hate New York. Then again, she'll say just about anything to keep me here. The woman has serious abandonment issues thanks to my deadbeat father.

I pause to stretch my hamstrings, bracing a hand on the car hood as the lingering pull from my earlier workout burns down my legs. Then I give the dog's leash a gentle tug and lead him down the long driveway and out the front gate.

He trots eagerly at my side as we head toward the pedestrian sidewalk that lines the streets of Hayes's prestigious private community. These hills are home to some of Laguna Hills's wealthiest residents—tech titans, real estate moguls, even a few Hollywood stars—and it shows. Towering heritage oak trees rise on both sides of the road, immaculately pruned and decades old. The pavement is flawless. Not a single pothole or piece of trash in sight.

There are some great hiking trails here, too. Quiet. Shaded. Just secluded enough to feel like your own secret world.

After a few minutes, we reach the entrance to my favorite one, a path that leads all the way down to the beach. I unhook the dog's leash so he can roam freely beside me. This trail is usually packed on weekend mornings, but by early evening, most people have cleared out. It's why I prefer coming at dusk, even though my mother's always warning me not to go places alone this close to dark.

My mother has always been a bit… obsessively cautious.

She doesn't think anywhere is safe, not even a private trail in one of the most exclusive, well-protected neighborhoods in all of California. And I'm not talking about the usual stuff most mothers worry about—kidnappers, serial killers, random creeps. Nope, my mother's fears run far deeper.

More… fantastical.

Ever since Amber and I were little kids, our mother has warned us about another world—a realm of shadows that exists right alongside our own. She calls it the "Underworld" and claims it's like a darker, twistier version of Alice's Wonderland. A hidden place, brimming with dangerous magic and full of ancient, powerful gods and monsters, the stuff of nightmares. Superhuman beings with the strength of a thousand men and the ability to live forever.

She always said Amber and I were "special"—though she never said how—and that if the wrong people ever found out about us, they'd come and drag us into the Underworld. This wasn't just some made-up cautionary bedtime story to keep us in line, like the Boogeyman or Krampus. She genuinely believed it.

Back in elementary school, she made us wear these ridiculous black tourmaline bracelets to ward off evil and tucked protection pouches made of special yarrow flowers under our pillows to keep us safe from "spiritual danger." They actually smelled kind of nice—like rosemary and oregano—but were so bulky it was hard to sleep on them.

It wasn't until sixth grade that I realized this wasn't normal. None of the other kids wore spelled crystal jewelry or kept emergency magic sachets in their backpacks. And their parents definitely didn't talk about deadly imaginary worlds.

I blame my father—whoever, wherever he is.

Mom said he was the one who first told her about the Underworld. He's the one who got her to believe.

When we were growing up, Amber and I used to ask about him all the time.

Who was he?

What was he like?

Mom would feed us scraps, but never enough to truly satisfy our curiosity. She shared little details, like how he had the same dark hair and fair skin I did. That he was athletic and strong and fast. Smart and well-read. But no matter how much we pestered, she'd never tell us anything important, like why he left us or where he went.

Her answer was always the same: we were too young to understand. One day, when we were older, she'd explain everything.

Eventually, we stopped asking.

Suddenly, a deep, thunderous bark jerks me out of my thoughts, and the dog bolts from my side. Ears pinned, teeth bared, he charges straight toward the overgrown woods to our left.

"Shit—*Dog!*"

I take off after him, cursing myself for letting him off leash. This is our third time on the trail this week —he's been solid so far, no issues—but I should've known better. We're still just getting to know each other.

"Hey! Come on!" I yell again, running to catch up.

Low-hanging branches whip against my legs as I tear through the woods after him. My sneakers crunch over leaves and loose rocks, the ground turning rough and uneven underneath my feet.

A gnarled tree root juts out of nowhere, and I trip, crashing to the ground. I cry out, curling forward and clutching my leg, trying to breathe through the sting. Tears spring to my eyes, uninvited.

"Dog, stop—*NOW!*"

My voice comes out sharp, cracked open with frustration as my patience snaps. The dog reappears instantly, racing back to my side and dropping to the ground in front of me.

His body trembles, tail tucked tight beneath his legs like he's bracing for punishment. A low, nervous whine escapes his throat as he looks up at me—wide-eyed, anxious, like he thinks I might hit him. The thought punches straight through my gut.

"I'm sorry, boy," I murmur, forcing a smile. "Didn't mean to scare you."

I brush bits of gravel and broken twigs from my skin and check the damage. Nothing major, just a few scrapes, some areas beginning to bruise. Still, I'll probably have to skip shorts for a few days.

"What got into you?" I ask as he edges closer, pressing his muzzle gently to my injured leg.

The dog had seemed perfectly fine one minute, and then he went full chaos gremlin the next, tearing into the woods like something was after him... or he was after something.

But what?

No squirrel. No rabbit. There hadn't been

anything in the woods with us. At least nothing I could see.

But then, the second I gave him a real command—not just yelled his name but actually told him to *stop*—he'd listened. Came right back to me, just like that day at Hayes's house.

It's almost like… he understands me?

An idea sparks.

"Sit," I say, soft but firm, testing him at first.

The dog drops onto his hind legs without hesitation.

"Lie down."

He lowers himself to the ground, those big golden eyes locked on me, like he's waiting for the next move.

"Good boy," I murmur, grinning as I scratch behind his ears, surprised—and thrilled—by how easily he obeys.

Still, that was pretty basic. Beginner stuff. Maybe I just got lucky.

With a grunt, I push off the ground and stand, wincing as pain flares in my ankle. It hurts a bit but it's not too terrible. Nothing a little ice and some ibuprofen won't fix.

I hold my palm out in front of the dog's face. "Stay."

He doesn't budge.

I slowly circle him. Aside from the occasional tail flick to swat a fly, he's still as a statue.

"Roll over."

He does—smooth and easy—then sits back up, ears alert, gaze steady.

"High five."

He lifts a paw and taps my palm.

Holy shit.

I think maybe he really does understand me.

"Fist bump."

I make a fist and hold it out to him. He hesitates, head tilting a fraction as he lifts a paw, slow and deliberate. Just when it looks like he's about to do it, he lunges at me instead. His teeth clamp down on my shoelaces, and he yanks so hard my left sneaker nearly flies off.

"Ugh," I groan. "No, not like that." I lean in, reaching for his paw to show him what I meant. "Here, look. Fist bump, got it?"

That's when he opens his mouth, bares his teeth—and growls.

I snatch my hand back, my heart slamming against my ribs.

"No! Bad boy!"

The sound he makes, low and threatening, scrapes along my spine like a rusted blade. For the first time, I really see him. Not the adorable, lovable mutt I brought home from Hayes's driveway. Not the dog I imagined walking down the beach with in our matching skulls and crossbones bandanas.

The creature in front of me now is something else. Tense. Dangerous. Muscles ripple beneath his fur, and his eyes—those bright golden eyes—don't look so playful anymore.

They look primal.

Predatory.

And his teeth—

God, his teeth look like they could rip straight through a person. Long and curved like daggers. Not just sharp—lethal.

Even though he's never acted aggressive toward me before, the realization hits me all at once. He could hurt me if he wanted to.

Badly.

Hell, he could *kill* me.

The growling intensifies, darker and heavier, vibrating in the air between us.

"Dog, no. Please…"

My voice trembles as I raise my hands, palms out, and slowly step back.

Hayes was right.

I should be afraid.

This animal is so big. So strong. I don't know where he came from. Don't know who owned him before me, or what he might've been trained to do.

Did he really get lost? Or did someone let him go… on purpose?

A shiver snakes up my spine as one of my mother's most terrifying stories slinks out from the dark crevices of memory—tales of monstrous canine creatures from the other world. Massive. Bloodthirsty. Bound to the will of the Underworld's rulers.

She called them hellhounds.

Their purpose: to hunt humans. Track them down on Earth and drag them, screaming, into the shadows below. She said once they caught your scent—once they smelled your blood—they never let go.

My breath catches.

What if—

But before I can really go there, logic kicks in. Followed by a sharp stab of embarrassment.

What the hell is wrong with me?

The dog isn't growling at me.

He isn't even looking at me anymore.

Instead, his gaze is fixed on the woods across the trail, ears twitching, body coiled tight, eyes locked on something I can't see.

I squint, scanning the trees, trying to make out what's got him so on edge. Probably just a coyote or a bobcat. Maybe a raccoon. It's too dark to tell.

All around us, the trees blur into a tangle of flickering shadows and shifting shapes. The sun's nearly gone, dipped behind the ridge, casting long streaks of dusk across the forest floor. Any second now, the last rays of daylight will vanish—and whatever's out there will have full cover of night.

Bad things happen in the dark.

My mother's voice—her constant warning— echoes in my ears as a loud snap cracks through the trees. Twigs splintering under the weight of... paws? Feet? Whatever it is, it's close.

Way too close.

My pulse spikes, adrenaline flooding my system and dulling the ache in my ankle as I stumble back a step, then another. It's not that I suddenly believe in my mother's crazy stories, but maybe there's something to be said for making it home before nightfall.

The dog and I bolt.

I run hard, barely feeling the pain, legs pumping, heart racing like it's trying to escape my chest.

We don't stop until Hayes's house is in sight—and even then, even after locking every door and flipping on every light—I still don't feel safe.

Because even as I tell myself it was probably nothing, just some stupid animal in the woods that spooked the dog, I can't shake the feeling that maybe it was something else. Something out there in the dark, watching us.

Watching.

And waiting…

CHAPTER 4

The Monday morning before classes officially start somehow turns into *The Amber Show*. Never mind that I'm starting freshman year of college—my first step into the real world. Because, of course, Amber has to make everything about her.

My sister prances around our tiny apartment like she's heading to a *Vogue* photo shoot, barking orders and demanding Mom hurry up with breakfast, so she won't be late for her first day of senior year. Mom rushes through the kitchen, flustered as she dutifully preps Amber's favorite green kale and cucumber smoothie and then pours the green sludge into two BPA-free plastic tumblers.

She hands the drinks to us with a big smile, and I try not to gag as I glance down at my liquid breakfast.

I *live* for sugar.

Pop-Tarts with frosting. Glazed donuts. Gooey sticky buns. Muffins oozing with chocolate chips.

My favorite breakfast is birthday cake pancakes, packed with rainbow sprinkles, drenched in syrup, and piled high with whipped cream. Basically, dessert disguised as breakfast. But I suppose that's a lot to ask for at 7 a.m., especially when Mom doesn't have to go to the Artists Co-op where she works until later this afternoon. Her wealthy, stay-at-home-mom clientele would never dream of being up this early on a

Monday morning. That's what nannies and house-keepers are for, obviously.

Still, I smile and thank her for the gross smoothie anyway, trying not to take it personally, even though it kind of is.

She knows I hate health food.

Sometimes it feels like my mother forgets she has two daughters, not just Amber, but I suppose I can afford to be magnanimous today. Hayes is picking me up and treating me to the Coffee Hut before class. It's my favorite breakfast spot near campus, and they have the best goddamn cinnamon rolls in town.

Right on cue, Hayes pulls up outside the apart-ment and gives a quick honk. He stayed at his parents' place last night, and even though I'm technically on his way to campus, it's still sweet that he offered to drive me this morning. He knows new things make me nervous. New people, especially.

"See you later!" I say, tightening my backpack straps as I head for the door.

"Have a nice day, dear." Mom waves absentmind-edly, rinsing out Amber's tumbler in the sink.

Amber trails after me, way too eager.

"Is that Hayes?" she asks.

"Mmm," I mutter, not slowing down.

"I think I'll go say hi before Brooke gets here. Do I look okay?" She fluffs her blonde curls and smooths the hem of her ballerina-pink chiffon skirt.

"You look gorgeous, sweetie," Mom says.

Amber eyes my outfit and lifts a judgy brow. "Wait

—Ally, you're not seriously wearing *that*, are you? You know Halloween isn't until October, right?"

I happen to love what I'm wearing: a black skater dress, ripped fishnets, and motorcycle boots. I even spent extra time on my makeup, layering thick mascara with sharp-winged eyeliner. My long black hair is tied into twin pigtails, my signature thin black choker cool against my throat. It's giving Nancy Downs, my favorite witch from *The Craft* movie.

"Oh yeah?" I pause at the door and glance back. "Well, you look like Barbie threw up on you."

Her cheeks flush. Or maybe it's just her too-bright, caked-on shimmery blush.

"I do not! Take that back!"

"Girls, please. It's too early for this."

A stress line creases the center of Mom's otherwise smooth forehead, and I feel a flicker of guilt. She's way too young for wrinkles.

Mom had us in her early twenties. She's petite like Amber, and just as blonde and beautiful. Men are constantly stopping her on the street to ask her out, but she always shuts them down with the same polite, uninterested smile. As far as I know, she hasn't dated anyone since my father left.

"Sorry, Mom," I say.

I glance over at Amber, considering a truce. Sure, she's an asshole, but maybe it wouldn't kill me to be a little more civil, at least for my mother's sake. Perhaps I could—

"Yeah, sorry, Mom." Amber's voice drips honey.

"Have a great first day of school, Ally." She smirks. "Oh, and good luck being a nobody all over again."

All thoughts of civility go right out of my head. It takes all my restraint not to hurl my backpack straight at her perfectly curled head.

"Go to hell, Ambrosia!"

"Alysander!" Mom yells, horrified, but I don't stick around for a lecture. I slam the front door behind me, blood boiling as I storm toward Hayes's SUV.

"I swear to God, I'm going to commit a felony," I say, climbing into the passenger seat and sinking into the buttery leather. My backpack hits the floor with a heavy thud.

Amusement sparkles in his blue eyes as he looks over and laughs. "Morning to you too, Alligator."

"I'm serious," I say as he whips out of the driveway, my voice climbing with irritation. "I hope you're not afraid of prison, because that's where you'll be visiting me. I'm this-close to murdering Amber with my bare hands."

"That right? What'd she do this time?"

I lean over and twist the dial on the stereo until it lands on "Supermassive Black Hole." Muse floods the car. God, I love Matt Bellamy—his vocal range is unreal.

"Actually, scratch that." I huff. "Why should I do time for her? I'll hire a hitman. How much you think those run?" I shoot Hayes a look, batting my lashes. "Can you spot me a few thousand, bestie?"

He turns to me, one hand on the wheel, flashing

that sexy, slow-burn grin—the one that always looks like it's hiding secrets… and probably a few sins. "Al, you know I'd do anything for you," he says, "but offing your sister would seriously mess with my love life."

"Ugh. Gross." I groan, flopping my head against the seat. "Please tell me you two aren't happening again."

"Still undecided." He shrugs. "But don't worry, you'll be the first to know."

"Oh goodie."

Well, shit.

I was really hoping this little break of theirs might actually stick this time, but it sounds like another reconciliation may already be on the horizon.

"Whatever," I say, crossing my arms. "I don't need your help anyway. I'll just sic the dog on her." I pause, then add, "Actually, I forgot to tell you. He kind of lost it the other night."

Hayes stiffens—barely, but I catch it.

"Lost it how?"

"It was so weird. He went full Cujo on something in the woods behind your house during our walk Saturday." The memory prickles under my skin. I still don't totally understand what happened. "He was fine one minute, then he just… snapped. Like, hackles up, growling-at-the-dark kind of thing. I thought he was about to attack me, but it was something in the trees, I guess. Something I couldn't see."

Hayes lifts a brow, smirking. "What—like one of your mom's little made-up Underworld monsters?"

"Ha ha. Very funny," I say. "I'm serious. The whole thing was creepy as hell, whatever it was."

"Probably a possum or something," he says, already turning away. "Woods are full of 'em."

I nod, but the weird feeling lingers. Because whatever was out there with us… I don't think it was just a possum.

After a quick stop at the Coffee Hut for our pastry and caffeine fix, we arrive at school.

Even though I've driven by LHU my entire life, it's different seeing it today—as an actual student. The campus is truly stunning, even I have to admit that.

From the cathedral-like buildings with their towering arches and intricate stone carvings, to the pristine lawns and palm fronds swaying lazily in the breeze, it all feels like something out of a movie set. Sunlight glints off the fountain in the main quad, and even the air smells expensive, like fresh-cut grass and money. Sure, it's not NYU, but I guess it's not the worst place to be stuck for a year.

We turn into the student parking lot, and Hayes glides into one of the reserved spots up front. Because apparently, being quarterback comes with valet-level parking privileges.

Please don't let this year suck.

I whisper the silent prayer as I step out of the car, slinging my backpack over one shoulder and trying to shake off the nerves coiling in my stomach. Hayes comes around to my side and casually hooks his elbow through mine, like it's the most natural thing in the world. His fingers settle into the crook of my arm, warm and steady. Anchoring me, like always.

"You okay?"

I take a slow breath, eyes fixed on the looming campus ahead. My throat tightens as a wave of overwhelm sweeps through me.

New faces. New classes. New professors. New everything.

"Not really."

"Just stick with me, kid. I promise, we'll make this our best year yet." He pulls me in, and his familiar scent—a delicious mix of cedar, dark amber, and fire-lit spice—envelops me, softening the sharp edge of my nerves.

"It's just... I'm still bummed about the play," I admit, my voice shakier than I'd like. "It felt like a fresh start, you know? Like maybe if I got the part, people might actually like me for once." I try to smile. "That's pathetic, huh?"

"People do like you, Al," he says softly.

"People like *you*. They merely tolerate me because I'm your friend."

"That's not true."

I snort. "Oh, come on. It is, and you know it."

"You're just... different, is all. That scares some people."

He lets go of my arm and steps back, giving me a look—half thoughtful, half amused—as his gaze slowly travels down my all-black, unapologetically goth outfit.

I know I look good.

I'm tall and toned, with just enough softness in the right places. I've got big boobs and a great ass, thanks to all those workout classes. But my outfit isn't the right style. Not like all the other fangirls giggling and waving at Hayes as they pass by, decked out in their pastel-ruffled skirts and designer shoes and bags.

"Okay, yeah, maybe you could blend in more if you tried," he says, fingers steepled against his lips as he continues to study me. "But then you'd be another plastic doll like everyone else around here. And that'd be a damn shame, because I think you're already perfect just the way you are."

I roll my eyes. "All right, cheeseball. No more Disney Channel for you."

"I'm serious, Al. I mean it."

"Oh please. You have to say that," I mutter. "You're my best friend."

His gaze lingers on me a beat too long.

"Doesn't mean it's not true."

Something flickers behind his eyes—something I can't name, but it makes my heart flutter in that stupid, dangerous way it shouldn't around him. Suddenly, I'm hyper-aware of *everything*. How close we're standing. The way his shoulder brushes mine. The heat radiating from his skin.

The hairs on my arms rise into little goosebumps. I shiver, blaming the ocean breeze. The chill of the wind. The lack of a proper sweater or jacket. Anything but the way he's looking at me.

"Let's get going, okay?" I clear my throat and step

back, shrugging off his touch. "I don't want to be late."

He blinks, and for the briefest moment, I see a crack. A flash of hurt. But it's gone in an instant, replaced by his usual easy grin.

"So, where to?" he asks casually as we walk across the quad toward the main campus building. "I've got Professor Grant for Intro to Business first."

"I'm Theater History and Visual Culture. Then Vocal Performance Studio." I shake my head with a grin. "And, of course, French this afternoon—the class you somehow talked me into. Still not sure why I agreed."

"Because you love seeing my pretty face," he says with a wink that's way too self-satisfied. "Besides, my father says knowing multiple languages is essential for business these days. You'll need it to communicate with your legion of international fans someday."

"Yeah, right." I scoff.

Spanish would've made way more sense, especially living this close to Mexico. But no, I signed up for French. It's not like I'm jetting off to Paris anytime soon. Not like Hayes's mom, who flies there every Christmas just to shop for holiday gifts, and again twice a year for Fashion Week.

But Hayes already speaks Spanish fluently. And Greek. And like five other European languages. He figured picking up another one would be "easy" and promised we'd study together. Said he'd make sure I got an A too.

"Yo, Vassilios! Over here!" someone yells from the steps of the student union.

I glance up and spot a cluster of good-looking guys in matching athletic hoodies and team slides loitering around. Hayes's football buddies. I'd met most of them over the summer at the workouts and practices Hayes dragged me to. Long, sweaty afternoons where I killed time reading horror novels in the bleachers.

Dylan Masterson waves at us. Star running back, party god, surrounded by sorority girls in Greek-letter tanks, their glossy hair bouncing like shampoo commercials. Truthfully, he gives me the ick. He's attractive, sure, but he knows it and wields those good looks like a sleazy used car salesman. Dylan is all jawline and overinflated ego, with a spray tan and zero self-awareness.

Next to him is Tony Hernandez, the team kicker. Tony is the complete opposite of Dylan. Warm, funny, effortlessly charming, with big, kind eyes. He came out recently, and even though we live in California, our small town still skews conservative. Some alumni grumbled about Tony's "locker room presence," whatever that was supposed to mean. Hayes— despite only being a freshman—shut it down fast, making it clear he had Tony's back. No room for debate. After that, everyone else fell in line.

"Go hang with your friends," I say, nudging Hayes lightly with my elbow.

He looks surprised. "You don't want me to walk you to class?"

"Nah, I'm on the opposite side of campus anyway."

"So?" He smiles, easy and warm. "I don't mind. I like walking with you."

I know he's just trying to be nice and probably feels bad I don't have friends like he does, but I don't need an escort across campus. I'm not ten years old.

"I'll be fine. Have fun."

"Al—"

"Jesus Christ, Hay. Just go." I give him a shove.

He chuckles, backing away. "Meet you at the dining hall at noon? Lunch on me?"

I nod, turning toward the Arts Complex without looking back.

My first class of the day goes well enough. I've always loved theater—the stories, the symbolism, the history. I'm hopeful Vocal Performance Studio with Professor Jones will be just as good.

I first met Professor Jones over the summer at an open house for accepted students. He spoke on the arts panel, then stuck around to chat afterward. We ended up talking for twenty minutes about everything from professional choirs to vocal strain. A few days later, I spotted him again at the *Hercules* auditions. He was in the audience, volunteering as a vocal coach, when I thought I'd nailed Megara… but apparently didn't.

"Hello, Ms. Smith!" he calls out as I slide into my seat for my second class of the day. "Nice and early. I like that."

"Hi, Professor."

I'm the first to arrive, so I take my time unpacking, pulling out my notebook and a handful of pens, arranging everything just so.

"Welcome to The Studio. I think you're going to enjoy my class." He gives me a kind look. "Shame about *Hercules*. You holding up okay?"

I look down, heat blooming in my cheeks.

"Ego's still a little bruised. But yeah, I'll live."

"That's the business, I'm afraid," he says with a shrug. "But don't let it stop you. You've got one of those rare voices, the kind that makes people forget to breathe. Best soprano I've heard in years."

I glance up, caught off guard. He says it like it's a fact, not just fake encouragement because he feels sorry for me.

"You really think so?"

"Absolutely. And I've got a feeling you're just getting started." He straightens, a smile spreading beneath the thick bristles of his mustache as he adjusts his bold bow tie, bright as a painting against his rich brown skin. "Speaking of, I do hope you're auditioning for the Fall Showcase today?"

Shit.

I totally forgot about that.

Every year, top students from Vocal Studio perform solos at the showcase. It's supposedly a huge deal on campus and exactly the kind of thing I need on my NYU transfer app. I'd meant to prep a piece, but between Hayes, the dog, Amber, and everything else, it completely slipped my mind.

Frustration knots in my throat.

"I don't think so, Professor. I don't have anything ready."

"Surely you've got something memorized from your *Hercules* audition you can sing for us?"

I mull over his suggestion as the room fills behind me. My confidence still feels paper-thin. Am I really ready to put myself out there so soon? What if I fail again? Or worse—what if everyone laughs at me?

And yet… I don't think Professor Jones would be pushing me unless he really thought I had a shot.

Just before class begins, Rebecca Choi slides into the seat beside me with a friendly wave. She's petite and always effortlessly put together, with silky dark hair that falls in neat layers around her face and preppy designer clothes that somehow never wrinkle.

Rebecca's a freshman too. She moved to Laguna Hills last year, and even though she's one of Amber's closest friends, she's not nearly as awful as the rest of them. She actually clapped for me during my Megara audition, while Amber and the others snickered in the back row.

To be fair, I don't know if they were laughing at me or something on Instagram. They were glued to their phones the entire time.

After a quick rundown of the syllabus, Professor Jones launches straight into showcase auditions. Each time he calls a name, my pulse spikes. I'm practically vibrating out of my seat. Then—he says mine.

For a second, I think about bolting. But no. I can't let fear stop me from doing what I love. Even if I suck, even if everyone really does laugh, I have to at least try.

Like my body's on autopilot, I walk to the front of the studio, open my mouth, and sing.

My voice wobbles at first—soft, unsure—but by the time I hit the chorus, I find my stride. I forget the room, the eyes, the pressure, and just let go, nerves melting away until all that's left is the song. It's just me and the music.

I belt out each new line, hitting notes no one else in class has even touched. A grin spreads across my face as I nail the final crescendo. Okay, maybe it wasn't the strongest start of all time—but the rest?

I crushed it.

Only Rebecca claps when I finish. The rest of the room stays silent. Maybe they're stunned. Or maybe just petty. I don't care. I don't need them to clap. All that matters is what Professor Jones thinks.

"There it is. That's the voice I was hoping to hear again." He nods, clearly impressed. "You're in the showcase, Ms. Smith."

Endorphins flood my body, and I feel it—that high of being heard. Of being seen. For once, I don't feel like the weird girl, or the loser who didn't get the part. For just a few minutes, it feels like maybe I'm enough, exactly as I am.

But deep down, I know better.

Nothing good in my life ever stays that way for long.

CHAPTER 5

The rest of my first week of college goes by as I expected. No surprises, at least.

Classes are interesting—nothing like what NYU probably offers, but still. Professor Jones's vocal studio is amazing, and I secretly love having French with Hayes. And yes, just like he said, seeing his pretty face in class kind of makes my day.

Not that I'd tell him that.

But beyond the more challenging coursework, college is exactly what I imagined: a slightly shinier version of high school. No new friends. No sudden shift in social gravity. No buzzing invites or spontaneous party offers. Just me, floating on the fringes like always, smiling politely while everyone else moves around me like I'm invisible.

It's not active hate or dislike or even avoidance. More like… irrelevant ambivalence. Maybe that's even worse.

Like yesterday. I passed a table in the quad where a group of sorority girls were handing out flyers for rush week. They gave one to every girl in sight—except me. I stood there for half a second, just long enough to feel the sting, then kept walking like I hadn't noticed.

Not that I really cared.

I'd never survive in a sorority. An entire house full of Ambers? No, thank you.

Still, it would've been nice for it to be my decision, not theirs.

Hayes, of course, is already thriving at LHU. Between football practices and fraternity pledging, I barely see him outside of French class. Most afternoons, I'm either holed up in the campus library or stretched out on his apartment couch with the dog, doing everything I can to avoid going to my own home and facing Amber.

She's living her dream—lead in the community theater play, queen bee at school, and on the verge of getting back with her hot college ex. The last thing I want to do is listen to her humblebrag every night at dinner about her amazing life. And honestly? Hanging out alone with my dog is fine by me. I like him better than most people anyway.

By Saturday afternoon, I'm more than ready for a much-needed movie date with Hayes. That morning, he threw the winning touchdown in the first game of the season, leading the LHU Chimeras to a blowout victory. The crowd went wild, chanting his name like he was some kind of god. I watched it all from the stands—alone—surrounded by screaming fans decked out in face paint and head-to-toe red and gold.

Now, hours later, the adrenaline has faded, and it's the two of us again, like old times. Just Hayes and me at his parents' house, the absolute best place to watch movies.

On the lower level of the house is not one, but two, state-of-the-art theaters. The "summer" outdoor theater is across from the Olympic-size pool and has heaters and a larger screen, but we choose the "indoor" theater because it has an industrial-size popcorn maker, and I'm starving.

We grab bottled waters from the kitchen first and then head toward the movie room, with Hayes pausing to scoop up a bowl of freshly stuffed olives off the counter. He pops a few into his mouth, then plucks one out and dangles it in front of my lips.

"Open up," he teases.

I duck away, swatting his hand. "Ew. You know I hate olives."

Something about the texture has always grossed me out. Too slick, too weirdly firm. Technically a fruit, but not even sweet or sugary. Basically useless.

"You sure? Even when I'm hand-feeding them to you?" he jokes, arching a dark brow.

"Especially then."

He just grins and pops the olive into his own mouth instead, chewing happily as we walk down the hall. It's harvest season, and the olive groves on the Vassilios estate are bursting. Hayes eats the stuff like candy, tossing back a few more as I follow him into the movie room.

It's one of my favorite places in the house. More luxury theater than anything you'd expect in a private home. A massive nineteen-foot screen dominates the front wall. Hayes's father calls it his pride and joy. I still can't believe the man left it behind for the summer to go to Greece. When they first installed the projector last Christmas, Hayes's dad didn't leave the room for an entire week.

Facing the screen are three rows of plush, stadium-style leather recliners, each one equipped with a built-in cup holder and adjustable headrest. Blackout curtains and a high-end surround sound system complete the meticulous design.

I load the popcorn machine in the back and the room fills with the rich, buttery scent—warm and familiar, like comfort wrapped in nostalgia.

After filling a bowl to the brim, I carry it to the front row and settle into one of the recliners. With a twist of the knob, the seat leans back, and the dog curls into a cozy ball at my feet, already dozing off. Before I even ask, Hayes tosses me my favorite cashmere blanket, the one I used to steal during sleepovers back in junior high.

We decide on *Evil Dead*, one of our favorites. It's a classic horror flick: college kids, remote cabin in the woods, bloodthirsty demons, plenty of gore.

With a single tap on the iPad, the lights dim, and the haunting opening notes of the movie begin. The screen fades in on a shadowy lake shrouded in mist just as Hayes drops into the seat beside me, even though there are two completely empty rows behind us.

I try to focus on the movie, but it's impossible.

He's so close.

Too close.

The kind of close that makes my whole body buzz with awareness.

Our arms and legs are nearly touching. Every time he reaches for the popcorn bowl lying between us, his fingers graze the bare skin of my knee. It's light enough that I know it's accidental, yet every brush sparks like a live wire, sending a shock straight through me. I feel all of it—his warmth, his scent, the casual ease of his presence—each sensation doing unspeakable things to my insides.

I sneak a quick glance over when I can tell he's focused on the movie. The flickering screen throws shadows across his face, making his cheekbones look almost too perfect, his jawline sharp as glass. He's so stupidly handsome, it's offensive.

His nearness is so distracting I consider moving to the back row, just to breathe and clear my head. But no—that would look weird. Besides, this isn't exactly new territory.

I've been doing this for years, pretending I don't feel anything when I'm around him. That I don't notice the way my heart gallops every time he's near, or the way my body leans into his like it's gravity.

Hayes, for his part, has never given me a single sign of mutual interest.

Not one.

In all these years, he's never shown any indication he sees me as anything more than a friend. Never looked at me the way I'm sure I look at him. Never paused just a second too long. Never leaned in like he might kiss me.

Nothing.

He's always been too preoccupied with other girls —dating my sister, flirting with strangers, falling into whatever girl is next in line.

I shift the blanket over my legs and try to concentrate on the movie. I need to stop thinking about Hayes like this. He's just another hot guy. Big deal. Southern California is crawling with them.

Not that I've ever met anyone else quite like him.

Or who matches my elite taste in rock music and scary movies.

Or who can beat me at *Resident Evil*.

But still.

"Where do they come up with this shit?" Hayes mutters with a low laugh, shaking his head as the girl on screen gets possessed, stabbed, reanimated, and then hacked up into little pieces with an axe.

"Oh, shut up. You love this movie."

"I used to." His voice shifts, thoughtful. "I don't remember it being so… over-the-top. It's kind of laughable."

"Hard disagree. Demons are terrifying."

"Uh, you know they're not real, right?"

"Says who?" I shoot back. "You don't believe in the devil? Heaven and hell and some epic showdown for our souls?"

He gives me a look—a smile that's soft, but also just a little sad. "Not really."

"You think there's nothing else then? Just us?"

"I didn't say that."

"Then what?" I press.

"Well, you know how my dad's always going on about Greek mythology?"

"Obviously." I grin. "Pretty sure the last time I

saw him he was telling me about some flying monster with six heads and a wicked vendetta."

"Yeah, that tracks." Hayes chuckles. "Anyway, he's always made a point of teaching me the old Greek ways. They didn't believe in a black-and-white, Judeo-Christian idea of good versus evil. There wasn't one god, but many, and they could do incredible good and terrible harm. Sometimes both at once. Like nature." He shrugs slightly. "And the Greeks believed in daemons, not demons. Spirits. Some helpful. Some… not so much." He pauses, gesturing toward the screen as a geyser of blood erupts from a body. "I believe in something, sure. Just not *this*."

I toss popcorn into my mouth, chewing slowly, thinking about the research I did over the summer for my *Hercules* audition.

"What about Hades then?" I ask. "Didn't the Greeks believe in him? Wasn't he basically Satan?"

Hayes groans. "I told you not to watch that stupid Disney movie. It's a complete bastardization of mythology."

I grin and lob a piece of popcorn at him.

"You're just salty your parents named you after the villain."

Hayes's mother once told me they picked his name because of the Greek god. That Hades was powerful, determined, and loyal to the end—qualities they hoped their son would one day grow into. I always thought being named after a god was cool. Way better than my own name anyway.

"Hades wasn't a villain." Hayes smirks, brushing

the popcorn off his lap. "He may have ruled the Underworld, but he wasn't evil. Didn't torture souls or any of that bullshit. Honestly? He was one of the better gods."

"Sure." I shake my head. "Just a regular ol' nice guy in charge of hordes of the dead."

He doesn't laugh, just holds my gaze a little too long.

"Hades was steady. Just. Fair," he says, voice low. "The world needs someone like that."

I press my lips together to keep from smiling. Hayes is more like his father than he realizes—just as fiercely proud of his Greek heritage, taking any slight against mythology as a personal attack. I don't really get it, but it's kind of adorable how worked up he gets.

"Oh yeah? Like how?" I ask, egging him on. Not because I need a mythology lesson but because I know he wants to give it.

"Well, like the story of Orpheus," he says, his whole posture shifting, energized. "His wife dies, right? So he goes to the Underworld to bring her back. Everyone paints Hades as this heartless monster, but he lets the wife go. He bends the rules because he respects Orpheus's music… and because he understands what it means to love someone so much you'd risk everything for them. Hades was absolutely crazy about his wife, Persephone."

There's something different in his voice. Softer. Like maybe the story means more to him than he's letting on.

"Yeah, I remember. Your dad told us that one." I

study him, something tightening in my chest. "But isn't it a tragedy? She doesn't make it out."

"That's because they didn't listen." Hayes shrugs. "Hades gave them one rule—don't look back. And what does the guy do? He looks." He grabs a handful of popcorn and turns back toward the screen. "That's on them."

I curl deeper into my seat, drawing the blanket tighter around me as gunshots ring out from the TV. Onscreen, the protagonist is now fleeing from more demons.

"Still. It's pretty romantic, huh? Going all the way to the Underworld for someone you love." I sigh, quiet and admittedly a little bitter. "No one would ever do that for me."

"I would."

His reply is instant.

No hesitation. No need to think it over. Like it's something he's considered before and the answer's always been yes.

"Really?" My voice barely rises above a whisper. "You'd risk your life for me?"

Something flickers across his face, shy, sweet, and dangerously sincere. "For you? There's nothing I wouldn't do." His eyes hold mine in the dark—steady, intense. "If you go, I go."

For one suspended beat, the world stills. And then—

"Besides, I gotta keep you alive to help me host all my wild parties, Alligator," he says, playful now, lobbing one of his mom's beaded throw pillows at my side. I dodge it, laughing too fast, trying to ignore the way my heart's still pounding in my chest. "Speaking of—what time are you coming over tonight?"

"Nope. Not happening."

Hayes is throwing his first college party tonight—a welcome bash for his new frat and the entire football team. Kegs. A DJ. Poolside bartenders. The works.

I know I should want to go. Most girls would kill for an invite, especially from Hayes himself. But me? I'm just not feeling it.

"C'mon, Al," he says. "I need my best girl by my side. You're the only one who won't let me get blackout wasted and end up in some sort of scandal."

I roll my eyes, half-smiling. "That sounds like a *you* problem."

"Pretty please?" He grins. "I'm not asking you to shotgun beers or dance on tables. Just show up. Keep me grounded. Help me survive the night."

"There is absolutely, positively, no way I'm—"

"Oh yes, you are." He launches another pillow straight at my face this time. "And I won't take no for an answer."

I shriek, swatting it away, and dissolve into laughter as we tumble sideways in a tangle of cushions and limbs, wrestling like we're twelve again. The dog lets out a startled yelp and scrambles to the other side of the room, getting as far away from us as possible.

"Let go, idiot!" I gasp, breathless from giggling as I jab at his ribs.

He catches my wrist with a fast, practiced grip and

twists it gently behind my back, his movements fast—too fast. Too smooth. And just like that, we're no longer tangled in a playful mess. I'm pinned helplessly to the floor, and he's on top of me.

The realization slams into me like a second heartbeat.

HAYES… IS ON TOP… OF ME.

Warmth radiates between us. His hair, just a little too long, brushes my cheek. Our bodies touch, lightly, but it's enough to send a current skimming across my nerves. Sharp and electric. Like we could set something on fire if either of us moved even a fraction. One shift closer and we'll both ignite.

I tilt my face toward him, slowly, like I'm drifting forward without meaning to.

He does the same.

My pulse races like a jet plane, not just from adrenaline, but from something deeper. Hungrier. My eyes fix on his mouth—those full lips, so close now, I can almost feel them on mine. If I moved just an inch closer… would he stop me?

Would he kiss me?

"Al. I really need you tonight."

His eyes are darker now. And hot. Molten hot. The blue is so deep it almost bruises violet at the edges.

Why does he have to look at me like that?

And why, oh why, does my body betray me every single time he's near?

NO. NO. NO.

Must stop fantasizing about my best friend.

Right. Now.

I tear my gaze away, fixating instead on a random spot above his left ear. The flickering light from the screen dances across his skin, golden and soft, too perfect to be real.

"Is it because of Amber?" he asks, watching me carefully. "Is that why you don't want to come?"

I stiffen. Just the mention of her name is enough to set my jaw.

"No."

I try to sound casual, like it's not a big deal. Like I hadn't immediately thought of Amber the second he told me about the party.

Because of course she'll be there.

Whether or not they're technically back together, there's no way my sister would miss tonight. And I'd rather not subject myself to Amber—or her flock of loyal minions—if I can help it.

"You know you're going to have to forgive her eventually, right?" he asks. "She is your sister."

"So you are inviting her," I say, too sharp, too accusing.

"Of course I am. But you can't skip out on me just because she's coming."

I can see the flicker of something behind his eyes —regret, maybe. Or disappointment.

"It's not about her." I force my body to move. To untangle and stand. "I just… don't want to go."

"Uh huh."

"It's not!"

I sink back onto the couch, tucking my legs underneath me as the dog curls up beside me again. Reaching for the popcorn, I shove a few kernels into my mouth, trying to come up with some excuse—anything—that sounds believable.

"I mean, we both know your parents would flip if they knew you were throwing a party," I say, forcing a shrug. "Maybe you don't care, but I do. I love them and want to stay on their good side."

Even to my own ears, it sounds flimsy. And we both already know the truth. Of course it's about her.

It's always been about her.

"My parents won't even notice," he says. "They're too busy launching new fleets or building skyscrapers or whatever they're doing in Athens."

Guilt pricks at me.

I've been so wrapped up in my own issues, I keep forgetting he's hurting too, just... in a different way than I am.

"I'm sorry they're not home yet," I say softly.

"Yeah, well, at least I've got Dimitra." He gives me a half-smile that doesn't quite reach his eyes. "And her homemade spanakopita."

Dimitra's been the Vassilioses' live-in housekeeper since forever. She came over with the family when they first moved here from Greece. She's more like family than staff.

But... she's not his parents.

The end credits roll, and Hayes clicks off the TV. He yawns, stretching, his broad arms arching overhead.

"It's getting late," he says, checking the time on

the new gold Rolex he recently got for his eighteenth birthday. "You need to go home and get dolled up for tonight. You know—cake your face, try on a hundred different outfits. Normal girl stuff."

"You forget. I'm not normal." I snort. "And I'm not trying to impress anyone."

"Not even me?" he asks, mock-wounded.

"Especially not you."

"Fine. Wear whatever you want. I don't care," he says. "Just please… change your mind."

He gives me that look—the one that always gets me. Gentle. Familiar. Like I'm the only person in the world who really matters. Something in my chest pulls, and against my better judgment, I sigh and throw my hands up.

"Okay, whatever. I'll come," I say. "Now stop harassing me."

"Deal." He grins. "Go get ready," he says, reaching over and yanking the lever on my recliner. The seat snaps upright with such force I nearly launch out of it.

On my way out, I kneel beside the dog and press a kiss to the tip of his black nose.

Hayes arches a brow. "Hey! Where's my kiss?"

"Oh please." I smirk. "I'm sure you'll get plenty of them tonight, lover boy."

"True."

My hand lingers on the dog's thick fur a moment longer. "About time we name this guy, don't you think?"

"It's only been a week. Someone might still come looking for him," Hayes says.

"It's a name, not a marriage proposal," I tease. "God, you really are allergic to commitment." I toss him a grin over my shoulder and head for the hallway.

"Just be here at nine sharp, smartass!" he yells after me. "And bring some of your mom's oatmeal lavender cookies. I'm seriously craving them."

By the time I reach my car, the weight of what I just agreed to is already sinking in. I can't believe I let Hayes talk me into the party. He just has this… power over me. Something impossible to fight. Like magic.

I already know tonight is going to hurt in all the ways I've been trying to avoid. Seeing Amber. Her friends. Their looks and whispers. Wondering if Hayes is still hers.

This has disaster written all over it.

CHAPTER 6

By the time I get home from Hayes's house, I've already convinced myself I'm not going to his party tonight under any circumstances. Pretending to be social and playing nice with Amber and a crowd of frat guys and sorority girls I have zero interest in isn't worth my energy. Even if Hayes is right and I do need to patch things up with my sister eventually, a few more days of space—and licking my wounds—won't kill anyone.

And as for Hayes, he probably won't even miss me.

Despite all his begging earlier, I doubt Hayes will notice I'm not there. With so many people around, he'll be too busy playing host to care. Better for me to spend the night working on my NYU transfer application anyway. At least that feels like forward motion. Something real I can control.

I need to make sure everything is perfect. Every word. Every detail. I can't afford to give them a single reason to say no this time.

When I walk into the apartment, it's predictably quiet. My mom usually works late on the weekends, juggling back-to-back clients at her downtown studio. This town has no shortage of wealthy women looking for someone to read their chakras or decode their star charts, anything to distract them from their unhappy marriages and unsatisfying lives.

My mother wasn't always like this, peddling New Age philosophies and alternative wellness to the wealthy and spiritually bored. Before she got pregnant with me, she was a fine arts major with an actual point of view.

She had vision.

Talent, too.

A few years ago, I found some of her old paintings stashed in the back of her closet. A handful of oil canvases filled with dark, visceral images of haunted worlds. Shadow-thin angels and bleeding red skies. Devils cloaked in smoke. They unsettled me, but in the best possible way. It was like she saw something the rest of us didn't. Those paintings meant something.

But I guess meaning doesn't pay the bills.

Amber's bedroom door is wide open as I pass by, everything inside aggressively pink, like a cupcake factory exploded. Last year, she convinced Mom to let her paint the walls, and now her ruffled bedding matches the same high-octane, bubblegum hue. A glowing neon "A" hangs above her bed, and right beside it, a peppy poster chirps: *Be So Happy That When Others Look At You, They Become Happy Too.* I get a headache just looking at it.

Thankfully, she's not inside.

Amber works weekends at Laguna Attire, a trendy boutique downtown, to fund her shopping addiction. They sell stuff I wouldn't be caught dead in—bedazzled fringe jackets, low-cut neon bodysuits, glitter cowboy boots. Amber and her friends go absolutely feral for that crap.

Once I get to my own room, I shut the door and settle at my black lacquer desk, ready to dive into my transfer applications. Unbidden, my eyes drift to the corkboard hanging above, covered in photo memories of Hayes and me through the years.

There we are on the first day of fifth grade, holding chalkboard signs with our ages and heights—Mom's idea. Then making s'mores on the beach the summer after sixth grade, both of us in matching Camp Crystal Lake hoodies, deep in our *Friday the 13th* phase. There's the flag football championship game in junior high. We won that night thanks to Hayes and his perfect spirals. And our first high school dance, the only one we went to together because he got lazy and couldn't decide who to bring as his date that year.

In the center is my favorite photo of all.

It's me and Hayes, of course, but Mom and Amber are there too. It's from an old karate tournament, back when Amber was still halfway normal and took classes with us. I'm clutching a trophy the size of my torso, grinning like my face might split in half. Amber's got her arm around my shoulder. I'd just won best all-around in the juniors' division, one of the only times I ever beat Amber at anything. Everyone's smiling for the camera—except Hayes.

He's smiling at me.

Next to the corkboard is a shelf lined with my most prized possessions. Front and center is Hayes's

Stranger Things Demogorgon Funko Pop, the one he gave me in sixth grade after I fell out of his treehouse and broke my wrist. Totally his fault. Pretty sure he cried more than I did that day.

Beside the Demogorgon sits the rainbow-hued Stephen King box set Mom got me for my last birthday. On the other end, my framed black-and-white print of David Bowie—the *Labyrinth* Goblin King himself. He looks unbothered and brilliant. I aspire to be both someday.

I grab my favorite chenille blanket and drape it over my legs, then open my clunky old MacBook. The thing weighs a hundred pounds and hums like a lawnmower as it boots up. It's basically an ancient relic. One of Mom's clients was going to donate it to Goodwill but gave it to us instead.

Once I'm on the now-familiar NYU admissions site, I pull up the two transfer applications required for Tisch. First is the Common App, the standard application everyone fills out: GPA, test scores, coursework. The easy stuff.

Second is the separate portfolio submission for the music school. That one's trickier. It requires a song portfolio and performance résumé. Which would be fine, except I don't have a single polished recording.

My résumé's not much better.

Aside from high school choir and a few arts-heavy classes I squeezed into this semester at LHU, my so-called "musical career" mostly consists of singing in the shower.

I take a deep breath, trying to slow the panic

rising in my chest, and decide to focus on the Common App first. Low-hanging fruit. No reason to have a heart attack just yet.

The academics section is a breeze. My high school GPA and test scores were well above the median when I applied last fall, even for a school as competitive as NYU. Grades have always come easy to me. It's everything else that's the problem.

I'm making decent progress, steadily moving through each section—until I reach "Parental Information."

Damn.

It's still blank.

I let out an annoyed sigh. I'd sent my mom the login weeks ago, and she'd promised she'd handle it. I know she's not thrilled that I'm already looking to transfer, especially since my semester at LHU has barely started, but she's going to have to get over it.

I debate calling her at work, but at this point, it might be faster to just do it myself. At least the parts I know.

I start to fill in the sections as best I can:

Name: Melinda Smith

Marital Status: Single

Occupation: Artist

(Because there's no way I'm putting "Aura Healer and Crystal Specialist" on a college application)

Education Level:

The question stops me cold.

I have no idea.

Did she go back to school after dropping out when

she got pregnant with me? Did she ever finish her degree?

I should be able to answer this. It's the kind of basic information someone should know about their own mother, but I don't.

Does that make me a shitty, self-centered daughter?

Possibly.

Unsure what to do next, I try calling. It goes straight to voicemail.

She must have a client. Even though there's zero scientific proof, my mom is fully convinced that radio frequencies from cell phones interfere with her "psychic energy" during readings, so she always turns hers off.

With no other options left, I shut the laptop and head for her bedroom closet, going straight to the purple, cosmic-swirl storage bin where she keeps all her important papers. Inside it, everything is filed into manila folders with tabbed labels scrawled in her messy cursive. There's one for each of us:

Melinda.

Alysander.

Ambrosia.

I flip through the "Melinda" folder, quickly scanning the contents: bills, lease papers, credit card statements, something titled "Empath Degree."

I bite back a laugh. God only knows what kind of shady online program handed that one out.

I'm almost to the end of the folder when something tucked way in the back catches my eye. A sealed, legal-size envelope. It's soft at the corners, slightly crumpled, and marked with a single letter:

"S."

I pause, fingers hovering. Then I slide it out.

I know I'm crossing a line. If the situation were reversed, I'd lose it if she went through my private things. But this is different. Because I know who "S" is.

"S" means Sonar.

My father.

I was barely a year old when he left, too young to remember him. No matter how many times I've asked, Mom never told me much about him, either. I know she gave up everything to raise us on her own and carried more than I probably realize, but none of that makes the questions go away.

He's still my dad.

I have the right to know who he was. To know where I come from.

My fingers tremble as I tear the envelope open, an uneasy feeling curling in my stomach. I suddenly remember the Greek myth Hayes's father told us about Pandora's jar.

Pandora was the first woman, given a sealed container full of the world's evils and warned never to open it. But curiosity got the better of her, and the moment she lifted the lid, all the suffering, disease, and hardships of life escaped into the world. I wonder if this is what she felt right before she opened it. Whatever I find inside—good or bad—there's no undoing it afterward.

Still, even knowing I might regret it, I dive in anyway.

The first thing I see is a small 4x6 photo tucked into the corner of the envelope. A man in his late twenties. Handsome. Thick black hair, the longest lashes I've ever seen, and a grin like he doesn't have a care in the world. He's standing in front of the Laguna Hills pier, head thrown back mid-laugh.

He looks like me.

I know instantly—this is my father.

Mom always said she didn't have any pictures of him. She claimed he hated cameras, and that since they never married, there were no engagement shots. No wedding photos.

Clearly, that was a lie.

But what really surprises me is how normal he looks. How… happy. He doesn't look like someone who'd abandon the woman he supposedly loved or their two baby girls.

I flip the photo over. Scrawled on the back is his full name—Sonar Delios—and a date around seventeen years ago. The picture must have been taken right before he left.

A weird flutter rises in my chest. After all these years, I finally know my father's last name. Mom would never tell us. I think she was always too afraid we'd try to find him—or worse, try to find his family.

Delios.

It sounds Greek. Does that mean I'm part Greek too?

I can't wait to tell Hayes. He's going to love this.

Beneath the photo is a slim stack of letters, bound with a gold ribbon. Each one is written in my mother's hand and addressed to my father. No stamps. No return address.

They were never sent.

I open the first one carefully. The paper is soft and yellowed at the edges, the date marked just a few months after Amber was born. My stomach twists as I begin to read.

My Dearest Sonar,

I know there's nowhere to send these letters, but I needed to write you anyway. Maybe somehow, wherever you are, you'll feel the words. I miss you. Every single day.

More than anything, I wish you could see our girls. Alysander and Ambrosia are happy and healthy. They grow bigger, and bolder, by the day. Alysander is already stringing together sentences and little Ambrosia has started crawling. They have your spark. They're so special, just like you said they'd be.

You'd be proud.

But, my love, it's been nearly a year since you left, returning home to that awful place I still can't bring myself to name out loud. You told me to watch for the signs. And to be careful. I've made the girls their amulets, like you instructed. Kept the protection stones under their pillows. I've stayed alert for hellhounds... for Watchers... for any Olympian emissaries.

But there's nothing.

I can't help but wonder if it's safe now. If maybe it's time for you to come back to us.

I hate the thought of you trapped there all alone, sacrificing your life for us, if the danger has passed. I know you believe this is the only way to keep us safe, but... what if it isn't true?

Please, Sonar. Come home. Our daughters need you. I need you.

Yours forever,

Mel

I continue on to the next letter, reading with a growing mixture of fascination and horror. This one is dated a few years later.

My Dearest Sonar,

Today, I had a birthday party for the girls. Alysander turned five and Ambrosia is now four. When it was time to make a wish, Alysander turned to me and asked for you to come home.

It nearly broke my heart.

She looks just like you. Beautiful pale skin.

Hair dark as a raven's wing. I wish I could tell her where her daddy really is, and why he can't come back. Of your bravery. Of the sacrifices you've made for us.

Except... well... I still don't understand it all myself.

I love you so much.

I want to trust you.

But why haven't you returned yet?

You told me you were one of the great Titan gods. That nothing could keep you away from our family once it was safe. But it's been years now, my love.

We are safe.

So where are you?

Yours forever,

Mel

My hands shake as I open the last letter. This one is dated eleven years ago.

My Dearest Sonar,

I am afraid.

Something terrible has happened.

Yesterday, the girls and I were out for a picnic at the beach. I know you always warned me not to go out after dark, but it's been so long. I almost forgot about the Under-world and those who wish to harm our family.

I heard the sound as the sun was setting. It was a howl so low and eerie, it sent shivers through my bones. It was like nothing I'd ever heard before, like it came from the very bowels of Hell.

It was the hellhounds.

You would've been proud of me. I didn't panic. I scooped up Ambrosia, grabbed Alysander's hand, and ran.

I could hear the pounding of paws behind us, monstrous, fast, closing in. I was so sure it would catch us. I thought it was all over. And then... I heard a squeal. A horrible sound I'll never forget. Like bones snapping.

And then... silence.

I didn't dare look back.

I still don't know what happened or how we escaped alive. I just got the girls in the car and drove away as fast as I could.

I'm so sorry I ever doubted you.

I believe, Sonar.

I believe EVERYTHING now.

Yours forever,

Mel

I lower the letter, my palms clammy and hot. I'm in a state of shock, not sure how to react or what to think.

The letters were written years ago, when my mother was still deep in the throes of grief, still grappling with the heartbreak of my father leaving. It would be easy to justify them as the wild ramblings of a broken woman. Something she wrote late at night after a bottle of wine, before crying herself to sleep. Her way of trying to make sense of why the love of her life walked out on her and her children.

Yes, that has to be it.

Because the alternative?

That my mother actually believes what she wrote in those letters? That she really thinks my father is some kind of ancient god, and that our family is in danger from monsters from another world?

That's... *insane*.

I'm still sitting cross-legged in her closet, reeling, when I hear the front door open.

I jump up and scramble to rewrap the letters, shoving them back inside the folder and burying it deep in the bin like it might catch fire. There's no way I can let my mother know I found them. She'd be mortified I read her love letters and furious I invaded her privacy.

And my sister?

Even if we were on speaking terms right now, she's the last person I'd share the letters with. There's no version of reality where she could handle any of this. Amber's all rose-colored glasses and rom-coms

and butterflies. She's not built for real-world prob-
lems, let alone grief, depression, or, god forbid, serious
mental illness.

No. This is my secret now to bear.

I creep back into my room and collapse onto my
futon, heart thudding, mind still racing. Maybe I can't
tell my mother or Amber about this, but I don't think
I can hold it in all alone. It's too big… too heavy. I
need to tell someone. Someone who won't think I've
lost my damn mind.

Luckily, there's one person I can always trust with
anything.

Even this.

And I know exactly where to find him.

CHAPTER 7

When I pull up to Hayes's house, the party is already in full swing. A caravan of Ubers winds through the electronic gate, and cars line the circular driveway, spilling out onto the lawn. Hip-hop pulses from the backyard like a second heartbeat, the air thick with excitement and the promise of bad decisions.

I park in a secluded spot near the vineyards, so I won't get blocked in. I want a clean escape route.

My plan is to find Hayes as quickly as possible, tell him about the letters I found in my mom's things, get his advice, and then get the hell out of there. I know he'll be busy—he always is at these parties—but if I can just steal a few minutes, I'll feel better. I always do after talking to him.

I step out of the car and follow the long drive toward the front door. A familiar silhouette fills the entryway. Hayes's football buddy Dylan lounges on the front porch, blocking the door.

He's dressed in a button-down shirt, ripped jeans, and designer sneakers, the unofficial uniform of every cocky campus fuckboy. Draped across his lap is Amber's friend Tiffany, giggling at whatever he just said. Tiffany's model-tall and stunning, with legs that go on for miles. She and my sister are practically conjoined, which means if Tiffany's here, Amber's not far behind.

For a split second, I consider turning around and driving straight back home.

But I need Hayes.

Just seeing his face, hearing his voice—it's the only thing that can quiet the anxious buzzing in my chest.

So instead of fleeing, I grit my teeth, smooth down the black velvet corset top I threw on over my baggy jeans and keep going. Thankfully, Tiffany chooses that exact moment to head inside, probably in search of a drink. Or my sister.

Perfect.

If I can get to Hayes without being spotted by Amber or her friends, this night might actually be survivable.

"Well… hey there, gorgeous," Dylan slurs as I approach. He hooks a finger through my belt loop and yanks, pulling me too close. His breath is hot and sour against my cheek. "Where you headed?"

"Hands off, Masterson." I twist out of his grasp. "I gotta go."

I try to sidestep him, but he swings an arm out and plants it against the doorframe, trapping me in place. He takes a drag from his blunt, then exhales in my direction. The sharp, skunky smell of marijuana hits me full in the face.

"What's the rush? Hang for a minute. Have some fun." He extends the joint toward me like it's a peace offering. "Here—take a hit. Uh… Alison, right?"

"It's Alysander."

Dylan has never gotten my name right, despite meeting me at least half a dozen times.

"Oh, right. Sorry."

"Where is he? Inside the house or out by the pool?"

Dylan runs his fingers down the doorframe, eyes glassy with whatever mix of alcohol and drugs is pumping through his system.

"Who?"

"Hayes," I bite out.

"Oh, that's right. Now I remember." He snaps his fingers like he's just solved some complicated puzzle. "You're Hayes's little friend. So… you here all alone tonight?"

He traps a loose strand of my hair between his fingers, twirling it slowly with a slimy little wink. I hold in a groan. Dear God. Talking to him is a complete waste of time.

"Never mind. I'll just find him myself."

I try to walk around the guy again, but he won't budge.

"You know the price of admission, right?" He gives me a sleazy grin. "Door tax is a kiss. House rules, babe."

"Not a chance."

I shift my weight, channeling every karate and boxing class I've ever taken, then bring my knee up sharply into the inside of his thigh. Not enough to do real damage. Just enough to make him yelp and instinctively step back.

"Ow—what the hell, Alison? Watch it!"

While he's off balance, I duck under his arm, pivot, and slip past him through the doorway before he can recover.

"See ya, *babe!*" I call out sweetly, blowing him a kiss as I go.

Inside the house, the party's already in full swing. The living room is packed, vibrating with energy and chaos. Music blasts from expensive speakers, so loud one of the oversized photos of Hayes's father posing with his beloved racehorses hangs crooked on the wall. A keg's been shoved up against the leather couches, and Tony and some of Hayes's other team-mates are taking turns doing keg stands, beer spraying across the hardwood floor. Surrounding them is a circle of pretty girls with Instagram-ready smiles, cheering them on like it's a sporting event.

On the other side of the room, the basketball team plays beer pong on top of the custom-designed pool table. I wince as a cup tips over, beer spilling dangerously close to the stainless-steel cable pockets. Hayes's father would have a coronary if he saw this.

I can't believe Hayes's parents are still gone. Especially Kora. She's always back from Greece by the time school starts.

I'm not allowed to call her Mrs. Vassilios—just Kora.

She's one of those effortlessly elegant, impossibly cool moms. A stunning, statuesque blonde, all sharp cheekbones and long, flowing limbs. Kora is like a supermodel who stepped off the runway and into real life. Her flawless skin looks ageless, like she could be 21 or 51, and she's always draped in the latest European fashions.

Yet, somehow, on top of all that beauty and wealth, she's also kind and unbelievably generous. The sort of person who remembers your favorite tea and stocks it in her cupboard just for you.

Hayes's mother has always been a steady presence in my life, like a second mother. When we were little, her chauffeur, Niccolò, would drive us all around town in her gleaming silver Rolls-Royce. Just Hayes, me, and Kora. She went everywhere with us. School carpool. Junior high dances. Karate classes.

She was the first to notice me lingering near Mr. Vassilios's horses, watching with silent longing whenever Hayes and I played outside near the paddocks. Without asking, she somehow knew what I secretly wanted and convinced her husband to let me ride Steopethe, their oldest, gentlest gelding.

From that very first time, I was hooked. I've been riding ever since.

Kora also single-handedly saved my eighth-grade graduation.

Our families were supposed to attend the cere-mony together, but everything fell apart when Mom showed up at Hayes's house in a tie-dyed caftan with neon tassels and wooden clogs. My mother has never blended in with the designer-clad moms of Laguna Hills—not like Kora, who wears crisp pantsuits to PTA meetings and tasteful cocktail dresses to school galas. Mom's tastes have always been more eccentric. Colored scarves. Long flowing skirts from bohemian thrift shops. Crochet clothing.

I'd been mortified.

I ran upstairs and hid in Hayes's closet, refusing to come out. These days, I try my best not to care what people think. But back then? I wanted to disappear.

Kora swooped in and worked her magic, convincing my mom to borrow one of her chic silk dresses and a pair of Chanel ballet flats, somehow without offending Mom or getting me grounded. Kora would've made a terrifyingly effective diplomat. She knows how to bend a situation to her will without anyone realizing she's the one pulling the strings.

My mother ended up loving the dress so much, Kora let her keep it. It's still hanging in her closet, reserved for special occasions.

A blast of cool air drags me back to the present as I step outside the sliding glass doors. Having no luck finding Hayes inside, I make my way toward the back-yard. LED lights in the Olympic-sized infinity pool pulse and shift colors in sync with the bass thumping from the outdoor speakers. The whole place is lit up with tiki torches and small clusters of fire pits are scat-tered across the lawn, their flames flickering against the night sky.

I pause for a moment, letting my eyes sweep over the space. Hayes's place has one of the best views in all of Laguna Hills. Rolling green hills on one side, and the Pacific Ocean on the other. If I squint hard enough, I can just make out where the dark sky meets the even darker sea. It's the kind of view that usually feels magical, but right now, it just feels like a distraction.

People I vaguely recognize from classes and Hayes's apartment complex hover around more kegs and the greasy pizza boxes piled high on the outdoor tables. I notice, with disgust, that all the pizzas are topped with revolting olives—Hayes's favorite. Because of course they are.

Unfortunately, none of the people stuffing their faces or the half-naked guys splashing around in the water are Hayes.

And he's not in the pool house either.

I bite back an annoyed grumble and retrace my steps, heading back inside. If he's not dominating at the pool table or flashing his abs in the hot tub, he must be in the kitchen, playing bartender. That's his other go-to move at parties.

On my way to the kitchen, I spot my sister.

It's exactly as I'd feared it would be. She's holding court on the main staircase. Her back is turned, but I'd know that mane of platinum-blonde hair anywhere, fluttering down her back as she tosses her head, laughing along with her friend Brooke. They're dressed almost identically—tiny, bright-colored skirts and low-cut tops. And standing right between them, like he belongs there, is Hayes.

My stomach dips.

Amber leans in, one manicured hand resting on his shoulder as she whispers something into his ear. Her body language is unmistakable. Smiling, flirty, far too close. She's clearly set her sights back on my best friend. And she'll get him too.

Amber always gets what she wants.

But that doesn't mean I have to stand around and watch it happen.

I spin toward the front door, head down, my dark hair falling forward like armor. If I can make it out of here without being seen, I'll count that as a win. I don't even care anymore about talking to Hayes about my mother, or if he thinks I bailed on his party. I just want out.

My hand is already on the doorknob, twisting, and then—

"Hey, Alligator! Get your ass over here!"

Shit.

I freeze.

Maybe if I move fast enough, I can still make it to my car and pretend I never heard him calling after me.

But before I can take another step, I feel a pair of arms wrap around my waist, and I'm lifted clean off the ground like I weigh nothing.

"Where you going?" Hayes asks, grinning as he sets me back down. "Didn't you hear me yelling your name?"

"Oh… hey," I say, my voice too bright, too fake. "Didn't realize that was you. How's the party?" I plaster on a smile. "You having fun?"

"I am now that you're here."

He gives me that look—the one that sends a

swarm of extremely unwelcome butterflies through my stomach.

"Now come on," he says, taking my hand and tugging me back inside. "Let's get you a drink."

He drops a cold beer in my hand and then steers me over to the staircase—right into enemy territory. Tiffany has now joined my sister and Brooke. Amber's friends glance at me with mild indifference, their polite nods just a step above lukewarm. Though I've never been close with them, they're cordial enough when we're forced to be around one another.

It's my sister I have to worry about.

"There you are, Ally!" Amber squeals in a saccharine-sweet voice that's as fake as her glued-on eyelashes. "I'm so glad you made it. Hayes said you might show up."

I muster up the phoniest smile I can manage. Two can play this game.

"Yep, here I am."

I wish her outsides were as messed up as her insides, but even I have to admit she looks unfairly gorgeous.

Her makeup is flawless, her shiny golden waves perfectly styled, and her outfit—while not my style— fits like it was made for her. The barely-there skirt and nude heels make her long, sun-kissed legs look incredible. Huge, fake pearls she insists are real to anyone who will listen sit in her earlobes to complete the look.

"I was just telling everyone how much I hoped you'd come. I've barely seen you all week," she says, all soft-eyed sincerity. She takes my hand in both of hers and gives it a gentle squeeze. "I've missed you."

Right.

What a load of crap.

Amber has been avoiding me just as much as I've been avoiding her, and we both know it. If she really wanted to see me, it wouldn't be hard. We share the same tiny apartment.

"I live right down the hall, Ambrosia."

Hayes chokes on a laugh.

Amber's expression darkens, just for a second, but she recovers quickly, brushing invisible lint off my shoulder like I'm the one who's ruffled.

"You're hilarious, Ally," she says with an exaggerated smile. "I just wanted to say, I really am sorry about Megara. You're such a great singer, but I can't help it if the director liked me better. What was I supposed to do? Not take the role?" She sighs softly, as if the whole thing has been so hard on her. "And besides, it's not like you told me how much you wanted it. You never tell me anything anymore. I didn't even know you were applying to NYU." She pauses, then adds one word sharp as a knife. "*Again.*"

I wince, the cut landing right where she wants it.

"Forget it," I say, all casual, biting back the reaction I know she's fishing for—a scream, a shove, something unhinged for her and her friends to laugh about. But I stay cool, giving her nothing. "I don't have time for a silly play anyway."

"You sure?" Hayes cuts in. "Because Ambs told me a role just opened up."

"Wait, really?" I step back. "I thought they were fully cast."

Amber nods eagerly, all glossy hair and confidence. "Someone dropped out last minute. It's not public yet, but I can put in a good word for you if you want."

I blink, genuinely surprised. "You'd really do that for me?"

"Of course I would. You're my sister, Ally."

For a second, I falter. She looks so genuine, I almost second-guess everything.

Maybe I've been too hard on her. Maybe she really didn't steal Megara just to spite me. Maybe—for once—Amber actually wants to help.

"What do you think?" Hayes offers a small smile, one of those careful, noncommittal ones that says he's watching this play out. "It'd look great on your NYU app. Could be the thing that gets you in."

"That's so sweet of you, Ambs," Tiffany says. "You're such a good sister."

"So good," Brooke echoes.

I know I should be grateful. Accept the offer. Say thank you. But all I can focus on is the way Amber shifts closer to Hayes, fingers trailing along his arm like they've done it a thousand times. She keeps glancing at me from the corner of her eye, like she's watching a game she already knows she's won. Measuring. Calculating.

And that's when I get it.

This isn't for me.

It never was.

This is all a well-timed gesture to polish her image, to look generous in front of Hayes and her friends. She's performing, tossing me crumbs just so she can shine. It all makes my stomach turn.

Or maybe that's just her nauseatingly sweet perfume.

"Thanks," I say. "But I'm going to pass."

Silence falls like a dropped glass.

"What?" Amber asks, blinking like I've just insulted her. "You don't want it?"

I flash a bright, fake smile. "Thanks for the offer, but I'm really focused on my songwriting right now. I can't afford any distractions."

"Seriously?"

Hayes stares at me like I've just gone totally insane.

Maybe I have.

Maybe it is crazy to turn this opportunity down, but I've got my pride. I don't need my little sister bailing me out with her backhanded charity. Or worse, using me as leverage in her relationship with Hayes.

"Good to see you guys, but I'm gonna head out," I say, handing the beer—still unopened—back to Hayes. "Catch you around!"

I'm halfway down the front steps, nearly to the driveway, when I hear footsteps pounding behind me. A hand clamps down on my shoulder and whirls me around.

"What the hell was that?" Hayes demands, eyes

blazing with twin violet-blue flames. "Why would you throw away your shot at NYU?"

The gas lamps lining the driveway cast a golden halo around him, making the white of his eyes seem impossibly bright. He looks almost unreal. Like something carved from myth and fury.

"I'm not throwing anything away. I just think the play's a dumb idea."

"Oh yeah?" His stare burns through me. "Since when?"

I cross my arms, jaw tight.

"Since now."

"You're a terrible liar. You know that, right?"

"I'm not—"

"Just tell me the truth, Al," he cuts me off angrily. "What's really going on."

I look away, fixating on the scuffed studs lining my motorcycle boots, doing anything I can to avoid those all-knowing eyes.

He means well. I know he does.

He *always* does.

But Hayes will never understand my life. He'll never know what it's like to always feel invisible. To feel like you never matter and never will. To always come in second place, constantly watching your little sister shine while you fade away into nothing.

And that's why he'll never get why I'd rather burn it all down—the play, NYU, my dreams—than take a damn handout from Amber. Especially if that handout brings them closer somehow, if it means I'm partly responsible for them getting back together.

Of course, I can't tell him any of this.

"She just… pisses me off, okay?"

I let out a long, frustrated sigh and yank open the car door, annoyed at myself for showing up tonight in the first place. I knew this was a mistake.

"I get it. I know you two aren't on great terms right now," he says carefully, "but can't you just try? I really think this is your ticket back in."

"Maybe I don't want back in."

"But Ambs is really trying to help. Can't you give her a chance?"

"I didn't ask for her help. Or yours," I say sharply. "So just stay out of it."

He groans, throwing his hands in the air.

"You're impossible, you know that? You've been torn up over this for days. I was fixing it for you."

"Well, maybe I don't need *fixing*!"

My chest burns hot with anger and embarrassment.

"That's not what I—"

"I'm not your pet project, Hayes!" I snap. "I am who I am, whether you like it or not. You don't get to mold me into whoever you think I should be."

"I wasn't—"

"You get everything," I cut in, the words tumbling out fast and ugly before I can stop them. "The money. The charm. The perfect family. The golden boy life. You win just by existing. Me?" I laugh, bitter and hollow. "I have nothing. No money. No dad. Probably no future. So forgive me, please, if I don't want your charity. Or *hers*."

The air between us goes still. His eyes flash with something raw—hurt, maybe frustration. Maybe both.

"That's not fair. You know I love you just the way you are." The anger drains from his face, replaced by something tender. Something more vulnerable. "I just…" He hesitates, eyes searching mine. "I want you to be happy, okay?"

"I am happy! So fucking drop it already!"

He jerks back, like I slapped him.

"Fine." His voice goes flat. "Got it. Sorry I bothered you."

He turns and walks away.

As I watch him retreat into the chaos of the party, regret and shame slam into me. Not slowly. Not gently. All at once. Sharp and immediate, like a punch to the ribs.

What the hell is wrong with me?

Hayes is the only one actually standing in my corner. The only one trying to help without wanting something in return. And I just treated him like he was the enemy.

Worse, I can already picture how this ends.

Hayes drifting back toward Amber because it's easy. Familiar. Safe. And me all alone, having pushed away the one person who never asked me to be anything other than myself.

"Hayes, wait—"

I rush after him, weaving through the crowd, my pulse racing. I just need to find him. Apologize. It's not his fault my sister makes me feel like I'm nothing, or that I might care about him in ways I shouldn't.

But when I finally see him again, he's already with Amber. Their fingers are laced together as they head up the stairs toward his bedroom. A door slams shut on the second floor, and my stomach hollows out painfully.

I stand there for a few moments, motionless, still watching the space where they disappeared. I know exactly what it means.

It's time for me to go.

On the way out, I cut through the kitchen, grabbing a bottle of water and a piece of Greek baklava for stress-eating. God bless Kora. She always makes sure her kitchen is stocked with everything I'm not allowed at home—sugar, gluten, all the good stuff. And she insists Dimitra keep a fresh tray of baklava ready for me at all times, just in case I get a craving.

I sink my teeth into the sweet pastry, letting the honeyed walnuts melt on my tongue. The first bite is warm and safe. It doesn't fix everything, but for a moment, it dulls the sting. Even from halfway across the world, Kora still manages to take care of me.

Pulling out my phone, I type a quick text to Hayes.

> I suck. Forgive me? 😅 🖤

I add a smiley face and a black heart, then stare at the screen while I chew, willing him to respond. But the message stays unread.

A sick feeling of dread crashes over me.

What if this was the last straw?

What if Hayes is finally done with me this time?

"Why so serious, Alysander?" Dylan slurs, stumbling up behind me. His hand brushes the back of my stool, just a little too close to my neck. He's clearly shit-faced, but at least he got my name right this time.

"Oh... hey, Dylan."

"Here," he says, handing me a red Solo cup and then dropping into the stool beside me. "This'll cheer you up."

"I'm driving. I really shouldn't—"

"Less talking. More drinking."

He grins and lifts a half-empty bottle of Kora's favorite wine, pouring generously into my cup, some of it sloshing onto the marble floor.

I stare at my drink for a moment, contemplating. The night has already gone to hell. Maybe a drink is exactly what I need. A little wine. A lot of water. Worst case, I'll Uber home and come back for my car tomorrow.

"Okay, sure." I shrug. "Why not?"

The mandarin and caramel notes flood my mouth as I take my first sip. Smooth. Dangerously sweet.

One cup turns into two. Two into three.

And then... I stop thinking altogether.

I forget Hayes is upstairs with Amber. I forget NYU. I forget the crazy letters to my father buried in the back of my mother's closet. I forget everything except the sharp, sweet rush of distraction.

Soon, everything becomes lovely and amazing.

Even Dylan.

I never liked him much before, but maybe I misjudged him. He's more charming than I remembered. Handsome, too. I feel weightless and light and happy as I laugh at all his jokes.

The rest of the night unspools in fragments.

Music.

Spinning lights.

Dylan's hand on my back—

And then nothing.

CHAPTER 8

Hours later, I wake in bed in an eerily quiet, dark room.

Well, quiet, except for the pounding in my skull.

Sports trophies and gleaming medals line the shelves of the matching oakwood desk and dresser across the room. Football and basketball championships. National archery titles. Fencing awards. Far more accolades than I can count. On the wall in front of me, a 90-inch flat screen is mounted. Beneath it, the latest gaming console and every video game money can buy.

Draped over windows are thick burgundy curtains that blot out the moonlight. A matching duvet and black sheets, silky and soft, drape over my body, woven from the finest Egyptian cotton. Everything here is effortlessly luxe. Perfectly curated. I've seen it all so many times before. I know exactly where I am.

Hayes's room.

Hayes's *bed*, technically.

I bolt upright, and a flash of pain slices through my skull.

"Shit, that hurts," I croak, one hand flying to my temples. My head feels like it's been dropped into a blender and set to purée.

Then—

Laughter. Low and familiar.

"Hayes? Is that you?"

More laughter.

Then… *snoring?*

I scramble to my feet, dragging half the comforter with me. Panic spikes as my mind spins through every worst-case scenario.

Did I somehow become an unconscious bystander in a tryst between Hayes and one of his countless female admirers and end up in the middle of a threesome?

Then, an even more alarming thought.

Please, please, please don't let it be Amber.

If I've just spent the night in the same bed as Hayes and my sister, I will literally launch myself right out of his second-story window.

"Who's in here?" I grit out.

"Relax, Sleeping Beauty. It's just us… and the dog."

My eyes adjust to the dark—and there he is. Hayes, smirking on the far side of the bed. He pulls back the covers to reveal the dog underneath, fast asleep, curled up like a baby and tucked snugly into Hayes's side.

Correction.

Tucked snugly into Hayes's shirtless, glorious, carved-from-freaking-marble side.

I swallow hard, watching as his chest rises in slow rhythm. Each breath traces the hard lines of his abs and the sharp, sinful V of muscle that disappears into low-slung pajama bottoms. My thoughts short-circuit and it takes everything in me to drag my gaze away.

"Uh… what am I doing in your bed?" I ask, blinking through my temporary, lust-induced haze. "Wait—what are you doing here?"

"Where else would I be? It's *my* room, genius." He chuckles, wrapping warm fingers around my wrist, and tugging—effortless, commanding—until I'm pulled right back down into the bed again. "Now shut up and go back to sleep."

His leg brushes mine under the covers and heat skims up my thigh. I freeze, nerves sparking to life, every cell in my body on high alert.

What the hell am I doing sleeping in my best friend's bed?

Should I leave?

I should leave, right?

But his sheets are so warm. His pillows so damn soft. And he smells so freaking good, like clean skin and the faintest hint of that addictive cedar scent I swear is designed to ruin me…

I let myself sink deeper into the mattress. We're so close I can feel the heat of his body, his presence melting the last of my resistance. It's late, I'm still drunk, and I'm so, so tired.

"Right… your room…" I mumble, settling into the silken bedding. "It's just—weren't you with Amber earlier? I thought I saw you guys heading upstairs."

He rolls over to face the wall.

"She wanted to use the bathroom so I let her. Then I kicked her out and crashed," he says, his voice muffled in the pillow. "Any other burning questions, Nancy Drew? Or can I go back to sleep now?"

Relief crashes over me like a wave. I exhale all at once, the tension draining from my limbs. I can't believe it. Nothing happened with my sister.

Or with anyone else tonight, from the look of things.

It's surprising, to say the least. Hayes doesn't exactly go to bed alone after these parties, and Amber's not the only one who's been circling.

Not that he's a player or anything.

Just… well. He's Hayden Vassilios. Stupidly hot. Effortlessly charming. He walks into a room and every girl looks up. Hell, most of the guys do too. He could have anyone he wants. So if he wasn't busy hooking up with my sister or anyone else, then—

I shoot upright again, heart suddenly racing again.

"Uh… we didn't, um…" I fumble, my words getting tied up in my dry throat. "Did we?"

He groans again, rolling halfway back toward me. "Did we what?"

The last few hours are a total blur. My head throbs. My mouth tastes like regret. I glance down— and freeze.

I'm not wearing my jeans anymore. All I've got on is just my underwear and the black velvet corset I wore to the party.

Did I kick them off in my sleep? Or… did someone take them off?

Alarm ripples through me.

I'm in Hayes's bed. He's half-naked. I'm half-naked. And I have no memory of how I got here.

Please, God, tell me I didn't do something humiliating. Or stupid. Or irreversible.

"You know..." My face is hot with embarrassment. "Hook up?"

He blinks. And then—bursts out laughing. Full-body, bed-shaking, asshole laughter.

"What?" he chokes out. "Are you serious right now?"

"I'm in your bed," I say, gesturing helplessly between us. "And you're shirtless! And—I seem to be missing pants?"

"Nothing happened, you lunatic." He snorts. "You pulled your jeans off yourself, climbed into my bed, and passed out like a toddler."

I drop my head back onto the pillow.

"Oh, thank God."

There's a pause.

Then, almost too quiet to hear, he asks, "Why? Did you want to?"

I freeze.

"Want to *what?*"

"You know... hook up?"

He laughs low and deep against the pillow, but there's something unreadable in his eyes when he glances over at me again. Something that doesn't feel like a joke at all.

My heart does this weird little flip in my chest. I mean... he's definitely joking.

Right?

"No, you idiot," I shoot back, trying to sound nonchalant. "I'm just shocked you didn't spend the night with Amber. Or some sorority girl with fake hair extensions and a spray tan."

His grin fades.

"Is that really what you think of me?" he asks, quieter now. "That I just hook up with whoever's in front of me?"

He doesn't sound angry—not exactly—more hurt. Now that I think about it, it was kind of a rude way to phrase it.

"I didn't mean it like that," I say quickly. "I just meant… you're a guy. A good-looking guy. And we're in college, and that's what good-looking guys do in college." I tug at the edge of the blanket. "I guess I was just surprised. That's all."

There. That sounds slightly more diplomatic and way less like I just called my best friend a manwhore.

He lets the silence stretch.

"So…" His mouth curves into a slow, smug grin. "You think I'm good-looking?"

I smack him under the covers.

"Oh, shut up."

The sheets rustle faintly as he shifts underneath, moving just a little closer to me. It's nothing, really, barely a movement, but suddenly the space between us feels smaller, tighter. Something in me stirs, sharp and wanting.

But then, a flash of memory—hours ago, me riffling through my mother's things—and a weight slams into my chest. An awful, gnawing twist of worry hits as I remember why I came to Hayes's party in the first place.

"Listen, Hay. I need to tell you something." I pause, forcing myself to breathe normally. "It's about my mom."

That gets his attention.

"What is it?" He glances over, his eyes wide open and alert. "Is Mel okay?"

The concern in his voice is so immediate, so genuine, it makes my chest ache. He's such a good friend to me, and he's always been especially fond of my mother. He knows what she means to me. How she's all I've ever had.

"I found something tonight. Something she's been hiding from me." I fiddle anxiously with the soft edges of the duvet. "Brace yourself, okay? It's really… weird."

He arches a brow. "Weirder than usual?"

Despite my nerves, my lips twitch with faint amusement. It's a perfectly fair question where my mother is concerned.

Hayes has witnessed more than his share of my mom's most unhinged moments, like the time she burned sage in the school parking lot to "cleanse my academic aura." Or when she insisted we all wear crystal amulets during flu season. And who could forget the Thanksgiving she canceled entirely because Mercury was in retrograde and she was convinced the day was cosmically doomed? We ended up eating peanut butter and jelly sandwiches in separate bedrooms, and I watched *The Nightmare Before Christmas* alone.

"I… I don't even know where to start." My throat tightens as I think about her letters to my father again. "I don't know what it all means."

"Alligator, relax," he says, gentler now. "Whatever it is, we'll figure it out together."

I open my mouth to respond, then freeze as a wave of sudden nausea slams into me, violent and powerful. My entire body lurches as baklava and wine start coming up.

"Oh God," I whisper, hand flying to my mouth. "I think I'm gonna be sick."

I bolt out of his bed and race to the bathroom, barely managing to slam the door in time. My stomach revolts as I collapse over the toilet, everything I foolishly consumed the last few hours erupting in waves.

I retch so hard, so thoroughly, my ribs scream in pain. It feels like I'm being turned inside out. For a moment, I think I might actually die.

Finally, mercifully, it ends.

I slump back, shaking, palms braced on the edge of the seat as Hayes's fancy Japanese toilet flushes automatically. A soft whir fills the room and the bowl cleans itself, like it's erasing every trace of my bad decisions. I wipe my mouth, watching my insides disappear without ever having to lift a hand.

Imagine… being so rich, your toilet flushes itself.

Once my wobbly legs are ready to cooperate again, I stand and rinse my mouth with the mouthwash Hayes keeps under the sink and splash cold water on my face.

Hayes's eyes are already closed when I crawl back into bed. He looks fast asleep—or at least pretending to be.

I reach for my phone on his nightstand and nearly have a heart attack when I see the time.

3:02 a.m.

Well… that's not good.

My mom is going to lose it.

Even though I'm nearly eighteen and already in college, she still worries about me like I'm made of glass. Like I might shatter if she looks away for too long.

In high school, I had a midnight curfew, even senior year. The one time I forgot to text her that I was crashing at Hayes's house in one of the spare bedrooms, she nearly called the police to report me missing.

I was an hour late.

Not a day. Not one week. One hour.

She grounded me for a month. Even Amber said she was being insane, and Amber never agrees with me. But once my mom's fear locks in, there's no reasoning with it. Safety and control are everything to her.

For years, I told myself I understood. I made excuses for her, rationalizing that trauma does that to people. My father walking out had to leave scars, and I figured this was just one of them. An overcorrection.

A mother clinging too tightly because she'd already lost too much.

But now I know better.

Of course, she panicked.

In her mind, when I break curfew, I'm not just out a little too late. I've been taken. Dragged somewhere dark and unforgiving, somewhere no one comes back from. Monsters. Gods. The Underworld itself.

I check my messages, bracing for nuclear fallout. Instead, I find something I never expected—an extremely civilized exchange from 11:30 p.m.:

> Hey Mel. Al fell asleep here. I'll take care of her. Don't worry. —H

> Thanks, hon. She's lucky to have you. Sleep tight!

I blink at the screen.

My best friend is a goddamn angel. Even after I'd been a total asshole to him earlier, he still had my back, still thought to cover for me.

"Thanks for texting my mom, Hay," I whisper, setting the phone back down on the nightstand. "You're the best."

He opens one sleepy eye and grins.

"I am, aren't I?" he says, eyes drifting lower. "Also, you might want to move that wine bottle before you kick it and break a toe."

I glance down.

Sure enough, there's an empty bottle of his mom's

fancy Greek wine tucked near my ankles. The glass is cool as I grab it, groaning under my breath.

"Shit. Did I seriously drink this whole thing?"

"No idea," he says with a massive yawn. "When I found you half-comatose on the couch downstairs, you were singing to the dog, asking if he wanted to share."

My cheeks burn with embarrassment.

"I did not!"

"You kept calling him Argyros."

"Argyros? What's that?"

He plucks the bottle from my hand and taps the beautiful gold-foiled label: *Vinsanto Santorini Argyros.*

"Ah." I grin. "Actually, that's kind of perfect. Regal. Let's call him that." Then, a little breathless, I add, "Wait… if I was downstairs, how did I get here?"

He flashes a slow, wicked grin, equal parts mischief and smug delight.

"I carried you."

The air leaves my lungs.

"You *carried* me?"

As in… all six feet plus of quarterback muscle scooped me up like some rom-com fever dream? Did I really hear that right?

"Of course," he says, as if it's obvious. "You passed out two seconds after you finished serenading the dog. Couldn't leave you there alone, all adorable and defenseless."

My body lights up, a quick, involuntary rush sparking through me as I imagine his arms around me. Did he look at me tenderly? Brush the hair from my face as he gently laid me down on his bed, tucking me into his impossibly soft sheets?

Goddamn.

Why couldn't I have been awake for *that*?

"Hay—"

But he's already asleep again, breathing slow and steady.

Meanwhile, I'm lying here wide awake now, heart thundering, skin buzzing. He's so close. One shift, one breath, and our bodies would be touching.

How am I supposed to sleep like this?

It's hard to believe that once upon a time, lying in bed next to Hayes felt completely normal. Natural. But it did.

When we were little kids, Kora used to make us popcorn and sweet treats while we watched spooky cartoons in Hayes's bedroom. We'd stay up late in our matching Scooby-Doo pajamas—mine had Velma and ghost footprints, his had Shaggy with glow-in-the-dark eyes. After the show, we'd curl up together, a tangle of blankets and sugar, as Kora quietly tucked us in for the night.

But that was years ago. We haven't shared a bed since sixth grade. Now, lying beside him again, everything feels different. Charged. Electric. Like the air between us has been rewired.

I keep sneaking glances at him, unable to help myself. He's fast asleep, but somehow still impossibly gorgeous. His lashes rest dark and thick against his cheekbones, lips parted just slightly. There's a softness to him like this—unguarded, peaceful—but also something dangerous, something magnetic. He looks like some dark fairy-tale prince. Beautiful but forbidden.

I wonder—what would happen if I reached out and touched him? Just one fingertip brushing that soft lock of hair off his forehead?

Would he stir? Would he lean into me? Would he—

Suddenly, he rolls toward me, his arm snaking around my waist in one sleepy, unthinking motion. His grip is warm, strong. Possessive. Like he's claiming me in his dreams without even realizing it.

He exhales softly, nuzzling into the curve of my neck, and I nearly detonate on the spot.

Oh. My. God.

I suck in a sharp breath, every inch of me frozen.

Does he know what he's doing?

Should I move?

If Amber walked in and saw us like this, she'd murder me on the spot.

I should move. I should absolutely move.

Except… I don't want to.

I don't want to do anything ever again except lie here in Hayes's bed, in his arms, forever.

My brain turns to mush. All I can think about is the way his fingers flex against my hip, the way my body is buzzing so hard I feel like I'm lit up from the inside. And I know there's no hope of me falling asleep now. Not like this. Not with this much of him touching this much of me. Not when every heartbeat feels like it's screaming his name.

Sometime just before dawn, he shifts again and rolls away. His arms fall slack, and the heat between us fades as space creeps in, cool and quiet.

Only then do I let myself exhale.

Heart slowing. Limbs uncoiling. My eyelids drift shut and somewhere in that hazy space between waking and dreaming, it hits me—

I never told him about the letters.

CHAPTER 9

The next morning, I wake to the soft snoring of Argyros curled at the foot of the bed. My skull feels like it's stuck between two warring nations, every throb a cannon blast. Pure agony. My throat is dry and raw, but the thought of leaving Hayes's bed for water—let alone trekking to the kitchen—feels like a Herculean task.

I burrow deeper under the silky sheets, shutting my eyes against the sliver of daylight sneaking past the thick blackout curtains.

Seriously, what kind of idiot goes shot-for-shot with a football player?

Me, that's who.

Fragments of last night stitch together in my mind, bright and disjointed flashes like fireworks.

Baklava.

Dylan.

Too much wine.

Shots with Dylan.

More wine.

And, oh yeah, somehow winding up in my best friend's bed without my pants.

My skin heats at the memory of a half-naked Hayes lying beside me. The rise and fall of his muscular chest. The easy weight of his arm around my waist, as if it belonged there. His cool breath on my neck. The way my heart slammed against my ribs from being so close to him.

But then I shove the memory aside, pushing the covers back and quickly yanking my hair into a makeshift ponytail. Thinking about Hayes that way… it's dangerous, for so, so many reasons.

I take a peek to my left to see if he's still asleep, but the space next to me is already empty.

Oh.

My stomach lurches in protest as I sit up too fast. I curl forward, arms wrapped around my midsection. It feels like an alien is trapped inside, clawing its way out through my intestines.

Last Halloween, Hayes thought it would be fun to have an *Alien* movie marathon. Neither of us had ever seen the early ones from the '80s.

I'll never forget watching the chestburster scene for the first time. I'd jumped about ten feet in the air when the alien exploded from a man's body, killing him in a bloody, gory massacre. Hayes, however, had laughed his ass off.

After the movies, I stayed for dinner. Right before dessert, Hayes started choking and gasping and then fell over backward across the dining room table like he was having a seizure. Then his chest erupted, a fountain of blood squirting everywhere.

His shirt.

The dinner table.

My face.

I nearly had a heart attack until I realized it was ketchup, not blood. The whole thing had been an elaborate prank. Hayes could be a real bastard when he wanted to. Suffice it to say, neither I nor his parents were amused.

After I recovered from wanting to kill him, I had to give him credit. It was kind of brilliant, though I still feel queasy every time I think about that dinner.

With great difficulty, I maneuver myself into a sitting position in Hayes's bed. My stomach makes a series of desperate, gurgling sounds. I'd better get up —and soon—before I throw up again, this time all over Hayes's expensive 800-thread-count sheets. Then he'd really regret having me spend the night. No way my pretty, polished little sister wakes up puking in bed.

I clutch my belly, rocking in place as I scan the room with blurry eyes. Both Hayes's car keys and the black *LHU Football* gym bag he keeps by his closet are gone.

Then I remember—it's Sunday. Practice day.

That means film review, rehab, light conditioning. Hayes never misses a Sunday team session, no matter how wrecked he might be from the weekend.

I shuffle into his bathroom with Argyros faithfully on my heels. The dog waits beside me while I empty what's left of last night into the toilet. Afterward, I flop around on the cold marble floor dramatically.

"I think I'm dying," I croak to the dog.

Argyros edges closer and licks my hands, then my cheeks, trying to comfort me while Hayes's fancy toilet flushes itself. I bury my face in the soft fur of his backside, moaning pathetically but too hungover to care.

I lie there for a good twenty minutes, clinging to

the dog like he's my life raft. Only when the nausea finally eases do I inch toward the sink like a zombie, splash cold water on my face, and rinse my mouth with minty mouthwash. Then I drink greedily from the faucet with cupped hands.

All I want is to crawl back into Hayes's bed and stay there, but that's not an option. I've got work to do, and the clock is ticking. Since I—definitely fool-ishly—turned down Amber's offer of help last night, I have to figure this NYU thing out on my own.

The play would've been helpful, but it isn't the only way to prove I'm worthy of admission. There's YouTube. TikTok. Spotify. Plenty of ways to showcase my music, if I'm willing to put myself out there. If I want to be taken seriously as an artist, I need to start acting like one. Real artists create. They take risks. They get rejected and then keep going.

And I need to talk to my mother, too.

Before I can fully commit to the idea of New York next year, I need to know what those letters to my father meant. If something snapped inside her after he left, I have to understand. I can't just pack up and move to the other side of the country without knowing what happened and if she'll be okay.

As I head out of Hayes's bedroom, I grab my jeans from a crumpled pile in the corner and pull them on, still mildly embarrassed I stripped them off in my drunken state even if I have no memory of it. Then I stop at Hayes's closet and grab an oversized hoodie that reads "Laguna Hills University Chimeras, Feel the Roar" in bold gold lamé. The school mascot—a snarling fusion of lion, goat, and serpent—stretches across the chest, ferocious. I slip the sweatshirt over my wrinkled top and push my hands into the sleeves, welcoming the warmth.

Argyros whines, tail low, giving me the saddest eyes imaginable when I get to the garage door. I try to say goodbye but he's not having it, so I decide to bring him home with me instead. He's just so darn cute. How could I not?

I figure I can sneak him into the apartment for a few hours while I work. With any luck, I can get him back to Hayes's place later this afternoon, before Mom or Amber show up. Amber's high school homecoming dance is coming up soon, which means she'll be working late, hustling for extra money to buy a new dress. No way my sister would be caught wearing the same thing twice.

As soon as I get home, I pop two Extra Strength Tylenol and down a bottle of Gatorade. Then I faceplant onto my futon, dragging the covers up to my chest.

I'd planned to use the quiet today to brainstorm material for my transfer application, but I still feel like roadkill. I tell myself I'll just rest for a bit—close my eyes, let the meds kick in—and work once I feel human again. NYU can wait a few more hours.

Argyros hops into bed beside me, curling into my side like a living furnace. He presses his warm snout to my stomach and immediately drifts off, snoring softly. I watch him twitch and yip in his sleep for a while, then shut my eyes, willing myself to do the same.

But sleep won't come.

Sunlight slices through the uncovered casement windows, searing straight through the midnight-blue sheets I've pulled over my head. What I wouldn't give for Hayes's blackout curtains. And—fine—maybe his warm body too.

I shake the thought loose before it spirals. That's another thing I need to get a handle on: no more sexy-time fantasies about Hayes.

Frustrated, I kick the covers off and grab my laptop. If I can't sleep, maybe some background noise will help.

I scroll through Netflix until I land on *Glee*. I find the flash-forward episode—the one where Rachel's finally made it to Broadway. It's my favorite. I've seen it at least a dozen times, and it always gets me. If only that were me…

Hours later, a loud knock jolts me awake.

"Alysander?"

My mother's voice drifts in from the hallway. I throw off the covers and squint toward the windows. The sun has vanished, leaving my bedroom cloaked in darkness except for the faint blue glow of my laptop's sleep screen.

Damn. I must've dozed off during the show and slept through the entire day.

"Honey?" The doorknob jiggles. "You in there?"

Beside me, Argyros stretches and yawns. I glance at him, my stomach sinking. So much for driving the dog home before anyone found out he'd been here. My mother is definitely not going to be happy about this.

Oh well.

Too late to do anything now. It's not like I can hide a hundred-pound wolf-dog in my bedroom the size of a broom closet.

"Come in," I say, bracing myself.

My mom steps inside, her eyes immediately narrowing at the sight of Argyros.

"Alysander Sage Smith!" Her mouth tightens into a frown. "What is that animal doing here?"

"Uh, what animal?" I deadpan, tugging the sheet over Argyros's head.

He paws it off, giving me a deeply unimpressed look.

"What part of *no dogs in my house* did you not understand?"

She tugs at the end of her long blonde fishtail braid, lips tight, like she's doing everything she can not to fully explode on me. Even riled up, she's still beautiful.

In her flowy cotton boho dress and glitter Birkenstocks, she looks more like Amber's older sister than someone's mom. Total flower-child vibes—the opposite of my gothy-punk aesthetic—but over time, I've come to respect it. At least she's true to herself. Comfortable in her own skin, no matter who's watching.

"Sorry. I fell asleep," I mutter. "I was going to take him back before you got home. I swear."

"And that's supposed to make me feel better?"

"Mom, come on." I push up onto my elbows. "This whole thing is ridiculous. I'm almost eighteen. I can smoke. I can vote. Hell, I can be drafted into war. I can have my own dog," I say. "If it's a money thing, I'll get a job. I'll cover everything myself."

"It's not about the money!"

Her voice falters, just for a second, and I know I've hit a nerve. Mom has always been sensitive about finances. Being a struggling single parent in our affluent town can't be easy.

Still, I've always assumed that cost was the reason why she'd resisted having a pet for so long. One more mouth to feed. But if it's not that...

"Then what is it about?"

She hesitates. "I just... don't need the extra responsibility."

"I already said *I'd* take care of him."

She sighs and crosses the room, easing down on the edge of my bed, careful to keep her distance from Argyros.

"And what about next year? You can't bring a dog with you to New York."

I roll my eyes.

"Pretty sure they allow dogs in Manhattan, Mom."

"Not in the NYU dorms they don't." Her face softens then, and she gives me a hopeful look. "But... if you stayed local. Laguna Hills University has a wonderful music program, you know. And we're so close to LA—lots of great opportunities to get involved with the arts here. If you stayed, *maybe* I'd reconsider the dog."

A familiar pang of sadness—of guilt—hits, low and sharp. There's a part of me that still feels like her little kid, not her grown daughter. New York is far, and it's not like we have the money for regular flights back and forth. I won't be able to come home often to see her. If I get into NYU, we'll go from seeing each other every day to just a few weeks a year, during school breaks. I know it will hurt her when I leave. It will hurt me too. But I can't let that be the reason I give up on my dreams.

"Mom, we've talked about this," I say gently, reaching for her hand. "If I'm going to do theater seriously, I have to go where the industry is. That's New York City."

Her fingers stiffen, then slip from mine.

"Fine," she says. "Go, then. But I'm not taking care of your ridiculous dog after you abandon us."

I groan. "You make it sound like I'm leaving forever. I'll be home for holidays. And summers," I say. "We'll FaceTime every day. I promise."

She blinks at me, eyes glistening.

"You're my baby. The thought of you so far away, in a place where I can't protect you—"

And there it is. The tears.

"Mom, please don't cry—"

"I just worry about you," she says, dabbing her nose with the oversized, fluffy sleeve of her dress. "There are dangers everywhere, Alysander. You can't see them like I can. You don't know what's *really* out there…"

I bite back a sigh.

Here we go again.

Of course, in her mind, this isn't just about normal mother-daughter safety concerns like getting mugged on the big-city streets or lost on the subway. No, she thinks I'll be abducted by Underworld shadow people on my way to class or chased through Central Park by demon hellhounds.

"It's New York. Not the Black Forest," I mutter. "Besides, it's not like I've gotten in yet."

"You will."

She says it firmly, like my fate's already sealed.

"You don't know that," I say, picking at some loose threads on my bedspread. "The competition's brutal. I've got good grades, but no résumé."

"You've got chorus."

"High school chorus," I say flatly. "What if I'm just… not good enough?"

She takes my hand, gripping it tightly.

"You're special, baby. More special than you realize." Her tone shifts, her eyes going glassy and wide. There's a hint of something, almost manic, in the way she's looking at me. My stomach knots, and suddenly, I'm thinking about the letters again.

"Mom… I need to ask you something." I lick my dry lips. "But you have to promise you won't get mad."

"Why would I get mad?"

"I just… don't think you're going to like it."

My shoulders stiffen, tension pulling tight across my chest. She's already on edge—about NYU, the dog, me leaving. And now I'm about to tell her I went through her private things. That I found intimate letters between her and my father that she never meant for me to see.

But it's more than that.

I'm scared of what she'll actually say about the letters when I ask. Scared I'm not ready to hear the truth. What if my mom isn't just quirky and spiritual and maybe a little too obsessed with her weird fairy tale stories, like I've always told myself? What if she's actually… unwell?

"You're making me nervous, Alysander. What is it?"

My fingers drift to my cuticles, picking at the skin. I wish I had one of her magical crystals—Tiger's Eye, maybe, for courage. I don't believe in any of it, but right now, I'd take anything that might help.

"First off, I didn't mean for this to happen," I begin. "But you didn't fill out the parent portion of my NYU application like you promised, so I figured I'd do it myself. I couldn't remember your college information—if you even graduated, or what year— so I went into your room…" I swallow hard. "Into the files in your closet—"

"Alysander!"

"I know, I know. I'm sorry." I lift my hands slightly, a small gesture of apology. "I was only looking for your college records, I swear. But then I found a folder tucked in the back of the box… the one labeled 'S'."

Her expression shifts—tightens. It's obvious she knows exactly what folder I'm talking about.

"I shouldn't have looked, I know that. But he's my father," I continue. "I read what you wrote in those letters. About gods. And monsters. The Underworld. You don't really believe all of that... do you?"

She draws back, her fingers drifting to the third eye pendant at her throat, the gold one with the blue stone at its center. The one that's supposed to ward off darkness.

"Oh, Alysander..." Her eyes glisten, but she doesn't look away. "This isn't how I wanted you to find out."

"Find out what?"

A wistful smile tugs at her lips. "You have his eyes, you know."

I'd suspected as much after seeing his photo but hearing her say it cracks something open in my chest. I wonder what it's been like for her—to look into my eyes every day and see his. To be reminded of the man who left.

Does it hurt her? Does it make her sad when she looks at me?

God, I hope not.

"You're right. It's time you knew the truth," she says.

Her eyes lock on mine with the eerie calm of someone about to detonate a bomb, and I brace myself for the implosion. Whatever she's been hiding, it must be bad. Really bad. Because what kind of man walks away from a woman like my mom? From two baby girls?

"Why did he really leave us?" I ask, heart thudding in my chest. "Was it drugs? Alcohol? An affair?"

"Oh no. Nothing like that." Her throat bobs as she swallows hard. "Your father was—*is*—the most amazing man I've ever known. We were happy. But he isn't like everyone else. He's… different."

"Different how?"

She leans in, voice dropping. "Your father's a Titan."

My skin prickles uneasily.

"A *what*?"

"A Titan," she repeats. "They're an ancient race of god-like beings who existed before the Olympians. You've heard of the Olympian gods, yes?"

"Like… from Greek mythology?"

"Exactly." She nods, looking pleased. "Many years ago, there was a great war between the Titans and the Olympians. The Olympians won, and your father— Sonar—was imprisoned in the Underworld by Zeus and his brothers Hades and Poseidon. But he escaped. Came here. Fell in love with a human woman… *Me*." She presses a hand to her heart. "And we had two daughters together."

I stare at her, willing the words to stop, a slow pressure building behind my ribs.

This cannot be happening…

"I was pregnant with your sister when they found out he'd escaped," she says. "Zeus sent the Watchers —Olympian guards—to drag your father back. He was terrified. Not for himself, but for us. Children with a mortal woman are forbidden, and he was afraid of what they'd do if they ever found out about you and your sister. He said he had to go, that he'd come back when it was safe."

Her voice catches, and a single tear slips down her cheek.

"I—I never saw him again." She draws a shaky breath. "But he was right. The danger, I'm afraid, is very real. It's why I've been so protective, so scared for you all these years."

My head spins as she finishes her story. I can't believe it; she's not denying any of it.

Crystals and aura paintings are one thing. Weird, sure, but harmless. Kooky. Eccentric. Something embarrassing to whine to Hayes about.

But this?

This is the kind of thing people get strapped into straitjackets for. The kind of thing that gets you committed.

"Mom… you know this isn't real, right? Titans? Olympians? They don't exist."

"Of course they do. Have you not been listening to me all these years?" She stiffens. "The tourmaline bracelets? The protection pouches? What did you think it was all for?"

"Those were just stories," I say, my voice faltering. "Silly little fairytales."

"I can assure you, Alysander, it's all as real as you and me."

I can only stare at her, stunned into silence.

My mother has held down a steady job, paid bills, raised two kids on her own. She functions in society, mostly. Yet all this time, she's genuinely believed she had children with a god from another realm. And somehow she's looking at me like I'm the one who's out of touch with reality.

"Mom... have you ever thought about talking to someone about this?" I ask gently.

"You mean a therapist?" She scoffs. "What for? So someone can tell me I'm crazy when I already know I'm not?"

I rub my temples, my headache from earlier returning with a fury.

"I really think it could help. I could even come with you," I offer.

"Alysander, I'm your mother. Please don't speak to me like I'm a child," she says, her tone clipped. "I know this is hard to hear. But you're half Titan— born of a god—whether you believe it or not. My only regret is not telling you sooner. Keeping it in has been eating me alive."

"Then why did you?"

"You wouldn't remember, but when you were little, you told me you were going to find your father and bring him home. You were five or six, but you were so sure. I panicked. I told you just enough to calm you down." Her jaw tightens, the movement sharp. "But the next day, you told your teacher, and the principal called me in. Asked if I was using drugs. I thought they'd take you away." She sniffles once, quick and fierce. "After that, I kept it all to myself."

I grab a tissue from my nightstand and hand it to her.

"Thanks, honey," she murmurs, dabbing at her eyes. "It's not easy being a single mom, being cut off by my own parents. No safety net. No support. No money for lawyers if anything went wrong. Keeping the truth buried felt like the safest option. I had to protect you and your sister. No matter what."

"Oh, Mom," I whisper, my throat tightening. "I'm so sorry."

I wrap my arms around her, pulling her in for a hug. She's been through so much. Whatever the truth is—whatever she's created to fill in the gaps—I don't doubt her love for me or Amber. Not for a second. Every overprotective impulse, every strange warning or superstition, it all comes from a place of fierce devotion.

As much as her misplaced belief in some crazy mythical delusion worries me, part of me understands why she clings to it. It's far less painful to believe my father left to protect our family than to admit the truth—he just didn't want to stay.

"I love you so much, baby," she murmurs. "I wish he could see the woman you've become. He'd be so proud."

"Uh huh… sure," I say, patting her hand noncommittally. The sentiment is sweet, but I'm not about to validate her fantasy. "Maybe we don't tell Amber about this just yet? Can it stay between us for now?"

Telling Amber would be like tossing a match into a powder keg. She'd lose her goddamn mind. Between college and everything else going on, I can only handle one unhinged family member at a time.

"Of course, honey." She nods, brushing away the last of her tears, then perks up with fragile optimism. "On the bright side, since you're half Titan, you can go to the Underworld someday."

I force a smile.

"Great, Mom. That sounds… really lovely."

But she's already gone, lost to a hope that sparks wildly in her eyes.

"Maybe enough time has passed. Maybe it's safe now for him to come home." She leans in, her voice trembling with fierce conviction. "And you're the one, Alysander. I just know it. You can bring him back to us. Just like you always said you would."

CHAPTER 10

By the time my mother finally leaves my room, it's already after 9 p.m. I'm more unsettled than ever and completely drained. All I want to do is crawl under the covers and pretend our crazy conversation never happened, but she insists I return Argyros to Hayes. Tonight. Which would be a whole lot easier if I knew where Hayes was.

Unfortunately, he isn't answering his phone.

I grab my car keys and head out, deciding to check his parents' place first. Worst case, Dimitra will be there and can keep an eye on Argyros until Hayes turns up.

On the drive over, I call him again. Still straight to voicemail, which is beyond weird. Unlike my mom with her electromagnetic interference paranoia, Hayes never turns off his phone. The guy practically has a panic attack if his battery dips below fifty percent.

So where the hell is he?

When I pull up to his parents' house, his sleek black Mercedes SUV is in the driveway, but no one answers the doorbell. I grab the heavy antique brass knocker that probably weighs more than I do and pound it against the door over and over.

Still nothing.

I'm just about to go through the garage using the code when the front door finally creaks open.

Hayes stands there in black sweats, eyes bloodshot

like he hasn't slept since I last saw him. His hair's a rumpled mess—unheard of, considering Hayes's hair is never anything but picture-perfect. The guy has more hair products than Target.

"Hey. Thanks for bringing him back," Hayes mumbles as Argyros noses past him into the foyer. He lifts a hand in a half-hearted wave and starts to close the door. "See you in French."

"Didn't you see my calls and texts?" I ask, body-checking him and pushing inside.

Argyros pads along after me, tail wagging happily as I head straight for the kitchen. I toss my bomber jacket onto the island and grab a handful of choco-late-covered almonds from the oversized candy bowl, popping a few into my mouth.

"Sorry, no," Hayes says, following me in. "I was busy."

"Doing what? Alphabetizing your cologne collection?"

I settle onto a barstool while Argyros flops down beside me on the hardwood. A quick scan of the gleaming kitchen shows... nothing. Not a single beer can. No crusty pizza boxes. No sign whatsoever that a full-blown rager happened here less than twenty-four hours ago.

"Wow. You got Dimitra to deep-clean on her day off?"

"It's late, Al," he says, voice low, rubbing his eyes. "What's going on? I know you didn't come barging in to talk about Dimitra's cleaning schedule."

My throat goes dry. Suddenly I'm nervous, unsure

how to tell Hayes about the letters and what my mom just told me. It's strange. I don't get nervous around Hayes. He's the one person I've always been able to tell anything.

Well—almost anything.

Just not the part where I'm halfway in love with him, like an idiot, obviously.

"Uh… can I get a water or something?" I ask.

Without a word, Hayes grabs a chilled Evian from the fridge, twists off the cap, and hands it to me.

I take a slow sip, using it as cover while I try to figure out how to explain this. It's not that I think Hayes will judge my mom. He already knows she's… unconventional. Quirky. A little out there. Whatever. But this is something else entirely.

And it's not just about her.

Mental illness runs in families. Genes, patterns, entire histories passed down like heirlooms. If my mother has some kind of mental disorder… what does that mean for me? Is this something buried in my DNA too? Could I lose my grip someday, just like she did?

"Al?" Hayes nudges my shoulder. "What's going on?"

My hands won't stop shaking. I shove them under the counter, hiding them in my lap, and close my eyes. And there it is again. My mother's messy handwriting looping across those pages, words I can't unread.

"I tried to tell you the other night. Before, you know, I got, uh, sick."

His expression shifts—serious now, tuned in. "Right. You said it was about your mom."

I swallow hard.

God, how do I even say this out loud?

"It's even worse than I thought, Hay."

He stays quiet, waiting.

"She thinks…" I falter, forcing the words through my teeth. "She thinks my father is from another world."

A beat passes. Then another.

"She *what*?"

He lowers himself onto the barstool beside me. His eyes stay locked on mine, steady and alert. Concerned. Not mocking. Not retreating.

"I know how it sounds," I say. "But this isn't one of her usual woo-woo moments. She's serious. She really believes it. And… I'm starting to wonder if she always has."

His gaze never wavers.

"Okay. Tell me everything," he says.

So I do.

In a breathless, rambling rush, I spill it all. The letters. The conversation. Titans, gods, the Under-world—every surreal detail tumbles out in sharp, uneven bursts, breaking on my tongue like shards of glass.

Hayes doesn't interrupt. He just listens.

When I finally stop, the silence stretches long enough that I start to regret saying anything at all.

But then he reaches across the counter and lays

his hand gently over mine. "It's okay," he says softly. "Everything's going to be all right, Alligator."

"But what's wrong with her? How can she believe those things? Who turns a deadbeat dad into some mythic hero from another universe?" I fight the wave of emotion clawing its way up my chest. "I want to *kill* him for doing this to her. She doesn't deserve it."

I reach for the water bottle, twisting it until the plastic buckles and warps in my hands. I wish it were him instead—my father, Sonar Delios—bruised and breakable in my grip, wherever the hell he is.

"I know. I'm really sorry."

"I just feel so bad for her," I say. "And I don't know how to help her. Or what to do."

Hayes offers me a small, sad smile. "Maybe you don't have to *do* anything."

I blink at him, the words not computing.

"What are you talking about? Of course I have to do something," I say. "She needs help. I can't just stand by and do nothing."

"Why not?" Hayes leans back, his tone measured. "Maybe it's not your job to fix it. She's managed this long on her own terms, right? If her beliefs bring her comfort, help her sleep at night, is that really such a bad thing?"

"I'm not following."

"Alright, sure, what she believes sounds crazy to you and me. But is it that different from other belief systems? Some people worship prophets. Some believe in virgin births and resurrections. People walking on water." He lifts a brow, eyes thoughtful. "Is

what your mom thinks really that much more unbe-
lievable?"

I stare at him incredulously, stunned he can sound
so cavalier about this, like my entire world hasn't been
turned upside down.

"She literally told me my father is from Hell,
Hayes!"

"Well… technically, she said the Underworld—"

"Oh my God. Are you serious right now?" I snap.
"My life is imploding and you're talking semantics?"

"You're right. I'm sorry." He shifts, rubbing the
back of his neck. "I just… don't know what the right
response is here. It's a lot to take in."

"No shit. That's the understatement of the year."

Suddenly, I feel ancient. Like the weight of the
entire day has settled into my bones, heavy and unrelenting. Everything aches. Mind, body, and soul.

"I'm tired. I don't want to think about this
anymore today." I push to my feet and stretch, arms
overhead, joints cracking like brittle branches. "Can
we finish talking in the morning?"

"Of course." Hayes nods, soft and understanding.
"I'll pick you up? Coffee Box?"

Despite everything, a faint smile tugs at my lips,
the first one all night.

"Breakfast on you?"

"Always."

I crouch low to hug Argyros goodbye, burying my
face in the warm, scruffy fur at his neck. He exhales a
contented, sleepy sigh as I press a kiss to his damp
nose, but he doesn't budge from the floor.

Hayes walks me to my car, his bare feet moving quietly across the driveway. He opens the door and leans in, one hand on my shoulder. His thumb grazes my collarbone, the faint spark of his touch almost enough to make me forget all my worries for a moment.

"I promise," he says. "Everything is going to be okay."

I lean into the warmth of him, clinging to those words.

"I'm… I'm really scared, Hay. She's all I have."

He pauses, just for a beat. Something flickers in his eyes, like there's more he wants to say. But then he swallows it back, his jaw tightening.

"Your mom's not crazy," he says. "She's just… dealing. The only way she knows how." Then, with a crooked smile that doesn't quite reach his eyes, he adds, "And hey—look on the bright side. Now we've got something new in common."

"Oh yeah? What's that?"

"We're both Greek, obviously."

He winks, then steps back, hands buried in his pockets, watching me closely as I pull away. Things are still far from okay, but somehow I feel lighter after confiding in him. As long as I have Hayes, I can handle anything.

But the next day, he breaks his promise and bails on me. Even worse than getting stood up for breakfast, though, is running into my sister and her insufferable friends on my way to my car. Amber, Tiffany, and Brooke are posted up in the apartment complex parking lot, drinking their matcha detox green teas, all glossy lips and judgmental stares as I walk by.

"Nice tats," Amber drawls, eyeing the temporary swallows on my arm as she props herself against Tiffany's cherry-red sports car.

"Thanks," I say, brushing past them. "They're temporary—unlike your shitty personality."

I know I look good, no matter what Amber thinks. I'm wearing my favorite black lace halter top, vegan leather shorts, and torn fishnets. The peel-off tattoos climbing up my arm look like curated artwork, and honestly, I wish they were permanent, like Hayes's tattoos. Maybe one day.

"Whoa. Someone woke up cranky." Amber raises an eyebrow. "Bad dream or just realizing NYU's never gonna happen?"

I grit my teeth but ignore the bait. Not worth it.

As I walk away, their voices trail behind me, snippets of mindless drama about Homecoming outfits and predictions for the Court. Apparently, Brooke's summer fling with someone else's boyfriend has earned her the unofficial title of *Class Homewrecker*, which is tanking her chances of making the ballot. Tiffany's struggling too, thanks to her well-earned reputation as an insufferable snob.

Amber, of course, is a shoo-in—again—but Beth Jones is having a moment. She's dating the quarterback, and she's likable in that bland, inoffensive way. Unthreateningly pretty. Which means, gasp, Amber might have to settle for Court Princess instead of Queen.

"What if you promise the senior class free Starbucks for a month?" Tiffany suggests, brow furrowed in genuine thought. "Beth's not that great. Kind of a suck-up, really."

"You can't just buy people's friendship, Tiff," my sister replies, flipping her long blonde hair over one shoulder. "It's not genuine. People can tell."

For just a moment, I'm weirdly impressed by my sister—and maybe even a little proud. That's shockingly grounded advice coming from Amber.

"I'll just start a rumor that Beth cheated on Brady," Amber adds. "Everyone loves Brady."

And she's back. There's the sister I know and loathe.

"Ooh, good idea." Brooke sips her green tea, nodding along.

"On it!" Tiffany says brightly, already scrolling through her Instagram feed, probably hunting for some half-suggestive photo to spin the narrative.

I open my car door, doing my best not to laugh. I thank every higher power there is that I never gave a shit about any of this silly Homecoming nonsense when I was still in high school.

"Hey, what's so funny?" Amber calls out, eyes narrowing as she zeroes in on me.

"You are." I smirk, shaking my head. "You guys are absolutely Machiavellian. And for what? It's a stupid school dance, not a presidential campaign."

Amber drops her backpack against Tiffany's car with a dramatic thud.

"Well, you don't have to mock us," she huffs. "Just

because it's not your thing doesn't mean it's not important."

I falter for a second.

Huh. Maybe… she's not entirely wrong.

Sure, I think Homecoming Court is ridiculous, but who am I to decide what matters to someone else? Just because I don't care about it doesn't make it meaningless. Writing something off as stupid simply because it doesn't matter to me—that's not insight. That's arrogance.

And even if Homecoming Court *is* performative bullshit, maybe that's the point. It gives shape to something otherwise formless: the need to be seen, to feel significant, to matter, even if only for a moment in time.

The truth is, I've spent so long rejecting that kind of validation—mocking it, distancing myself from it —that I sometimes forget I'm not immune to the same ache. The same quiet desire to be chosen. To fit in.

Even if I'd rather die than admit it.

"You know what? You're right."

Her mouth falls open. "Seriously? I am?"

"Yeah. I'm sorry," I say. "I hope it works out for you."

"Oh. Uh… thanks?" Her expression shifts—suspicious but intrigued. "So, what would it take for someone like you to vote for me?"

"Someone like me?" I draw back slightly. "What's that supposed to mean?"

"Nothing bad." She waves me off. "Just… you're

not like us. You're one of the Regulars. The common people. You get what they care about. You know how they think."

She says it with all the gravitas of royalty. It's absurd, but also, I suppose, kind of true. And the fact she said it with total sincerity rather than malice is weirdly disarming. I have to respect her honesty.

I laugh. "I guess I do."

"You're really smart too, Ally." For once, there's no sarcasm, no smug twist to her voice. Just a rare flicker of respect. "You have good ideas."

I pause, momentarily stunned by an honest-to-God compliment from my sister.

"Yeah, tell us, Alysander," Tiffany chimes in, her eyes wide and earnest. "What should we do to get votes?"

Amber and her friends actually lean in, suddenly attentive, like I'm some kind of expert campaign strategist instead of the person they barely notice most days.

I hesitate.

Not because I don't have an answer, but because the real ones—the ones that actually work—aren't the kind people want to hear. Anyone can offer flash: empty promises, shallow charm, performative virtue. That's what most people do. Say what sounds good in the moment, even if it's meaningless. Politicians. Royals. Influencers. Half the candidates for Homecoming Court probably do it too—promising free pizza they'll never pay for, pretending to care about causes they Googled that morning.

But being decent to people? Actually treating them with kindness, with basic respect?

That isn't transactional. It doesn't expire after voting week or get walked back in a campaign speech. It's not flashy, but it's real. And real matters.

"Have you tried just being nice to everyone?" I offer. "People like nice people."

"That's it?" Amber frowns, looking disappointed. "Be *nice*?"

"Hey, it worked for Cinderella."

I flash a grin and slide into my car.

But as I pull away, the smile slips. Whatever brief warmth I felt toward Amber during those few minutes of almost-normal conversation fades under a slow, simmering resentment. She gets to spend her morning scheming over tiaras and tulle, while I'm stuck unraveling our mother's mental health issues.

Not exactly fair.

At least Theater History offers a temporary reprieve, and today's lecture on dramatic adaptations of Dante Alighieri's *The Divine Comedy* is just engaging enough to keep my brain occupied.

"*The Divine Comedy* traces Dante's journey through Hell, Purgatory, and Paradise," Professor Guppy explains, pushing smudged rectangular glasses up her nose.

Professor Guppy is squat and round, with the voice of a sitcom aunt and the wardrobe of someone constantly under siege by lint. She always looks one strong breeze away from being buried alive in cat hair. Case in point: she's already retrieved a lint roller from her desk drawer and is running it briskly over her pants, collecting a fresh coat of fuzz. Rumor has it she lives alone with five cats.

Not that there's anything wrong with that. I have a creeping suspicion I'm destined for the same fate.

"The poem is divided into three canticas, essentially, three books," she continues, waving the lint brush now like a conductor's baton. "*Inferno* takes place in Hell. *Purgatorio* is Purgatory. And *Paradiso* is Paradise, or Heaven. We open on Dante lost in a dark wood, pursued by three beasts—a lion, a leopard, and a she-wolf. Of course, this is all allegory." She paces theatrically, her voice gaining momentum. "Can anyone tell me what the three beasts represent?"

Hands shoot up around the room.

I sink lower in my seat, avoiding eye contact. Between everything else going on, I completely spaced on the required reading for the week. Which is a shame because obscure ancient poetry about eternal suffering is right up my alley.

Thankfully, she calls on Tony, Hayes's football buddy.

"The beasts represent three types of sin—self-indulgent, violent, and malicious," he says, all easy confidence, like he's been waiting all day to show that off.

Who knew? The school's game-winning kicker is apparently a low-key theater-nerd aficionado.

"Very good." She beams. "And why sin?"

"Because Dante was obsessed with moral redemption." Tony smiles wider, reveling in the attention of the professor. "The entire poem is about the soul's journey toward God."

"Precisely!" Professor Guppy punctuates the moment with an emphatic finger in the air, like a human exclamation point. "Each of the nine circles of Hell also represent a specific sin. We'll unpack those later this week."

From there, she pivots to the parallels between *The Divine Comedy* and Greek mythology, noting how mythological references were part of the cultural fabric in Dante's time, like how pop culture references are today. That's why he encounters so many familiar mythical figures, like Charon, the ferryman who delivers souls across the River Acheron, and Cerberus, the three-headed hound that guards the gates of the Underworld.

She moves briskly, highlighting a few other terrifying creatures: the Furies, winged goddesses who exact vengeance on the guilty, and Geryon, a dragon-like monster with a man's face and a scorpion's tail.

At some point in the middle of her monologue, my thoughts drift, uninvited, to my father.

Of course I know he's not really trapped in some imaginary underworld realm like the one Professor Guppy's rambling about from *The Divine Comedy*. But then… where is he? Where has he been the last sixteen—almost seventeen—years?

Did he stay in California? Disappear into another state? Another country?

Wherever he is, I hope he stays there.

After what he did to my mother, he forfeited any

right to ever walk back into our lives. His absence didn't just leave a hole. It hollowed something out in her, carved a wound so deep she's still trying to cauterize it.

After class ends, I drift through Vocal Performance and then lunch, counting the minutes until French—until Hayes.

But when I get to the lecture hall, his seat is empty.

I text him—once, twice, three times.

Nothing.

Just like yesterday.

I don't understand. Even when he's buried in football and school, Hayes always responds to my texts. It's not just the missed class or bailing on coffee this morning without any notice, either. Last night at his house, before I unleashed my family drama, something felt… off. Like something was eating at him, something he didn't want to say. I don't want to jump to conclusions, but I know Hayes.

Something is wrong.

And whatever it is, he's not telling me, which worries me most of all.

CHAPTER 11

I don't see Hayes much over the next few days.

First, he's out with the flu. Then he's buried in makeup assignments and extra practices for the upcoming LHU Homecoming game. We barely exchange more than a few quick words in French class.

Without my best friend around to anchor me, my thoughts spiral, my brain switching to full doomsday mode. I can't stop obsessing over my mother's delusions. Though I should be spending my evenings prepping for my NYU transfer—polishing my music résumé, recording audition clips, tightening my portfolio—instead, I find myself diving into the internet's darkest corners, trawling through articles and academic journals on mental illness. Diagnoses. Case studies. Firsthand accounts. Trying to find an answer that makes sense.

From what I can piece together, it seems like my mom may have experienced a brief psychotic episode triggered by intense stress or trauma. A break from reality where the mind short-circuits under pressure. It can cause hallucinations and delusions, like thinking your long-lost ex is an immortal god from Greek mythology. If left untreated, the psychosis can progress into something more serious, like schizophrenia or other schizoaffective disorders.

Or worse.

The more I read, the more unsettled I become.

It makes sense that being abandoned with two small children and no support system would trigger a breakdown. I get that. But then other things don't add up.

Most people with psychosis experience other symptoms too. Personality shifts. Social withdrawal. Sleep disturbances. As far as I can tell, my mother doesn't have any of that. Sure, she's whimsical and free-spirited—if not a little flighty—but she's been that way forever.

And the timeline doesn't track, either.

It's not like there's been a sudden behavioral shift, the way most psychotic breaks seem to happen. If my mother is to be believed, she's been having these delusions about my father since before I was born. That's seventeen years, at least.

Isn't that too long?

Wouldn't the illness have progressed by now into something more pronounced? More dangerous? Especially with zero treatment?

But if it's not a psychotic disorder... then what is it?

Between my obsessive research and worrying—and the growing fear I might somehow be genetically wired for the same kind of psychotic break as my mother—I'm not exactly in a party mood when LHU Homecoming rolls around. I don't even want to get out of bed, let alone plaster on a fake smile and sit in a packed stadium for hours. But skipping the game isn't an option. I've never missed any of Hayes's home games, and Homecoming is the biggest one of the year.

Growing up so close to LHU, I've watched our town turn Homecoming into a full-on production for years. Even though it's a small college, the hype is huge. There's tailgating and a live DJ blasting pop remixes in front of the stadium. Food trucks. Parties up and down frat row. And, of course, the parade down Main Street, complete with cheerleaders, marching bands, and the football team strutting around like gods heading off to war. The whole day feels like one giant town-wide celebration.

A few hours before kickoff, Amber barges into my room without so much as a knock. She plops down in front of my mirrored closet doors, a brand-new red and gold bodycon dress riding up her thighs, and unzips her makeup bag. A glitter explosion of foundation sticks, compacts, and lip glosses spills onto the carpet.

"Seriously?" I glare from my bed. "You have your own mirror. Use it."

"Yeah, but the lighting's better in here. You've got the west-facing windows."

She says it like it's some kind of universal truth, but I know better. Amber couldn't care less about natural light. She has that ridiculous three-way lighted vanity mirror Mom caved and bought her last Christmas. What Amber wants is an audience.

She props her cell phone against the wall and cues up a hair tutorial from Nia Williams—her favorite beauty blogger—and then proceeds to curl her hair while I watch on in mild horror.

The Instagram influencer is even more insufferable than my sister—a too-perfect Florida girl with bleached teeth, zero self-awareness, and an unhealthy obsession with her ever-growing follower count. Amber, however, follows every step of the tutorial like she's prepping for brain surgery. Brows furrowed, lips pouting in focus. It's honestly kind of impressive how committed she is.

As she curls and sprays, she prattles on nonstop about the latest high school gossip. Who's hooking up with who, who got dumped, which girls are fighting over which guys. I pretend to care, inserting little head nods where appropriate, but I can't stop thinking about Mom.

"Ally!" Amber snaps. "Are you even listening?"

I yawn, unbothered, and stretch my legs across the futon.

"Sorry, did you ask me something?"

She groans, loud and dramatic.

"I asked who Hayes is taking to the Alpha Delts party tomorrow."

"How should I know? Ask him yourself."

"I can't do that." She scowls, scandalized. "I'd look totally clingy. We're not, like, officially back together—yet," she says, slicking on her shiniest pink lip gloss while checking her reflection. "But if he shows up with someone else, I swear I'll lose it."

I narrow my eyes, watching her spritz her hair until she gleams like a pageant queen. Then she fastens an oversized gold bow to the top of her head to match her dress.

"I don't get it," I say. "You're the one who dumped him. I thought being 'free' senior year was the whole point."

"I blame temporary insanity." She sighs, all tragic. "He's Hayden Vassilios, Ally. What girl wouldn't want him back?"

She's not wrong.

But her on-again, off-again saga with my best friend isn't something I'm eager to unpack.

"Can we please not talk about Hayes?"

"But now that he's single, everyone's circling. The cheer team. The dance girls. Practically all of sorority row. I was an idiot to let him go." Her voice trembles, teetering toward panic. "You'd tell me, right? If Hayes was seeing someone? You're the only one I can trust."

She looks up, mascara wand shaking in her hand, all wide-eyed and raw. A sudden rush of protectiveness hits me, sharp and unwanted. Even if she's a complete asshole most of the time, I'm still her big sister. It's my job to protect her... isn't it? Especially when she's like this. Insecure. Vulnerable. Almost... sweet.

For a moment, she reminds me of the old Amber.

When we were younger, before junior high and everything changed, my sister and I used to be close. We'd ride our bikes down by the boardwalk, doing little jumps and wheelies. Go kneeboarding together, catching waves in the ocean. Dress up as matching Disney Princesses and put on talent shows for Mom in the living room. I'd sing. Amber would dance. She even took karate with me and Hayes. She was pretty good at it, too, but then some cute boy at competition told her girls shouldn't fight. She quit the very next day and signed up for cheer camp instead.

I suppose it would be nice to get along again, like we used to. If things go as planned, I'll be in New York next year and then I'll hardly ever see her. Maybe we shouldn't waste whatever time we still have left together.

And I guess it's not her fault that everyone adores her.

Even the guys like Hayes, the ones you'd think would go for someone less cookie-cutter. Someone with layers. With depth. Originality. Someone like… well… me.

"Sorry, Ambs. If I knew, I'd tell you," I say, managing an actual smile. "But Hay and I have barely talked this week."

She shoots me a look, all smug amusement.

"Ahhh… so that's why you've been such a bitch. You and Hayes are fighting, huh?"

I sit up straighter.

"We are not fighting."

"Uh huh. Sure."

"You're so annoying." I chuck a contraband Hershey's bar at her from the stash I keep hidden from my mom behind my bed.

She snatches it midair, completely unfazed, and sets it aside with a look of pure disgust.

"Say what you want, but you always go full emo when things are off with you two. You've got a seriously unhealthy attachment to a guy you swear is just a friend." She pauses a beat, her gaze sharpening as she studies my face, like she's sizing me up. "Then again, I've always thought you had a thing for him."

"Good thing no one asked you."

I grab a hair tie and stalk toward the mirror, scowling at my reflection. I basically resemble a sleep-deprived raccoon. Smudged eyeliner, dark circles, and a tangled mess in the back of my hair that looks borderline aggressive.

"You can't go to the game looking like that," Amber tsks, shaking her head. "Sit—I'll fix you."

She goes to work, her acrylic nails sharper than they look. I wince as she tugs them through the snarls near my scalp, but the pain is brief.

When she's done, she beams at her handiwork and tells me to close my eyes as she douses me in hairspray.

"Ta da!" she says, spinning me toward the mirror.

I blink at my reflection. The knot on the back of my head is gone, replaced by two long, elaborate fishtail braids. My hair actually looks… incredible.

"You know," she says, her voice catching a little as she studies my reflection, "when I was little, I used to wish I looked just like you."

"Seriously?"

She nods, her soft blue eyes crinkling as she

reaches up to brush my widow's peak with surprising gentleness. "You're like Snow White come to life. All pale and mysterious and fairy-tale."

For the first time in weeks, the anger I've been clinging to loosens its grip. Just a little. In its place, something warmer slips in before I have the chance to brace against it.

"I bet some guys would even like you," she adds breezily, "if you weren't so scary."

And just like that—poof—there goes the warmth.

"Geez. Thanks."

"Listen, Ally, I think it's great you've got this whole 'independent woman' thing going on, but it's time for a little tough love." She eyes me critically, gaze sweeping down my outfit—faded dark-wash Levi's, scuffed combat boots, and one of Hayes's old football jerseys that swallows me whole. "I'll try to put this delicately. You think being smart and moody makes you intriguing and cool, but to everyone else, you just come off as... hard to love. If you ever want an actual boyfriend, you're going to have to make some changes. You can't just keep being..." She wrinkles her nose. "You."

I snort. "That was delicate?"

"You know what I mean."

She claps her hands together and tilts her head, already scheming.

"I have a great idea!" she says. "I just bought this sexy red tube top. It would look so good on you. You should wear it today."

"I like what I'm wearing," I say, but the bite in my

voice is softer than usual. Even though it's infuriating to hear her suggest I change the very parts of myself I actually like—the ones that make me *me* and different from everyone else—I can tell she thinks she's helping.

And so, for some inexplicable reason, I allow her to grab the top from her bedroom and wrestle it over my head. She yanks it down into place, smoothing it just so. The material is red and sparkly, all shiny sequins and bows. Not something I'd ever buy in a million years, but I'll admit it shows off my toned abs nicely.

"What you have to understand, Ally, is that life is like a rom-com," she explains, turning me around so she can button up the back of the top. "Like that movie *My Best Friend's Wedding.* Remember the part where Julia Roberts compares men's taste in women to desserts—"

"You know I hate rom-coms—"

"Just hush and listen," she orders, grabbing the only skirt I own from my closet—black vegan leather —and tossing it at me to put on. "Say you're Hayes. You're in a fancy restaurant ordering dessert. You want something special, so you order crème brûlée. It's beautiful. Sweet. Perfect. You don't order boring, plain ol' Jell-O."

"Let me guess. I'm the Jell-O in this metaphor?" I ask dryly, zipping up the skirt. "And you're crème brûlée? The dessert everyone wants?"

"Exactly!" She nods along. "That's why Dermot Mulroney passes on uptight Julia Roberts—the best friend who's secretly in love with him—and marries blonde, bubbly Cameron Diaz. She's the crème brûlée." She smiles brightly. "Like me."

I snort, rolling my eyes.

"First off, pretty sure I should be offended. But also? I like Jell-O. So whatever." I tug the skirt down a notch so it's not too short and check the laces on my boots. "But more importantly, I don't care what dessert Hayes picks because, for the millionth time, I'm not into Hayes."

Okay… maybe that's a little white lie.

But it's necessary.

Even if my feelings for Hayes blur the line between platonic and something else, I'm certainly not going to admit that to Amber. She's the last person on Earth I'd tell.

Well—second to last. Hayes still takes the crown there.

"Good," she says, flipping her hair. "Because Hayes is mine."

I open my mouth to argue, because Hayes isn't a purse or a pair of shoes she can slap a claim on. He's a person. A complex, thinking, feeling human being.

But then I stop myself, because as much as I might want to say it, it's not really my place. Hayes may have been mine first. I was his friend when no one else wanted to be. Even Amber used to make fun of him behind his back when we were little, just like everyone else. She didn't really notice him until his glow-up and the rest of the world suddenly decided he was worth paying attention to.

Still, that doesn't entitle me to anything. I don't

own him. I don't get to dictate who he dates. If Amber genuinely loves him—and he loves her back—then their relationship isn't any of my business. Wanting him for myself probably crosses a line I have no business even toeing.

"Ambs?" I glance at her, my voice quieter now. "What do you actually like about Hayes?"

She blinks, taken aback.

"What kind of question is that?"

"You could have any guy you want—why him?"

She shrugs, not even taking a moment to think about it.

"He's hot. I'm hot. We're easily the best-looking couple in Laguna Hills. People stare when we walk into a room, like we're famous or something. It's a rush, being that girl everyone wants to be." She smiles at me like it's all so obvious. "Who wouldn't want that?"

My eyes drop down to Hayes's old jersey now lying crumpled on the floor where Amber discarded it. Soft from years of wear. Frayed at the collar. It's been mine since ninth grade, when he handed it to me at football practice because he saw me shivering in the bleachers.

I never gave it back.

Not because it made me feel important to wear the star quarterback's jersey, but because it made me feel seen. In the middle of a touchdown play, Hayes saw me, and somehow noticed I was freezing in the stands.

He always notices me.

Amber wants the spotlight. But me?

I want the person who sees me when no one else does. I just want *him*.

I want the awkward, lanky boy from junior high who got nosebleeds during dodgeball and stayed up all night helping me build a papier-mâché volcano for the science fair. I want the boy from before the model jawline, before the abs, before everyone else started noticing him, too. And I'd still love him even if he were invisible, even if he wore a paper bag on his head and worked the drive-thru at Taco Bell.

"Anyway"—Amber adjusts the straps on her dress—"just stay in your lane, okay? I don't need some 'plot twist' where you embarrass yourself trying to steal him from me. Got it, Jell-O?"

That does it.

"Oh my God. You're such a narcissist," I snap. "I'm honestly shocked you haven't married your own reflection."

"At least I'd be married." Amber snatches a pillow off my bed and hurls it at my face. "No one's ever gonna marry you."

The pillow whizzes past me and lands with a muffled *thwack* against the bed. In retaliation, I snatch her hairbrush from the floor and fling it at her. She shrieks and ducks as it ricochets off the mirror and clatters to the ground—just as Mom bursts in.

"What on earth is going on in here?" she asks, eyes wide, arms folding across her gauzy white peasant blouse. She's dressed for the game in full boho regalia—giant gold hoops, stacks of bangles, and a tie-dye scarf wrapped around her hair like Stevie Nicks's long-lost twin.

"She started it," Amber says, pointing one manicured finger at me.

"Alysander Sage Smith." Mom whirls to face me, her voice like tempered steel. "You're too old for this nonsense."

"Of course you'd take her side." I snatch my belt bag from the floor and fasten it around my waist, heat rising in my chest, fast and sharp.

It's always like this. Amber gets away with murder, and I'm the one who gets scolded.

In moments like these, I can't help but wonder what life might've been like if my father had stuck around. Now that I know we look alike, I can't stop thinking about what else we might've shared. Would he have understood me? Backed me up?

It doesn't seem fair that I'll never know the truth. That all I have are my mother's hazy stories and half-baked delusions.

But this definitely isn't the time to bring any of that up.

"Can't you two ever get along?" Mom sighs, exasperated. "Your auras are all clouded and red. This kind of deep-seated anger is toxic."

"You're absolutely right, Mom," Amber says, syrupy sweet. "I will if you will, Ally?"

God, she's such a fake.

"Thanks, sweetie," Mom says. "I knew I could count on you."

"Seriously? She doesn't mean it."

Mom turns to me, her face hardening. "I'm not dealing with this attitude all day, Alysander. Fix your mindset or you can stay home while your sister and I go to the game."

"Stay home?" My voice spikes. "This is *my* Homecoming. You stay home."

"I don't like your tone, young lady." Her lips flatten. "You're lucky you have a mother and sister who want to go with you. I don't see anyone else volunteering."

Ouch.

That one lands harder than it should. Nothing like your own mother casually implying you're a social pariah.

I try to let it roll off. I know she doesn't mean it, not really. She just hates the constant bickering.

Still. It stings.

"It's okay, Mom," Amber says softly, taking our mother's hand. "Ally's just having a bad week. We should go easy on her."

I pause, unsure whether she's genuinely trying to defend me or just racking up more brownie points with Mom. I'm leaning toward the latter, but before I can fully decide, a knock sounds at the door. Amber's on her feet instantly, practically sprinting toward it, leaving behind her usual cloud of overly sweet, floral perfume.

Mom lingers, turning to give me one last long, disappointed look.

"I just don't know what to do with you sometimes,

Alysander," she says, and then turns on her heel, following after Amber.

I groan and flop back onto my bed for half a second before grabbing my phone and heading after them. My mother can be so damn sensitive. I get that it's part of what makes her such an intuitive empath —and so good at her job reading people—but she really can't take even a flicker of heat without wilting.

And now that I know about the letters and her mental health spirals, I worry even more. One wrong move and she might shatter.

As I join them in the living room, Argyros comes barreling through the front door like a missile, tail wagging. He launches himself at me, paws slamming into my chest with enough force to knock me backward. I suddenly forget I'm annoyed and collapse in a pile of fur and dog kisses, laughing as I bury my face in his soft coat.

And then I see him.

Hayes.

He follows Argyros inside looking like a walking fantasy—sun-kissed and all sharp edges, in fitted denim and a crimson football jersey that clings to him like it was custom-stitched for every muscle. His leather jacket is slung casually over one shoulder, and he's wearing that irresistible, traffic-stopping smile.

Amber squeals and throws herself into his arms.

"I'm so glad you're here!" she gushes, kissing him —so much for playing it cool—and loops her arm through his.

I don't get it.

Hayes has ghosted me all week. Barely any texts. No coffee. Skipping French class. And now he shows up at our apartment… for her?

"What are you doing here?" I ask, sharper than I mean to.

"Hey, Alligator." He nudges my foot with his, a quiet tap like a peace offering. "Good to see you too."

"You know what I mean. Shouldn't you be at the stadium?"

"All the guys are meeting their families first, for the parade." He scratches the back of his neck, looking almost nervous. "Since my parents are still out of town, Ambs thought maybe your family could come instead?"

Amber grins up at him adoringly. "We'd love to!"

"You're sure? I don't want to be a hassle or anything," he says, glancing toward my mom.

She steps forward with a warm smile. "We'd be honored, Hayden dear," she says, pulling him into a hug.

It still catches me off guard, how much she's softened toward him over the years. She used to warn me about getting too close. *All men leave, Alysander,* she'd say. But now she treats Hayes like he's the son she never had.

"Al?"

His eyes meet mine, searching.

I say nothing.

He hesitates, hand brushing the doorknob. "Or I can just skip the parade…"

"Yeah, why don't you?" I snap.

I know I'm being rude, but I can't help it. Amber keeps grinning at him like he's a prize she just won back, and it's making something sour and sharp coil in my chest. He barely has time for me anymore as it is. I don't want to share him with her.

Not again.

"Alysander, knock it off. Of course we'll all go to the parade." Mom grabs her purse off the table and pulls out a leather cord with a rough, metallic stone dangling from the end—dull gold, jagged, like something chipped from a cave wall. "Here, hun," she says, handing it to Hayes. "I made this for you, for the game."

"Pyrite, right? For protection?" He grins, taking it from her with both hands. "Awesome."

"That's right."

Mom lights up. She's made him one every season since he started playing football.

Amber makes a face. "He's not gonna wear that ugly rock, Mom," she says.

"Course I am. Thanks, Mel." Hayes winks and slips it over his head, tucking the stone beneath his shirt. "I'll take all the help I can get."

We head outside. Amber and Mom walk arm in arm while I rush ahead, Argyros trotting at my side like my own personal shadow. Hayes falls into step beside me, his shoulder brushing mine.

"Hey, grumpy," he says, tugging gently at my braids. "You look different today. Where's my jersey? You mad at me or something?"

"Nope. Just didn't feel like wearing it."

"If you say so." He scans my outfit with a crooked half-smile. "This is good too. You look hot."

"Yeah right."

"I'm serious."

I tug at the hem of the sparkly red top, suddenly self-conscious. "You sure? I kind of feel like a sequined tomato."

His gaze sweeps over me then fully, slow and deliberate, lingering on the strip of bare skin between my tube top and skirt. He doesn't even try to hide it. When he swallows, thick and slow, I forget how to breathe.

"Jesus, Al…" His voice is low as his eyes flick back up to meet mine—darker now, unreadable. "You really don't see it, do you?"

My pulse flutters in my throat.

"See what?"

A full beat passes. Then another. Until the air between us stretches taut, electric.

"How gorgeous you are."

I freeze.

The world seems to shift around me, everything narrowing to the space between us. My heart thuds so loudly I'm sure he can hear it. And for a second, I wonder if—

"Shotgun!"

Amber shatters the moment, sprinting past us and flinging herself into the front seat of Hayes's G-Wagon. Argyros follows after her, barking madly, ears flopping as he skids to the back passenger door, waiting for Hayes to let him in. The dog and Amber exchange a brief look of mutual disinterest. Then both immediately pretend the other doesn't exist.

"The dog's coming in the car with us?" Mom asks, looking visibly uneasy.

"What, you thought he was riding on the roof?" I deadpan.

She gives me a withering look.

"No, I just… is he even allowed at the game?" she asks.

"He'll stay in the car," Hayes explains. "He just hates being left alone at my place."

"Hm. I think I'll take my own car, if that's alright," Mom says, already fishing out her keys from her purse. It's not a question. She's not about to share air with a hulking beast of a dog.

"I'll ride with you," I offer, following after her and hopping inside her old Toyota even though I'd much rather be in the G-Wagon with Hayes, curled up in the backseat with my dog. But this is my shot to patch things up with her. Earn back some goodwill. Truth is, maybe she's not the only sensitive one in this family. I hate it when she's mad at me too.

As Mom puts the car in drive, I glance back longingly at Hayes's SUV. Amber leans into Hayes, laughing at something he just said. She tucks a strand of shiny blonde hair behind her ear, her whole body tilted toward him like she's already picturing the wedding.

I huff and sink lower in my seat, my attention snagging on the black tourmaline charm swinging from Mom's rearview mirror. It's supposed to ward off evil spirits. She gave me one once too—for protection—but it mysteriously "disappeared" after I tossed it in a trash can behind the school gym.

I glare at her stupid amulet now, dangling and useless.

Ward off evil, my ass.

If it actually worked, then why the hell was my sister still here?

CHAPTER 12

After the Homecoming game is over, we wait outside the locker room for Hayes, along with the other families of the football team. The air hums with celebration. Students and fans rush past us, singing the LHU fight song at the top of their lungs and high-fiving each other like they personally threw all of Hayes's touchdowns in the 47–0 shutout against Southern Cal State.

A few of Hayes's Alpha Delta brothers spot Amber and call out, inviting her to go with them to the big Homecoming weekend dayger at the frat house tomorrow. She just giggles and waves them off. I get the sinking feeling she's already planning to go with someone—Hayes.

Moments later, the team appears.

The crowd erupts as the players jog over, rowdy and triumphant, grinning like warriors fresh off the battlefield. Dylan and Tony fist bump each other while the rest of the team piles on Hayes, slapping his back as if he's the second coming. That's what happens when you throw six touchdowns in a single game.

I notice Hayes's jersey is soaked with Gatorade, because of course it is. Over the years, I've learned that football teams love nothing more than dumping coolers over the MVP. I've watched Hayes get doused with more neon sports drinks than I can remember.

Still, even dripping wet and flushed from adrenaline, he's annoyingly attractive. Like he just walked off a film set. Night-black hair clings to his forehead in damp waves, droplets trailing down the sharp line of his jaw. His jersey is plastered to his chest, outlining every muscle, and his piercing blue eyes spark with the thrill of conquest—alive, electric, dangerous. He looks like trouble.

The good kind.

The kind you want to run to, even when you know you should be running away.

He scans the crowd, searching, until his eyes find mine. Our gazes catch and the noise around me fades. It's just him and me, standing on opposite sides of a raucous mob, tethered by something we never seem able to name.

He grins that crooked, devastating smile I know by heart and lifts a hand in a slow wave. For just a moment, it feels like high school again. Back when everything between us was simpler. Before he started pulling away, and I never had to wonder if he'd make time for me.

But then—

Amber barrels through the crowd, squealing as she launches herself at him. He catches her with ease, arms wrapping around her in a full-body embrace. The moment she realizes he's drenched, she lets out a dramatic shriek. He just laughs and shakes his wet hair at her, flinging droplets across her dress like it's some inside joke between them.

Something petty and sharp uncoils inside me. It

looks like my sister has everything back on track. And judging by the smile tugging at Hayes's mouth, he doesn't seem to mind.

Amber laces her fingers through his and leads him over to where Mom and I wait. I glance away, forcing the jealousy down, reminding myself there are bigger things to worry about than my sister's attempts to resurrect an old romance. Even if it's with the one person I care about in a way I wish I didn't.

"Good game, Hay," I manage, the words catching in my throat.

"Thanks, Alligator."

He grins—and before I can react, scoops me into his arms and lifts me off the ground, spinning me around in a blur of lights and cheers. The world tilts and vanishes. All I feel is *him*. Strong and solid. Arms locked around me like I belong there. He holds me almost like I'm his.

Even if I never really will be.

Unlike my sister, I don't care that he's drenched in some sticky sports drink or messing up my outfit. I lean in closer, greedy for him and for the feeling of being held like this. I could stay wrapped in this moment forever.

He sets me back down all too soon. My feet hit the pavement though my heart's still somewhere up in the clouds. I stumble back, lightheaded and a bit giddy.

"Whoa. Careful," he says, steadying me. His hands linger on my shoulders—strong, grounding.

"Great game!" my mom says brightly. "I'm so proud of you, Hayden."

"Thanks, Mel." He pats his chest where her lumpy necklace is still tucked beneath his jersey and pads. "I owe it all to your good luck charm."

"My pleasure, hun," she says, smoothing down her hair. Then she leans in like she's revealing top-secret intel. "I saw some men in suits in the stands. I think they were NFL scouts."

"Probably." He shrugs. "I try not to focus on that stuff."

"Must be nice," I say, only half joking.

Hayes was recruited by every top school in the country without even trying. He could've gone anywhere he wanted. Ivy League. Full Division 1 football powerhouse. But no. He chose to stay here at a tiny college in our hometown.

I still think he's insane, but his parents wanted him close. His family's old-school, deeply traditional. His father is expecting Hayes to eventually take over their billion-dollar international shipping empire. As the only son and heir, Hayes is expected to run the family business one day.

"I still can't believe you're both in college now. And Amber's next." Mom sighs, a little wistfully. "Sometimes I wish I'd finished school. Gotten my art degree," she says, getting misty-eyed as she tousles Amber's hair. "But then I got knocked up with Alysander and then Ambrosia, and, well… there went that."

"Mom!" Amber jerks away, horrified. "How many times do I have to tell you—it's *Amber*!"

Up ahead, the coach gives Hayes a wave and jerks

his thumb toward the locker room. A few players start jogging toward the doors.

"I should head in," Hayes says, hesitating. There's something in his eyes that looks reluctant, like he's not ready to leave just yet. "Thanks for coming tonight. Really—it means a lot."

His smile falters for a beat, just long enough to twist something in my chest. I still can't believe his parents missed his first college Homecoming game. It's so unlike them. Especially Kora. She never misses anything important.

It makes me wonder again if there's more going on with his family than he's let on. He hasn't said much about it to me, but then again, I haven't exactly asked much, either.

"Of course, silly. I wouldn't have missed this for anything." Amber's voice is light and annoyingly possessive, like his words were meant only for her. "So, where to after? Anything going on at the frat house?" she asks, slipping her hand into his and giving him a suggestive look. "Or… we could head back to your place?"

He glances down at his feet.

"Actually, I'm beat," he says, his cleats shuffling over the concrete. "Think I'll just head home after Coach's recap."

I glance at him, surprised, but he's still staring at the ground.

This is… unexpected. Hayes doesn't do too tired to party—especially not on a Saturday night. And definitely not during Homecoming weekend.

"But I thought we were going out tonight?" Panic creeps into Amber's voice.

"Sorry. Not feeling it." He shrugs. "But I'll see you at the Alpha Delts party tomorrow, right?"

"Well… duh!" She forces a laugh that lands a little too sharp. I can hear the crack of disappointment behind the fake cheer.

Meanwhile, I'm ecstatic.

I shouldn't be. I know that. But I can't help the little smile tugging at my lips. Maybe Hayes and I won't hang out tonight like I'd hoped, but at least he's not spending the evening with her, either.

"Have a great night, Hay!" I chirp, looping my arm through Mom's and tugging her toward the parking lot. "Catch you later!"

"Actually, Al—hold up."

He catches my wrist, pulling me back gently.

"Yeah?"

"Can I give you a ride home?"

"What?" Amber gasps. "I thought we were riding home together?"

"Al and I need to talk," he says. "Argy stuff."

"Oh. Okay, sure." Her shoulders drop, interest evaporating the second the conversation turns to the dog. "Call me later, handsome. Can't wait for tomorrow!"

She leans in to kiss his cheek, smile tight. I notice the way her steps falter slightly as she heads for Mom's car—alone now, no longer riding shotgun with the star quarterback. But I don't feel too bad for her. She'll bounce back.

She always does.

"See you back home, sweetie," Mom says, pulling me into a hug. "Let me know if you're going to be out late."

I let her hold me a little longer than I normally would because I still feel guilty about our argument earlier. Even when she sides with Amber, I know she means well. She's not malicious. She just wants peace. It really does hurt her to see us constantly at odds. Mom believes family should stick together, especially one as small and fractured as ours. It's just the three of us, after all. It makes sense to cling tight to what's left.

I don't necessarily disagree.

It'd just be a lot easier if Amber weren't such a little shit most of the time.

Hayes tosses me his car keys, and I walk back toward the parking lot with Mom and Amber, say my goodbyes, and head for his SUV.

I find the G-Wagon easily enough—it's parked right up front, in the VIP spots. Argyros spots me through the open moonroof and loses his mind, barking and thrashing around in the backseat.

The second I'm inside, the dog launches himself on me, half-jumping, half-climbing into my lap. I laugh, pushing him gently into the backseat, where he finally settles, tongue lolling as he curls up contentedly. Then I plug in my phone and cue up Paramore.

The opening chords fill the car. Angsty, punchy, perfect. I sing along softly to emo girl rock music as Argy drifts off.

I'm halfway through the *Riot!* album when a figure finally emerges from the shadows. Black joggers. Faded black hoodie. Worn leather jacket on top.

"About time," I say as Hayes climbs into the driver's seat. "I was just about to file a missing person's report."

"Sorry." He laughs, starting the engine. "Couldn't find my hair gel."

"Oh no. Sounds like a real crisis."

"You have no idea," he says, throwing the SUV into drive and pulling out of the school parking lot.

I switch the music to his favorite Muse track, and soon we're scream-singing "Supermassive Black Hole" at the top of our lungs while Argy snores in the backseat. Hayes is obsessed with Muse. He dragged me all the way to the Forum in LA last spring to see them live.

Not that I minded.

I'd go anywhere with him.

We take the winding coastal highway home, the SUV hugging cliff edges above the Pacific Ocean. I roll the windows down, letting the cool, salt-laced air whip through my braids. Overhead, the full moon rises—huge and molten orange.

The Harvest Moon.

The name always makes me think of that old '80s horror flick *Children of the Corn*. The one where the kids in a creepy small town kill off all the adults to guarantee a successful harvest. Hayes and I watched it together in junior high. I remember Kora joking afterward that a good harvest is worth a few sacrifices.

She was kidding, of course.

At least, I think she was.

It was one of the few times I remember Hayes's mom talking about her past. She grew up in a small farming village in Eastern Europe with her mother, working the land from a young age. She talked about the harvest like it was sacred.

Kora rarely mentions her childhood.

No talk of siblings. No extended family. No funny uncle stories or crazy aunts. I don't even know what happened to her mother. It's like Kora moved to Athens, met Hayes's father, and that was the end of the narrative.

Hayes's father is the same. No talk of where he's from, no relatives, no roots. It's as if the two of them just appeared one day—fully formed, incredibly successful, and inexplicably private.

In that way, I guess Hayes and I aren't so different. Neither of us comes from big, sprawling families.

"On a scale of one to ten," Hayes says, grinning as we pull off the highway, "how pissed do you think Ambs is that I bailed on her tonight?"

I laugh, the sound catching in my throat.

"Eleven."

He tosses me a wink. "Your sister wants me— bad."

"A little full of yourself, aren't you?"

He pauses, the mood in the car shifting just slightly. "You think she's serious this time? Or just playing games again?"

"No clue." I shrug. "She says the breakup was a

mistake, but… who knows. Still—do you really think getting back together is a good idea?"

"Aw, no need to be jealous," he teases. "You know you'll always be my number one girl."

I punch his shoulder, maybe harder than necessary.

"I'm not jealous, you moron."

"Sure you aren't."

"I'm not! I couldn't care less about you and my damn sister!"

Hayes goes quiet for a beat, his hands tightening on the wheel.

"Relax," he finally says. "I was just messing around. I know you're not jealous. I'd probably die of shock if you ever showed real interest in a guy—especially me."

I fold my arms and look away.

"I like guys just fine. They just don't like me."

"That's the dumbest thing I've ever heard." He scoffs. "My friends all think you're hot. Dylan wouldn't shut up about you last weekend."

I grimace.

"You're not seriously suggesting I go for Dylan Masterson, are you?"

"Definitely not." His lips twitch. "I'm just saying, if you wanted to date someone, you could. A lot of someones." He glances at me again, slower this time —more searching, more curious, a flicker of something unguarded in his eyes. "So… why don't you?"

"Because I don't want *someone*. I want a guy I actually like."

"Okay, but how do you know who that is if you never try?"

I roll my eyes.

"Oh, is that why you date every girl who smiles at you?"

"I don't date every girl," he protests, then smirks. "Haven't hooked up with anyone on dance team—yet."

"You're such an idiot." I laugh, shaking my head. "So is that the logic behind dating Amber again? Just trying to see if you 'like her'?"

"Ha ha. Funny."

"Honestly, I don't get it." My voice tightens. "Sure, she's beautiful, but what do you even have in common? She doesn't like our music, she refuses to hike or box or do anything that might ruin her nails. She hates anything even remotely spooky—she won't even watch *Beetlejuice*, and that's basically a comedy." I turn to him, my jaw clenching. "Also? She's still in high school, Hayes. She's a kid."

"She's one year younger than us."

"Whatever."

The car goes quiet for a moment as he stares out the windshield, eyes fixed on the road. He takes his time, thinking hard.

"I can't explain it," he says, turning the SUV into my apartment complex. "Amber just… fits into my life."

"She's a superficial cream puff!"

He lifts a brow. "Maybe I like cream puffs."

"Then you should open a fucking bakery."

I stare out the window, biting the inside of my cheek. How could someone like Hayes—smart, deep, complex—want someone like my sister? It doesn't make any sense. It never has.

"Do you guys even talk about anything real? Like we do?"

"Sure."

"Like what? Hair products?" I shoot him a look.

He throws the car in park and turns toward me, his movements sharp and clipped. His eyes blaze with frustration—and something else. Darker. Rawer.

"Why does this matter so much to you?" he asks, voice rough. "Why do you even care?"

The air thickens between us.

"I don't—"

"I like Amber, okay?" he cuts me off. "I have fun with her. She's a cool girl. So what if we don't sit around unpacking our childhood traumas and swapping our deepest dreams or doing whatever bullshit you seem to think makes a relationship real?"

"Is that what you think you and I are?" I ask, my voice suddenly brittle. "Bullshit?"

He rakes a hand through his dark hair, tugging hard at the roots.

"That's not what I meant." He exhales hard, leaning back in his seat, gripping at the wheel like he needs the anchor. "This isn't about you and me. How I feel about Amber has nothing to do with you. I care about you both, just in different ways. What's wrong with that?"

His words hit me like an uppercut. I knew it, sure,

but to hear him say it out loud stings even more than I thought.

He still wants *her*.

"It doesn't work like that," I say. "Amber doesn't share. Sooner or later, she'll want all of you. And I'll get even less than I do now, which is basically nothing."

"We'll make it work."

"How?" My voice rises, jagged and sharp. "You'll squeeze me in for a few seconds between frat parties and football and hooking up with my sister? Am I supposed to be grateful for whatever scraps you toss my way?"

"That's not fair."

I laugh bitterly. "Yeah, well, life's not fair."

He slams a hand against the dashboard. "Seriously? What's your fucking problem, Al? You want me to choose, is that it? You or Amber?"

Panic tightens around my chest.

Shit—no. That's not what I want at all.

I didn't mean to push an ultimatum on him. Because if I force him to choose, he won't pick me. He'll choose her.

"No," I say, backpedaling hard. I can't lose my best friend. Even sharing half of Hayes is better than none at all. "That's not what I'm saying."

"Everyone keeps acting like I'm supposed to have my whole damn life figured out." His voice cracks. "But I'm only eighteen, and I just fucking don't, alright? I don't have anything figured out."

I look at him then. Really look.

The tension in his jaw. The tremble in his hands, still clenched on the wheel. The pain in his eyes that he's trying—and failing—to hide. This isn't just about Amber.

Something is very, very wrong.

"Hayes? What's going on?" I ask softly. "Are you okay?"

He exhales through his nose.

"It's my dad. If I don't go to Europe next year to help with the business expansion, he's cutting me off."

"You mean go for the summer?"

He shakes his head. "I mean for good."

My jaw drops.

"He wants you to drop out of college?"

A hollow, humorless laugh. "No football. No degree. No *me*, basically."

"But he can't... actually make you do that, can he?"

He's quiet for a long moment, like even answering is too painful.

"Mom promised to talk to him," he says. "But yeah, he can. He can do whatever he wants. It's his empire. And at the end of the day, she'll stand by him, no matter what."

"But what about what you want?"

He scoffs. "You know my dad. Legacy. Family. Tradition. That's what matters to him." He stares down at his knuckles, white from how hard he's holding the wheel. "What I want doesn't even make the list."

"That's not fair," I say. "You have to stand up to him. Fight for your future."

His parents have always seemed reasonable to me. I know how much they love him. Maybe if he just tells them how much this means to him, they'll meet him halfway. Work out some sort of compromise.

"You don't get it. It's not that simple."

"You don't have to do this alone." I reach out. My hand finds his thigh, the muscles tense, coiled like a spring. "I can talk to Kora. I'll make her understand. Your dad, too—"

He flinches, pulling back like my touch has scorched him.

"I don't want you to do that. It's not your problem," he says. "Just drop it."

"But, Hay, I want to help—"

"I said *no*." His voice slices through the air like a blade. "This is why I like your sister—at least she knows when to shut up."

The words hit like a slap. I jerk back, breath caught, throat tight.

"Fine," I whisper, reaching for the door handle. "If that's how you really feel, I'll go."

His hand shoots across the console, locking around my wrist before I can open the door. His grip tightens, his eyes wide with regret.

"Al, wait—I'm sorry. You know I didn't mean that," he says. "Please don't be mad at me. I couldn't handle that right now. Not with everything else."

"I'm not mad," I say, even though something inside me is already bruising. "I just hate that you keep shutting me out. Whatever's happening, I want to be there for you. I just wish you'd let me."

"Believe me," he murmurs, his voice thick, "there's a lot of things I wish were different, too."

"Like what?"

His expression flickers, like he's balancing on the edge of a confession. Like he wants to tell me everything.

Then he leans in, slow and deliberate, until the heat of him sinks into my skin. His comforting scent —that warm cedar smoke and something darker, spicier—folds around me, tugging at something low in my stomach.

My breath catches. Every muscle in my body goes taut, waiting, straining toward him before I can stop myself. His eyes flick to my mouth for the briefest heartbeat, and the air between us tightens, charged enough to make my pulse stumble.

For a suspended second, I think—hope—he might kiss me.

But he doesn't.

Instead, he veers higher, his lips brushing the side of my temple, feather-light. Gentle. Far too gentle to mean anything.

Then he reaches past me and opens the door.

"It doesn't matter," he says, his voice rough with restraint. "There are things you don't know. Things I can't tell you. And I can't change any of it, no matter how much I wish I could… and neither can you."

CHAPTER 13

I decide to skip the Alpha Delta dayger at Hayes's frat house the next day.

After last night, I'm not exactly sure where Hayes and I stand, and showing up to a frat party to find him tangled up with my sister doesn't strike me as the smartest way to find out.

He'd said he wanted to talk about Argy after the game, but it'd felt like something else. Like he was fishing for information. Testing my reaction to his getting back together with Amber, maybe. And then he shut me out the second I pushed too hard about her and his family.

Yes, he apologized, but there was distance in it. A quiet kind of retreat that told me not to push again.

I feel like giving him some space is a good idea right now. Maybe I'm giving myself space, too.

Still, I'd be lying if I said I wasn't thinking about the consequences of staying home today. If Amber goes and they spend the whole day together—laughing, drinking, reconnecting—what then? Would that be all it takes to seal the deal? To make whatever's between them official again? Hayes barely has time for me as it is. If he gets a girlfriend, especially one as clingy as Amber, that time is going to drop to zero.

What did he say again last night?

Oh, right.

She just "fits into his life."

Does that mean I don't anymore?

Of course, he also dropped that life-altering bombshell about being forced to move to Greece after the school year. Not for a semester abroad. Not for summer break. Move permanently—as in, pack up and go. So maybe he's just trying to keep his head above water, focusing on how to handle his parents and his future. Maybe Amber, and whatever's left between them, isn't even on his mind right now.

Sometime after lunch, I hear Amber's heels clacking across the tile as she heads out. I'm sprawled on my futon, door shut, bingeing old *Buffy the Vampire Slayer* reruns. I've seen every episode a dozen times, but I never get tired of them. Buffy was everything— smart, fierce, brave even when she was terrified. Outnumbered or not, she never backed down. She always ran toward the monsters. There's just some- thing about that kind of courage that sticks with you.

"Come on, let's go," my sister says, barging in my bedroom and plopping down beside me. "The party's already started."

I don't even look up from the laptop screen.

"I'm not going."

"Don't be ridiculous. It'll be fun, Ally." She elbows me lightly. "You can ride with me and the girls."

She sounds sweet and sincere, but I know her too well. I'd bet money Mom sent her in here to try and convince me, probably bribed her with one of those Sephora gift cards her clients hand out instead of tips.

Typical Mom.

She's already tried twice this morning herself. This has her fingerprints all over it.

"No, thanks."

"But Mom says—"

Bingo.

I knew it.

"I don't care what Mom says," I say flatly. "I already told her I'm not going, and I'm not changing my mind. So you can both just back off, okay?"

I finally look up—and instantly regret it.

Amber's wearing a brand-new dress I've never seen before: pale Cinderella blue, body-skimming, with flutter sleeves and a cutout at the waist. I know she already blew her last paycheck on her Homecoming dress, which means Mom must've caved and bought her this one.

Her blonde hair is curled into perfect, bouncy waves, her skin still glowing from a fresh spray tan. She looks like she belongs on the cover of a magazine. Every guy at that party is going to lose their mind when they see her.

Including Hayes.

A hot knot of envy twists under my ribs. I don't want to care. I *shouldn't* care.

But I do.

I hate how easy it all is for her. How she gets to sparkle and be adored and doesn't even have to try.

"I just thought it might be fun to hang out today," she says, almost shyly. "You know… like we used to."

I hesitate, something in me softening a bit.

It's not just the words—it's her expression. She's not smirking. Not performing for once.

Maybe there is a Sephora gift card in it for her, but this part is real. She genuinely wants me to come out and spend time with her. And I don't know why, but that gets me.

"You look really pretty, Ambs," I say, reaching out and tucking a shiny curl behind her ear. It's awkward and unfamiliar, big sister energy I didn't know I still had. "Have a great time today."

"Ally—"

"Please, just go. I'll be fine."

I turn away, cranking up the volume on *Buffy* until the sound drowns everything else out.

After she leaves, I search for something darker to watch. Something to match my mood.

I scroll through Netflix until I land on some old horror movie about a creepy kid who might be the Antichrist. Apparently, he kills people just by looking at them. The plot feels vaguely familiar, though I'm not sure I've seen it before. Probably just the usual trope. There are so many devil-child stories—*Rosemary's Baby*, *Little Evil*, *Deliver Us*. This one isn't half bad, from what I can tell, but I'm too distracted to really follow.

All I can think about is Hayes.

Sometime after a mysterious dog shows up and a Catholic priest starts warning the parents their child might not be human, I shut my laptop and drift off to sleep.

I'm running.

My bare feet slap against wet sand, lungs burning, heart pounding like a war drum. The wind howls, tugging at my hair. I can smell the ocean, taste the salt, feel the dusk thick and heavy on my skin.

I'm little—maybe five or six. My mother is screaming something I can't quite hear, clutching Amber to her chest with one arm, the other gripping my wrist so tightly it hurts.

Behind us, something snarls.

The sound makes my blood freeze. It's low and savage and not like any animal I've ever heard. It's wrong. Unnatural.

I glance back, and the shadows stretch, flickering. There are eyes in the dark, low to the ground. Glowing red. Hunting us.

"Faster, Alysander!" Mom cries. "Don't stop. Don't look back!"

I run harder, tears streaking down my cheeks.

Then—out of nowhere—he's there.

Hayes.

Standing at the edge of the rocks. Hair wind-tossed, face mostly hidden by the twilight. He steps forward and raises one hand, palm out, like he's telling the monsters to stop.

And they do.

They squeal in fear… and then everything goes still.

I blink—and Hayes is gone. The monsters, too.

And then I'm in Mom's car speeding away. Just road and sky and darkness…

I wake with a start, Mom's screams still echoing in my head.

The room is dim now, my laptop dark beside me. For a second, I'm not sure what's real. The air still smells faintly of wind and sea salt.

Just a weird dream, I tell myself. But the image of the monsters with the red eyes… and Hayes—his face, his hand raised like a command—lingers longer than it should.

I roll over, re-fluffing my pillow. It was probably that stupid horror movie. Or something I read in my mother's letters—that last one, the one about the beach and running from hellhounds.

Still… it felt so real.

Too real.

More like memory than dream. It didn't feel imagined. It felt remembered.

I shake it off and force myself to fall back asleep.

When I wake again hours later, something in me has shifted. I feel lighter. Clearer.

I decide I'm done lying around, obsessing over what Hayes might be doing with my sister or whatever mess is happening with his family. None of it is within my control. Especially if he won't let me in.

Instead, I'm choosing to focus on me. My wants. My goals. My future. If no one's going to choose me, I'll choose myself.

Maybe I didn't land the role I wanted in *Hercules*, but there are other ways to build my résumé. Other ways to boost my shot at NYU. I remember reading about a girl who grew her YouTube following to nearly a million subscribers. She turned down a record deal and still got accepted to both NYU and USC, which has the best pop vocal program in the country. And she didn't even write her own music. She just covered old Britney Spears tracks.

Surely, I can do better than that.

A burst of resolve moves through me as I turn my laptop back on and create my own YouTube channel. I choose a name that's simple and low-key. Catchy enough to stand out, but subtle enough that no one from school will immediately know it's me if they stumble across it.

Sander Sings.

With the account set up, I reach for my steel-string Yamaha acoustic guitar, the one always leaning against my nightstand. My mother bought it for me on my thirteenth birthday from a thrift shop near her studio. It's still the best gift I've ever received.

I sit cross-legged on my bed and strum a few chords, playing with the tune. I already know which song I want to upload first.

It's an angsty breakup anthem I wrote last year about a girl who falls for a guy she's never meant to have. A little punk, a little rock-and-roll. Maybe more autobiographical than I care to admit. I'm especially proud of the hook, though the melody still needs some work.

I run through the song a few times, adjusting the lyrics here and there, but I can't record yet because my stomach is growling so loudly I'm pretty sure the mic would pick it up. Not exactly the vibe I'm going for. The background of my first admissions track can't sound like a dying whale.

Unfortunately, there's nothing edible in the kitchen.

All I can find is Mom's vile wheatgrass smoothies and a container of homemade kale chips that taste like seaweed and cardboard had a disgusting baby. Mom usually saves grocery runs for Mondays, since she doesn't go into the Artists Co-op until later in the afternoon. Which means I have no choice but to wash my face, twist my greasy hair into a bun, and crawl out of my cave in search of real food.

A few minutes later, I pull my car out of the apartment parking lot and crank the volume all the way up, bopping my head along to an old Nirvana song. My adrenaline is still buzzing from all the singing. For once, it feels like maybe I'm not just reacting to my life but actually steering it.

I feel so good, in fact, that I decide to be generous and stop at Hayes's favorite Greek restaurant, Souvlaki's, to grab him dinner too. He's probably wasted at the frat party by now and could use something to soak up the damage.

Souvlaki's is pricier than I normally allow myself, which is why I usually only go when Hayes insists on paying. Still, I want to do something kind. Something uncomplicated. I even text Mom and Amber after I park, asking if they want anything.

See? You can do this. You can still be Hayes's friend, I tell myself. *Even if it feels like he's slipping further away each day.*

The pep talk almost works too—right up until I walk inside.

What the hell?

Hayes is here.

His black hair is damp, curling slightly at the ends like he just showered. He's in jeans and his favorite Nikes, looking far too put together for someone who is supposed to be spending the afternoon getting wrecked with his frat brothers.

He sits alone in our usual booth beneath a framed photo of the cliffs of Santorini. Half the image shows the iconic, blue-domed buildings that cling to the hillside of the Greek island. The other half is the Aegean Sea, impossibly blue, dotted with sailboats near the shore.

One afternoon out on the archery fields, Hayes's father told us of the Greek myth about how Santorini came to be. Jason and the Argonauts, a band of heroes sailing through the Aegean Sea, were on a quest to help Jason reclaim his rightful throne from a usurping uncle. During their journey, they landed on the island of Anafi. There, one of the men fell in love with a sea nymph who became pregnant and needed a safe place to give birth. To help her, the Argonauts threw a clod of earth into the sea, and the island of Santorini emerged.

Back then, I believed in stories like that. Magic pulled from nothing. Miracles born of love and desperation.

Now, I believe in science.

And I later learned that Santorini was formed by

a volcanic eruption, not some ridiculous romantic myth.

"Hay?" I call out, walking toward the table.

"Alysander?" He looks up, startled, like he's been caught doing something he shouldn't. The blue-and-white checked menu slips from his hand. "What are you doing here?"

I don't love the way he's looking at me, like I've intruded. And maybe I have. Showing up at his favorite restaurant alone could come off as… odd.

"I could ask you the same thing," I say. "Why aren't you at the party?"

He shrugs, his eyes sliding away. "I got bored."

Hayes ditching a party? That's not like him at all. Whatever's going on with his family must be worse than I thought.

"Actually, I'm glad I ran into you." I slide into the booth, pretending not to notice the way his posture stiffens. "I feel awful about last night. I didn't mean to push. I'm sorry. I just—I want you to know I'm here. For whatever you need, whenever you're ready to talk."

I offer a small, hopeful smile.

"That's great," he says, too quickly. "But can we do this later? I'm kind of here with someone." His eyes flick toward the back of the restaurant, to the bathroom.

A cold tendril of intuition curls at the base of my skull, slick and unwelcome.

Then I see it.

The extra place setting. The half-empty Diet

Coke, a pink lip gloss stain bleeding into the straw. The combo appetizer platter Hayes always orders for us—hummus, baba ghanoush, tabbouleh, dolmas—barely touched.

Hayes isn't alone.

He's waiting for someone.

Someone who isn't me.

Of course, I think, feeling stupid. *He's here on a date.*

"Right." My voice comes out brittle as I scramble to my feet. "I'll just go, then."

"I'll call you later, okay?" His eyes flick toward the back of the restaurant again, like he's worried whoever he's here with might come out at any moment and catch us talking.

Which is… strange.

Hayes has never cared before if I was around his dates.

Not that I enjoyed it, but I've third-wheeled through more of his flirtations than I can count. We've even joked about it—how he'd split his fries with me while ignoring some poor girl he had zero plans of ever asking out again.

But this?

He's jumpy. On edge. Acting guilty. Something about his behavior sets off alarm bells in my head.

I glance at the lipstick stain again, heart plummeting because, suddenly, *I know.*

I know exactly who he's here with.

And then, like a cosmic punchline I should have seen coming, my sister walks out of the bathroom, smiling and waving as she heads toward us.

"Don't be mad," Hayes says, his voice just a little too smooth, a little too rehearsed. "This isn't what it looks like. It's just dinner. I really needed a friend tonight."

He needed *Amber*?

She's the friend he turned to?

Like I'm not the one who's known him since we were five and has always been there for him.

"*I'm* your friend, Hayes. *Me*."

The words come out hot and sharp, and maybe a little desperate.

"Al, come on. Please." His voice is soft, almost pleading. "I don't want to fight with you again."

"But, Hay—"

"I just can't. Not today."

His fists clench the table edges, his knuckles going white. He won't even look at me anymore.

And that's when I know.

Really know.

It doesn't matter what I say or do. He's already chosen her.

He always chooses her.

I was a damn fool to think this time would be any different.

Heat stings the corners of my eyes as I step away from the table. I don't walk—I flee. Because if I stay, I'll shatter in front of both of them, crack open and bleed all over the floor. And I can't let that happen. I can't let them see what this is really doing to me.

I make it to my car, dive inside, and yank the door

shut just in time. An instant later, the tears come. Hot, stinging, unstoppable.

Rejection.

Humiliation.

Loss.

A part of me always knew this day would come. I just didn't realize it would come so soon.

My shoulders shake as I slump forward, burying my face against the steering wheel. The ache inside me swells until it spills over, raw, relentless, and hollow. It eats at everything in me, scraping me clean, until there's nothing left but exhaustion, followed fast by a crushing emptiness.

And then I remember.

Shit.

I forgot the damn food.

Because of course I did. As if the night wasn't already a complete disaster, now I'm going to starve.

Fucking perfect.

CHAPTER 14

I don't hear from Hayes after our run-in at Souvlaki's. He skips French on Monday, and I don't spot him anywhere on campus—not in the quad, not at the student union, not even lurking by the dining hall.

He's definitely avoiding me. No question about it.

Until now, the longest we'd ever gone without talking was twenty-three hours and fifteen minutes. We were twelve. I'd broken my wrist falling out of his treehouse after he dared me to climb up without using the ladder. I never could say no to a dare.

I don't remember much. Not the climb. Not the moment I slipped and fell. Not the drop. Just a flash of sky, a rush of wind, and then… nothing. I blacked out.

When I came to, Hayes was there, holding me, eyes wide and terrified. One hand was clutching mine, the other pressed firmly against my back to keep me upright. My wrist was already swelling, my whole body aching. But somehow, I was alive.

My mom had to leave work to take me to the emergency room. She yelled at us the entire drive while I sat in the backseat with Hayes, crying as he held my hand—the good, uninjured one.

It wasn't until later that I learned how serious it really was. The doctor said if I'd landed just a few inches differently, I could've broken my neck and been paralyzed. Maybe worse.

I was lucky. A miracle, apparently. Hayes helped to break my fall.

Naturally, Mom was convinced a guardian angel must've been watching over me that day. One from the Underworld, I suppose.

I was so furious about my broken wrist I refused to speak to Hayes, even though I was the idiot who took the dare and should've known better. Back then, I didn't know you didn't have to prove yourself just because someone told you to do something reckless.

Hayes didn't argue. He just looked miserable. I think he felt even worse than I did.

The next day, he bought my forgiveness by handing over his limited-edition Demogorgon Funko Pop. It was his favorite. He was obsessed with the show *Stranger Things*—not just for the monsters and jump scares, but he loved the idea of the Upside Down, a shadow world running parallel to our own, only darker and more dangerous. The vinyl figure was his version of a peace offering. My broken bone in exchange for the best creepy monster on TV.

The gift ended our fight almost instantly. It wasn't even a full day.

So, yeah. I'm not used to going this long without Hayes making his daily appearance in my life, but maybe a little space isn't the worst thing. If anything, his absence gives me room to focus on what actually matters for my future. Time for my music. Time to work on my transfer applications. Maybe even time to figure out who I am without him.

After classes that week, I head home each day, grab my guitar and songwriting journal, and get to work. Maybe it's all the pent-up emotion, worrying about Mom and about Hayes and his inevitable reconciliation with Amber, but the music pours out of me like it's been waiting for this. As if it's been building up inside me for years and just needed the silence and space to finally surface.

Even the melodies, which are usually the hardest part for me, come easily for once. It's like they already exist somewhere in me, quiet and fully formed, just waiting for permission. It feels like something's cracked open inside me.

I record a brand-new track and upload it to my YouTube channel. It's like nothing I've ever written before. More real, more raw. It's got legs and edge— angry girl rock, pure Olivia Rodrigo energy. I fall asleep that night with my guitar still beside me and a flicker of hope burning in my chest.

When I wake the next morning, the first thing I do is check *Sander Sings*—and I nearly drop my phone. My new song already has hundreds of likes, pushing toward a thousand. My heart stumbles as I blink at the screen, rereading the number like it might disappear.

I'm still buzzing when I walk into Vocal Performance Studio later that morning. The room is mostly empty. A few students are gathered in the back, and Professor Jones is at his desk, flipping through a songbook. He's wearing one of his signature bow ties, red with pink polka dots, paired with a crisp white button-up and khakis.

"Uh, Professor Jones?" I ask, walking over. "Can I talk to you for a second?"

He looks up, his brown eyes crinkling at the corners. "Of course, Ms. Smith," he says, closing his songbook and setting it aside. "What's on your mind?"

"I, um… started a YouTube channel. For my music." The words tumble out in a nervous rush. "I was wondering if you'd maybe take a look. Tell me what you think?"

I slide my phone across the desk and hit play before I can second-guess myself. Guitar chords spill out of the tiny speaker as he leans in closer and bumps up the volume. My voice fills the quiet theater, and a wave of panic spikes through me.

Do I sound pitchy?

Are the lyrics too simplistic?

My confidence unravels with every note.

I look away, pretending to study the faded theater production posters from past performances on the wall, anything to avoid meeting his eyes. The longer he listens, the more convinced I am he's about to tell me I'm not cut out for this. The high I felt last night after hitting upload? Completely gone.

When the song finally ends, my skin burns with embarrassment. I want to grab the phone and bury it under a rock.

But then… Professor Jones claps.

"Wonderful! Truly wonderful," he says, eyes bright. He taps the screen and lifts a bushy brow. "And look at that—already thousands of likes. Impressive."

I blink. "Wait, what?"

I take the phone back and check the screen. Sure enough, there are over 4,000 likes and climbing. Hundreds of comments too, most of them kind. Praise for the lyrics. Fire emojis. People asking for more.

"I'm proud of you. Putting yourself out there takes guts," he says. "How does it feel?"

"Good," I say, sliding the phone into my backpack. "I think."

His stomach growls just then, and he reaches into his desk drawer for a brown paper bag. "Do you mind?" he asks, holding it up like an apology.

"Oh—no, of course not."

He hums softly as he dumps the contents onto the desk: a sad little cup of oatmeal—no toppings, not even brown sugar—and one hard-boiled egg. It's barely enough food for a toddler.

"That's your lunch?"

"Wife's got me on a new diet," he says, patting at his rounded belly. "No sugar. No salt. She doesn't even season the eggs. Can you imagine?"

I stifle a laugh as he takes a bite and grimaces.

"Here's my advice." He chews slowly, thoughtfully. "The song's great, truly. But the bridge drags a bit. Tighten it up. Add a third verse. I think there's more story here to tell." He gives me a pointed look. "Don't ever hold back. The best artists never hold back."

If he only knew. Holding things back has basically been my life's defining skill.

"Thanks, Professor. I'll work on it."

"And keep going," he says, a note of encouragement in his voice. "Maybe we can make it your solo for the Fall Showcase."

A quiet thrill pulses through me. So far, all the solos are covers.

"Wow. That would be… really amazing."

I rummage through my backpack and pull out the Ziploc bag of brownies Mom packed for me this morning. She still makes my lunch like I'm five years old, but sometimes it works in my favor, like now.

"Here," I say, offering him the bag. "They're vegan, but I swear they're actually good. My mom's kind of a health-nut baking wizard."

"Well, thank you." He unwraps one like it's treasure. "I keep telling you, Ms. Smith, you've got real talent. You just have to start believing it, too." He smiles, warm and genuine. "And I'm not just saying that because of the brownies. Though they definitely don't hurt."

After that, class begins, and Professor Jones introduces our new assignment, due next week. We have to pair up and deliver a presentation on a pop artist of our choice, analyzing their musical evolution, cultural impact, and key contributions to the industry. The concept is actually kind of cool, but I hate partner assignments. I never have any friends to pair up with and always end up doing all the work.

I'm caught off guard when Amber's friend

Rebecca slides her desk next to mine and turns toward me.

"Want to be my partner?" she asks. "We could do Lady Gaga?"

"Sure," I say, a bit surprised but not opposed.

We pull out our notebooks, and she exhales softly.

"She's so talented, right?"

"Her artistry is definitely next level." I nod. "Tisch is my dream school—that's where she went. I applied last year but didn't get in." I glance down, cheeks warming, unsure why I'm telling her all this and wishing I hadn't. "It's probably stupid, but I'm trying again. Hoping to transfer next year."

"That's really cool," she says, and her expression is surprisingly earnest. "And hey, you never know. Gaga dealt with rejection too. All the greats have. And now look at her." She leans in slightly, voice softening. "No one else gets to decide what you're capable of. That's up to you."

"Yeah. Maybe."

I turn back to my notebook, dragging my pen through the margin like I'm focused, but really I'm just buying space. It's not that I don't appreciate what she said. It's just strange opening up to someone I barely know. Especially one of Amber's friends.

"So," I say, steering us toward safer ground, "what song should we cover?"

"'Born This Way.' For sure."

"You don't want to pick something more... mainstream?"

I expected her to suggest "Poker Face" or "Bad

Romance." Something glossy and pop-forward. Bubblegum music like Amber would pick. Not a song that's basically a gay rights anthem.

"I love that song. It's a powerful track about owning who you are no matter what," she says, glancing down at her two-toned Prada loafers. "That means a lot to some of us… to people like me."

Oh.

"That's cool," I say gently. Her expression wavers, like she's wondering if she said too much, but I've never cared who someone loves. "Love is love, right?"

"Thanks, Alysander," she says, a big smile on her face as she places a hand lightly over mine.

We spend the rest of class mapping out our presentation and dividing up work. I take Gaga's early life—her childhood in New York, her time at Tisch, everything leading up to *The Fame*. Rebecca takes the later albums, her foundation, and all her activism.

"Should we meet Saturday to finalize the slides?" I ask as class wraps up, copying our outline into my notebook. "After the game? There's a lot to pull together before Monday."

"But Saturday's the Alpha Delts Heaven & Hell party. Aren't you going?"

I school my face into neutrality.

"Right," I say, summoning a smile that feels passable. "The party. Of course."

I can't believe it.

There's an Alpha Delts party this weekend, and I didn't even know. Hayes hasn't said a single word to me about it. Was he ever planning to?

Or… was I just not invited?

Rebecca studies me, her expression sharpening. "Hayes didn't tell you?"

"Of course he did," I say, a little sharp, even though Rebecca isn't the one I'm mad at.

Thirteen years of friendship, and I have to find out about his parties now from someone who barely knows him?

"I meant Sunday, obviously," I say, forcing my voice calmer. "Let's meet then."

The rest of the week passes in a strange sort of limbo. I keep expecting to run into Hayes, maybe on campus or at his apartment when I stop by to see Argy, thinking he'll act normal again and casually mention the party. But our paths never cross.

By Saturday night, I'm simmering with the kind of anger and frustration that has nowhere to go. The worst part is I can't even call Hayes to yell about it without looking unhinged. The last time I saw him, I practically fled a restaurant in tears. Adding more drama isn't going to fix anything.

I sit at the dinner table with my mom and Amber, keeping my head down and focusing on the food so I don't say something to my sister I'll regret.

Tonight's meal feels like another gastrointestinal insult: Caesar salad without dressing or croutons, fake-meat meatballs over spaghetti squash instead of actual pasta, and a parade of steamed green vegetables, no sauce in sight. It's a full spread of Amber's clean-eating favorites.

If anyone had bothered to ask what I wanted, I'd

have said fried chicken and mashed potatoes. Or maybe a greasy, cheese-loaded pepperoni pizza. Something that doesn't taste like penance.

But of course, no one asked me.

"You look beautiful, honey," Mom says, smiling at Amber who looks like some kind of goddess come to life. She's still in her robe, but her hair's already curled and pinned with crystal barrettes. Makeup dewy and flawless.

"Thanks, Mom," Amber says sweetly, squeezing lemon into her seltzer.

Mom turns to me, eyeing my oversized hoodie and sweatpants with mild disapproval.

"When are you getting ready for Hayden's party?" she asks. "I assume you're not wearing that."

"I'm not going."

I stab a meatball and shovel it into my mouth, not even caring how disgusting it is. The last thing I want to talk about right now is Hayes.

"But Ambrosia said it's a big costume party." Mom blinks, clearly confused. "She said everyone would be there."

Amber groans. "Mom, I told you—they're not speaking."

"*Still?*"

My fork slips from my hand and hits the floor with a loud, metallic clang. "Can you please stop talking about me like I'm not sitting right here?"

"Sorry, honey." Mom winces and takes a long sip of her honey-lavender tea. "I'm just surprised. You and Hayden hardly ever fight."

I push my plate away.

"We're not fighting."

"Sure seems like it," Amber chirps, happily twirling her squash noodles like they're actual pasta.

"Oh my God, shut up, Amber."

"Alysander," Mom says sternly. "Don't speak to your sister that way."

"But she's antagonizing me on purpose," I say. "Hayes and I are fine."

Except we're not.

For the first time in years, I genuinely don't know where I stand with him. The silence between us no longer feels like just a pause. I'm starting to wonder if it might be an end.

"Did you say something to upset him?" Mom asks gently, her voice cautious.

I cross my arms, jaw tight.

"Mom, no."

"Well, maybe—"

"Can you not?" I push my chair back, the legs scraping loudly against the floor. "I don't want to talk about it."

"Fine," she says, like *I'm* the one being difficult. "It would just be nice if you and your sister could get along for once. I love Hayden like he's my own son, but it feels like he's always coming between you two."

"Oh, this isn't Hayes's fault," Amber cuts in, all wide-eyed innocence. "He's still talking to me. Ally's the one he's ignoring."

"For the last time, we're fine!" I yell.

They exchange a look—tight-lipped, patronizing, as if I'm being dramatic.

Maybe I am.

But I've hit my limit, and right now, it's easier to blow up at them than at Hayes. At least they're here. He's not. To unload on him, he'd have to actually show up.

"Thanks for dinner," I grit out. "Can I please be excused? I've lost my appetite."

Mom nods, and I scrape my plate into the sink, rinse it, and shove it into the dishwasher. While they're still whispering about me and distracted, I grab a few leftover sweet potato brownies off the counter and stuff them into my hoodie pocket.

Okay, so I lied about that too.

I'm still hungry, but I can't sit at that table another second.

"She's just so sensitive," Amber says loud enough to make sure I hear as I walk past them. "You can't even say his name without her losing it."

Once I'm inside the safety of my bedroom, I throw on my headphones and crank my music until it drowns out everything else. It's not like I even care about stupid parties or staying in alone on a Saturday night, but it's always been my decision. Hayes has never purposely excluded me from anything before.

Well, maybe excluded isn't the right word.

It's not as if he banned me from the frat party or told me not to come. He just… didn't invite me.

Maybe I'm reading too much into things. He's under a lot of pressure. Maybe he just needs space.

Except... why doesn't he need space from Amber, too?

Sometime after 8 p.m., there's a knock at my door. For once, Amber actually waits to be invited in, peeking her head through the crack like she expects to get it bitten off.

She's fully dressed now in a tight white dress, matching thigh-high boots, fluffy wings, and a shiny halo headband. An angel costume. Irony at its finest.

I rip off my headphones.

"Get out."

"Relax, okay?" She lifts her hands in surrender. "I come in peace."

"What do you want, Ambrosia? To rub it in some more? I get it—you're going to Hayes's party. And I'm not."

She ducks her head, surprisingly meek.

"I just... wanted to see if you wanted to come with me tonight."

I stare at her, thrown. Did Mom bribe her with another gift card to guilt-trip me out of bed?

"Why? What's in it for you?"

Amber rolls her eyes. "You really think I need a reason to do something nice?"

"Yes. Absolutely."

"You're my sister, Ally," she says, almost sounding wounded. "Did it ever occur to you that maybe I don't like seeing you upset?"

"No."

I burrow deeper under my covers, pulling them up

like a shield. Wishing—begging—for her to take the hint and leave.

She doesn't.

"Why do you hate me so much? What did I do?" she asks quietly. "We used to be friends, remember?"

I glance over, ready to snap again—but then I see her expression. Her eyes are glassy. She blinks quickly, and I see she's practically on the verge of tears.

"I don't hate you, dummy." I let out a frustrated breath. "I'm just… angry with Hayes."

"I'm sorry you guys are fighting. I didn't mean for this to happen."

"It's okay. It's not your fault."

She nods, a flicker of relief crossing her face. It almost feels like we're having a moment, like we're real sisters again. Like we used to be.

"I didn't tell him to pick me—he just did," she adds with a little shrug. "You can't be mad at me for that."

The words hit like a gunshot.

Of course.

Even when she's trying to be nice, she still has to win.

"Out!" I point at the door.

"Ally, come on. You know what I meant—"

I throw one of my balled-up socks, hitting her shoulder with absolutely zero force but maximum attitude.

"NOW."

She stumbles back, then finally leaves, probably off to find Mom and play the victim again.

Time passes slowly.

I lie in bed, fists clenched, staring at the ceiling.

How did things get so tangled between me and Hayes? I've replayed it a hundred times and still can't make sense of it. He's at a party right now, surrounded by half of LHU's campus. I'm the only person he's avoiding.

How am I supposed to not take that personally?

It *is* personal.

Does Hayes really think he can just cut me out without any explanation, like I never mattered? Like all our years of friendship don't earn me even a goodbye?

No.

He doesn't get to do that.

He doesn't get to treat me like one of his random hookups and just toss me aside. If nothing else, I deserve to know why he's doing this. After everything we've been through, the very least he owes me is the truth.

And I'm going to get it.

CHAPTER 15

Thirty minutes later, I swing open the front door of the Alpha Delta frat house, ready to crash the Heaven & Hell party and finally corner Hayes to get some answers.

I'm wearing the only red thing I own in my wardrobe of black—an old dress I haven't touched since I was eleven. It was part of a Little Red Riding Hood costume I wore trick-or-treating with Hayes in junior high. I was Red. He was the Big Bad Wolf. The cape and wicker basket are long gone, but somehow the dress survived, stuffed in the back of my closet like a relic from another life.

My costume did *not* look like this back then.

What used to hit my knees now barely skims the tops of my thighs. The once-loose cotton bodice clings tightly to me, framing more cleavage than I usually show and hugging every inch like it knows exactly what it's doing. I wasn't trying to be sexy. It just turned out that way.

I didn't have a backup, so it was either show up in a slightly scandalous costume or don't wear one at all, and for a college frat party, that felt like the worse choice. I already stood out enough without making it look like I didn't get the memo.

Feeling self-conscious, I threw on my black vegan leather jacket and knee-high lace-up boots to toughen it up. I left my choker on, the familiar band steady and grounding like armor. A swipe of my mom's red lipstick finishes the look. If Amber's playing the angel in her head-to-toe white ensemble, then I guess that makes me the devil.

The smell of beer, weed, and too-strong body spray hits me like a wall the second I step into the common room where the party is in full swing. The DJ blasts AC/DC's "Highway to Hell," bass thumping so hard I feel it in my ribs.

The Alpha Delt's house has been completely transformed for the Heaven & Hell theme. All around me, red string lights coil over the furniture like glowing vines, casting everything in a low, infernal glow. Smoke machines puff steady, hazy clouds from the corners, curling around my boots as I walk past. Half the ceiling is rigged with fake icicle chandeliers, while flickering red bulbs cover the rest. Heaven on one side, Hell on the other, apparently.

I scan the crowd for Hayes, weaving through all the bodies pressed and dancing together like one giant, writhing organism under pulsing strobe lights. Half-naked angels float past me in white lace and rhinestone halos, sipping neon jungle juice from plastic cups. The devils are even bolder in their tight red vinyl, glitter fishnets, and sky-high scarlet stilettos. I duck around a half-angel, half-devil couple making out under an archway of red and white balloons, then cut toward the back of the room.

No sign of Hayes anywhere.

Either he hasn't arrived yet—or worse, he's already upstairs in one of the bedrooms with some random girl. Or possibly my sister, who's also mysteriously missing.

The thought makes my stomach twist, but I force myself to stay optimistic. Maybe he's just out back, flirting with one of the barely-dressed sorority girls I saw heading that way. Not ideal, but still better than the alternative—him off somewhere, tangled up with Amber.

I step through the sliding glass doors onto the back patio, the thud of bass muffled as it closes behind me. The air is sharp with the bite of early October. A cluster of guys lounge in teak chairs near the deck, doing shots, the white linen cushions stained with spilled drinks. On the grass, a giant inflatable pool sloshes beneath a tangle of drunk freshmen I vaguely recognize from class, stripped down to their bras and angel-themed underwear, wings abandoned in the dirt. They shriek and splash around like overexcited hyenas.

A flicker of warmth blooms in my chest as I spot Argy curled up beside one of the fire pits. At this point, the dog has basically become the frat's unofficial mascot. Someone apparently felt inspired and tried to dress him up. A pair of red devil horns lies abandoned beside him, and he rests his head on his paws, yawning like he's deeply unimpressed with everyone's life choices.

"Argy!" I drop to my knees and clap my hands. "Come here, baby!"

His ears perk up, and he's on his feet and in my arms before I can brace for it, tail whipping back and forth like he's been waiting all night for me to arrive. He covers my face in wet, enthusiastic kisses, whining softly. I laugh, holding him close and pressing my face into his fur. It's nice to know at least he still wants me around.

"Aw, don't you two make an adorable couple?"

I look up to find Amber standing there, flanked by Tiffany and Brooke, who giggle at her stupid joke. Rebecca lingers off to the side, arms crossed, offering me an awkward little wave. They're all wearing slightly different versions of the same angel costume Amber has on—tight white dresses, glittery halo headbands, and feathered wings.

"Hilarious, Ambs," I mutter, biting my tongue. I'm not here for drama. "Have you seen Hayes? I can't find him."

Amber tilts her head, all wide eyes and mock surprise. "Thought you weren't coming tonight."

"Changed my mind." I shrug, scratching behind Argy's ears. "Have you seen him or not?"

I rise to my feet, brushing grass from the hem of my dress, and something in Amber's face changes. Her eyes sweep over my outfit—the red dress, the boots, the lipstick—and her mouth tightens, caught between jealousy and judgment. A few guys nearby are staring openly now. Appreciatively.

Not at her. At me.

I feel the difference immediately. And so does Amber.

"Oh my God," she says, loud enough for everyone

around us to hear. "What are you wearing? You look like Little Red Riding Slut."

Tiffany and Brooke laugh on cue, loud and performative, always hungry for Amber's approval.

Rebecca shifts awkwardly beside them. "Amber, come on." She offers me a small, watery smile. "I think you look nice, Alysander."

"Oh, relax." Amber waves her off with a breezy flick of her wrist. "She knows I'm just joking."

"And so witty," I say. "Ever consider a career in stand-up?"

Amber leans in, close enough that it almost feels private. "Look, I know you're hurting," she says, a tight, uneasy edge beneath her voice. "But throwing on the tightest thing you own and showing up here like some psycho ex isn't going to make Hayes suddenly want you around again. You're better than this, Ally. And if he doesn't see that, maybe it's time to stop chasing him."

I step back, my stomach flipping uncomfortably. Her words sting, mostly because I've already thought them myself. That maybe I came here hoping for something that isn't going to happen. That this is exactly how humiliation looks.

"Thanks for the life advice, Oprah," I say.

"I'm just saying, you're giving off a sad, last-ditch-effort vibe." Amber tilts her head, and there's actual sympathy in her eyes now, which somehow makes it even worse. "And it's not a good look."

"Got it. I'm a pathetic loser," I deadpan. "Any

other pearls of wisdom you want to drop before you go?"

She lets out a frustrated groan. "That's not what I meant. You always twist everything around. I'm actually trying to help you here," she says, reaching for me like she's offering some benevolent hand of mercy. "Look—instead of running around after Hayes all night, come hang with us instead. I promise we'll have fun."

I bat her away.

"Thanks for the super tempting offer, but I'd rather swallow a box of razors."

Two red blotches bloom across her perfectly bronzed skin, and for a second, she doesn't have a comeback.

Rebecca glances nervously between us. "Maybe we should just go inside, Ambs," she says, rubbing at her bare arms. "It's freezing out here."

I shrug off my leather jacket. "Here," I say, holding it out to Rebecca. "You can borrow it. I'm heading back inside to find Hayes anyway."

"You sure?" she asks, her fingers brushing mine as she takes it from me. There's a flicker of something in her smile. Hesitant, almost shy. "That's really nice of you."

"Becca, gross. Quit flirting with my sister," Amber says with a nasty smirk. "Ally's not here to be your gay awakening. She's too busy obsessing over Hayes to notice anyone else."

Brooke and Tiffany erupt into laughter, and

Rebecca goes rigid. Her smile evaporates as she shrinks back, pale skin flushing fiercely.

A hot pulse of anger hits me. Not because I think Rebecca is actually flirting with me, but because of what she shared with me the other day about her sexuality. Amber twisting that into a joke seems like a shitty thing to do.

"Jesus, Amber. Don't be an asshole," I say before turning to Rebecca, smiling apologetically. "Sorry. She got dropped on her head one too many times as a baby."

Something shifts in Rebecca's face, her expression curdling. "Mind your own business, Alysander," she says, her voice suddenly cool. "I didn't ask for your help."

"I wasn't—"

"And I don't need your pity," she cuts me off. "Or your ugly coat."

"I'm sorry. I just thought—"

"You thought what?" She lets out a brittle laugh, her eyes sweeping over me with slow, surgical precision. "You thought I needed saving? Please. Have you looked in a mirror? That dress and that lipstick? You're trying so hard, it's honestly tragic."

A knot tightens in my throat.

I can brush off Amber and the other girls. They've never pretended to be anything else. But Rebecca? Some part of me really believed she might be different. That maybe, in the middle of all this, I'd found someone who might actually become a friend.

"Here—take it," she says and hurls the jacket back at my face like it burns.

Argyros's ears flatten. A deep growl rumbles from his chest, low and warning, as he steps in front of me and bares his teeth at her.

Rebecca stumbles back, eyes wide. "Jesus! What the hell's wrong with that dog?"

"Argy, no!" I grab his collar just as his jaws snap in her direction. Huge, gnashing teeth catch the moonlight like razor-sharp silver knives.

Rebecca stumbles back, hands up, face pale with horror. "Get that psycho mutt away from me!" she cries. "He's feral!"

"Just like my sister," Amber says, shooting me a smug, satisfied smile as she loops an arm around Rebecca's shoulders. "Come on, Becca. Let's go."

"Did you see that?" Rebecca hisses as they retreat toward the patio doors. "She tried to have that *thing* attack me."

They disappear into the frat house, their laughter trailing behind them like poison. My hands tremble at my sides, fists clenched with the effort it takes not to scream.

What was I even thinking defending Rebecca? Believing, even for one stupid second, that she might actually want to be my friend?

God, how embarrassingly naïve.

So she showed me a few moments of kindness in class. Big deal. That doesn't make her different. She's just as fake as the rest of them. Plastic smiles. Vicious tongues. They're all the same.

I exhale slowly, the bitterness catching in my throat as I curl into Argy. I bury my face in his warm fur to hide the sting, but one tear escapes, carving a hot line down my cheek. I swipe it away quickly before anyone can see.

I know I shouldn't care what Rebecca thinks. Or Amber. Or any of them. But the truth is, it's not just about them. It's everything.

No matter what I do, nothing ever seems to change. It's like I'm forever stuck in place—unwanted, unchosen, invisible.

I never should've come here tonight.

"You look like you could use a drink."

Dylan's hand lands on my shoulder as he stands over me, clutching two beers in one hand and a lit joint in the other. He's wearing a halo—unironically, I'm pretty sure—and his white Prada fleece is freckled with beer stains.

"Thanks," I say, taking one of the beers. "Actually, I really could."

I raise it in a mock toast, then down the entire thing fast enough to make his eyes widen. I burp softly, and he laughs.

"Nice. How about some shots?"

I consider it for a second. Hayes is nowhere to be found, and I've just been humiliated by my sister and her stupid friends—again. My night's a complete disaster. So, yeah, shots sound like a solid plan.

"You're on."

Three shots and two beers later, I've got a warm, buzzing haze going. Dylan and I are the only ones still lingering outside. The rest of the party has migrated indoors to escape the cold. Argyros is stretched out near the fire pit, eyes half-lidded, ears giving the occasional lazy flick. Dylan hands me another shot, and the dog's ears suddenly perk. A beat later, he's on his feet, trotting toward the patio doors.

"Argy!"

The dog doesn't even glance back.

"Probably smells food," Dylan says with a lazy grin.

I shrug, watching as Argy disappears inside, then I throw back the vodka. It goes down almost too easily, like water.

The stars begin to blur above me. Everything spins.

I chase another shot with beer and look at Dylan through double vision, thinking about how cute both of him are. I don't even mind that he's a little puffy from alcohol, or the beer dribbling down his chin. He's still quite handsome. Nice, too. He's laughed at everything I've said tonight like I'm genuinely funny.

Maybe I am.

I don't plan to kiss him. It just happens.

Hayes is off somewhere ignoring me, probably with Amber, and something in me snaps. I deserve this. Someone who wants me. If nothing else, Hayes will hear about it. Maybe it'll make him jealous.

Dylan and I end up horizontal in the grass, his tongue darting sloppily in and out of my mouth. His rough lips on mine aren't exactly what dreams are made of, but it isn't terrible, either.

I feel light.

Unburdened.

At least… I think I do.

Then he shifts, his body pressing into mine. Arms touching arms, legs tangling. I don't feel any of the light-your-body-on-fire electricity I do whenever I'm with Hayes, but I'm not surprised. No other guy has ever made me feel that way. Maybe no guy ever will.

"Wanna go upstairs?" Dylan slurs against my mouth, his finger trailing across my neckline. "It's more… private."

I hesitate. The sky tilts, stars swirling again.

"Uh, no thanks."

"Ohhh. I get it." His grin shifts, something sleazy creeping in as his hand tugs at the hem of my dress. "You're one of those girls who likes to do it out in the open. I can work with that."

I swat his hand away.

"No. Stop."

"What's wrong? Aren't you having fun?"

Before I can answer, his mouth crushes against mine again. Hard. I try to stay still, hoping he'll stop. That he'll get bored and pass out. That I can just wait it out.

But then his hands are everywhere. Rough, greedy. He reaches for the edge of my dress again, and I shove at his chest, nausea clawing at my throat.

"I said no!" I try to sit up. "I… I think I drank too much. I need to go home."

He grabs my wrist, his nails digging into my skin.

"Don't be a tease, babe," he says. "We're just getting started."

"No. I want to go," I mumble, fumbling through the grass for my phone.

Shit.

Where the hell is my goddamn phone?

His lips are on my neck now, wet and urgent. "You're so sexy. I just wanna—"

"Dylan, stop!"

I try to push him away again, but he yanks my arms behind me, pinning them down.

"Quit fighting me. Just relax," he says. "You'll like it."

Pain flares in my wrists.

"Dylan—ow! You're hurting me!"

"Shut up already," he spits, pressing down harder. His mouth crashes into my neck, hot and suffocating, and terror blooms in my chest. I can't move. I can't get free. He's got me trapped.

"GET OFF ME!"

And then suddenly, he's *gone*—ripped away like a rag doll.

I whip around, breathless.

"Touch her again, and I swear it will be the last thing you ever fucking do."

Hayes is there.

Fury is carved into every line of his face, his eyes swirling like a storm barely contained. Beautiful. Lethal. He looks like the devil himself, cloaked in shadows and rage. Argyros is at his side, snarling so viciously that foam strings from his teeth and spatters onto the grass.

Hayes wrenches Dylan's arm behind his back and pins him to the ground with effortless, terrifying strength.

"What the hell, man?" Dylan thrashes around pathetically. "That hurts!"

"Good," Hayes growls.

I stare at him, dazed. Where did he come from?

"Let go! What's your fucking problem?" Dylan shouts.

"My *problem*?" Hayes leans in, voice dropping to something dark and deadly. "When a woman tells you to stop—you stop, asshole."

"We were having fun," Dylan sneers. "Believe me, she was asking for it—"

Argyros lunges with a savage bark, ready to tear him apart, but Hayes is just faster.

Impossibly fast.

His fist slams into Dylan's jaw in one brutal blow that sends all one hundred seventy pounds of Dylan Masterson flying across the yard. He hits the side of the frat house hard enough that the windows rattle.

"You son of a bitch!" Dylan wheezes, clutching his elbow. "I think you broke my arm!"

His expression twists from shock to fury, but with Hayes's glare locked on him and Argyros circling him like a shark, he doesn't dare move. Hayes stands there, chest heaving, fists still clenched, like he's one breath away from slugging Dylan again.

I scramble to my feet, swaying.

"Hay?" I ask. "What… what are you doing here?"

He turns to me as if suddenly remembering I'm there, and all that fury drains away instantly.

"Are you okay?" His voice softens into something raw and gentle.

"I—I'm…"

My chest tightens, the night collapsing in on itself, and I bolt from the backyard. I sprint inside, ducking into the first open bathroom I see, hands shaking as I slam the door behind me and twist the lock. Then I check it again, just to be sure.

I turn on the cold water and splash my face, catching my reflection in the mirror. Mascara streaks down my cheeks, and there's a smear of dirt on my skin, like I crawled out of something primal.

The girl in the mirror doesn't even look like me.

Oh God…

My stomach lurches and I sink to the floor.

What the hell just happened?

And Hayes.

How did he get to me so fast? We were all alone outside. I'm sure of it. And the way his punch sent Dylan flying into the wall? It wasn't possible…

A flicker of memory hits me then without warning, like a freight train. Suddenly, I'm twelve again, looking up at Hayes's treehouse. Then falling, pitching backward, knowing with absolute certainty that I'm about to die. Hayes calling my name—and then… waking up in his arms. Safe. Whole. Like he'd always been there.

Except… that can't be right.

Another fragment of buried memory surfaces, sharper this time, and I remember. Hayes was still at the top of the treehouse when I fell. There's no way he could've gotten down fast enough to catch me—

"Al?" Hayes knocks softly on the bathroom door. "It's me. Can I come in?"

All thoughts of the treehouse slip away instantly, dissolving like mist.

I don't know if I can face Hayes right now.

My eyes dart around the bathroom, searching for an escape. There's a narrow window behind the toilet, barely wide enough to squeeze through. Even if I could get it open, where would I go? I can't drive. Not after everything I drank. And my phone is gone.

"Alligator?" he asks, his voice gentle. "Please let me in. I want to make sure you're okay."

I weigh my options.

I could keep ignoring him, but that only ends two ways. Either he eventually gives up and I spend the night sleeping on the sticky floor of a frat house bathroom, still in my costume… or, far more likely, Hayes breaks down the door in front of everyone, which might be even more humiliating.

"Okay," I whisper. "But I don't want to talk about it."

I unlock the door. Argyros pushes in first, pressing his cold nose to my knee with a soft whimper. Hayes follows close behind, his presence steady and grounding, a quiet, comforting force.

He takes my hands in his, gently, and his mouth parts—first in shock, then in slow-burning fury—as he sees the red marks circling my wrists. His thumb brushes over the welts with a feather-light touch. Careful. Reverent.

"Does it hurt?"

"A little."

His jaw flexes, rage coiling beneath the surface. "I'm going to *kill* that bastard."

He rises, shoulders tensing, and turns for the door, ready to track Dylan down and finish what he started. He looks ready to unleash hell.

Maybe it should comfort me to see how much he truly does care about me, but right now, I'm just too shaken. My body aches. My eyes burn. All I want is to disappear into sleep and forget this night ever happened.

"Please, Hayes, I just want to go."

He grabs a clean towel and runs it under cold water, pressing it gently to my wrists. His touch is soothing. Steady.

Slowly, he helps me to my feet, his hand never leaving the small of my back.

"I'll take you home."

"No, not home."

I don't want my mom to see me like this. Besides, she won't understand. She's the one who always told me to be careful, always be on guard. That monsters are everywhere and you can't trust anyone, especially men.

"What do you need, Al? Tell me what to do."

The anger still burns in his eyes, but underneath it, there's something else, something unspoken and fiercely protective.

"How did you know I was in trouble?" I ask. "One second, it was just me and Dylan, all alone. And then… you…" My voice wavers. "And the way you hit him. My God, Hay, he *flew* through the air—"

"You're drunk. You're not remembering things correctly."

Maybe.

Probably.

"Come on," he says, opening the door and taking my hand. "Let's get you back to my place."

The walk to his apartment is a blur. I barely register the pavement beneath my feet or the sharp bite of October air on my skin. There's only Hayes's arm wrapped around my waist, his warmth tethering me to reality.

He doesn't speak, just keeps me close, guiding me through the quiet streets. Argyros trots at our side, bristling whenever anyone passes too near.

When we finally reach the apartment, Hayes leads me straight to his room and lifts me like I weigh nothing, lowering me gently into bed. The mattress dips beneath me, soft and comforting.

"Sleep, Al. I won't let anything happen to you," he murmurs, pulling the blanket up around me with the kind of care reserved for something fragile. As if even the slightest draft might undo me.

Argyros hops onto the bed and curls tightly against my side, his warm body forming a small, protective wall between me and the rest of the world.

His gaze locks on the door as if daring anyone to try getting past him.

As sleep creeps in, Hayes settles into the chair across from me. His arms fold across his chest, muscles still tense, his eyes never leaving mine. Steady. Watchful. Like guarding me isn't just a choice.

It's a promise.

I know I should feel safe with Hayes—and I do.

But the treehouse…

Something about the memory just won't let go. Hayes wasn't at the bottom when I started climbing, I'm sure of it.

So who the hell caught me?

CHAPTER 16

Warm, wet dog kisses greet me as I blink awake in Hayes's bed. My eyes crack open to narrow slits, the dim light of early morning bleeding in around the edges of blackout curtains. Argyros hovers above me, his rough tongue swiping across my forehead and cheeks like he's checking for injuries.

"Morning, boy." I gently nudge him aside, wiping slobber off my face with the back of my hand.

I slowly peel back the covers and glance around. The makeshift bed Hayes used last night—a pile of pillows and spare blankets on the floor—is empty. Miraculously, my missing phone sits on the nightstand beside me. Hayes must've found it.

Of course he did.

I tap the screen and scroll the text log. The last outgoing message is to my mom, sent sometime after midnight, letting her know I was safe and staying over so she wouldn't worry.

Hayes again.

Of course he thought of that, too.

The time glows 7:02 a.m. Too early for him to be gone already, even for Sunday practice. Which means he's still here, somewhere in the apartment.

I try to sit up, which is a mistake. A spike of pain drills through my skull, sharp and punishing, as the hangover hits full force. And with it, the memories of last night come rushing back in a brutal, unrelenting wave.

Flirting with Dylan.

Too many shots.

Laughing.

Kissing.

Pretending it was harmless fun, until it wasn't. Until his hands turned rough and my "no" wasn't enough.

My stomach pitches violently, my hands shaking with fury as the image of him on top of me snaps into focus. Pinning me down. Stealing my breath. Freezing me in place so completely I couldn't move. If Hayes hadn't shown up when he did… I don't know what would have happened.

My God.

What was I thinking? I never should've kissed that asshole in the first place.

Not that I blame myself for what happened.

I know it wasn't my fault. Still, the regret burns under my skin like acid. Not because of what I did, but because I knew better.

How did I let myself be alone with someone like that? It's not as if Dylan's reputation was a secret. Everyone on campus knew what kind of guy he was. Even someone like me, who usually stayed oblivious to that kind of thing.

Watching Hayes pull away, thinking I was losing him, made me reckless. Desperate. I lashed out in the only way I knew how in the moment. I let myself use

Dylan to feel wanted, because some fractured, impulsive part of me figured that if Hayes was going to act like I didn't matter, I'd prove someone else thought I did.

How could I have been so foolish?

My bare feet sink into the soft carpet as I slide out of bed, doing my best to ignore the blistering ache behind my eyes. I need to find Hayes and talk to him.

I'm still so confused. Everything between us feels unresolved, tangled. He ignores me for days, makes me believe he's pulled away, outgrown our friendship, outgrown me. And then he shows up like last night, out of nowhere, ready to burn the world down for me.

He *saved* me.

That has to mean something. Right?

Argyros trails faithfully at my side as I step out of Hayes's bedroom and trudge into the kitchen. Sunlight spills through the windows in sharp, golden slants, catching on sleek countertops and gleaming stainless-steel appliances that look like they've never been used. The whole space feels more like a luxury condo than a college apartment—minimalist, spotless, and expensive in a quiet, understated way.

Hayes stands at the fridge, shirtless, the morning light tracing the lines of his back and shoulders like a sculpture come to life. His pajama pants ride low on his hips, hinting at the cut of smooth muscle that disappears beneath the waistband.

I know I should say something, but I can't stop staring.

God, he's beautiful.

I hover at the edge of the kitchen, just inside the wide archway. My mouth opens, then closes—useless. Whatever I meant to say evaporates, my thoughts dissolving into static. Every nerve ending buzzes as I watch him.

He turns, catching me mid-stare.

"Going somewhere, Alligator?"

"No," I blurt, too fast, the back of my neck burning. "Just… looking for you."

"I was on my way back to the bedroom." He shuts the fridge with a casual bump of his hip, then crosses the room barefoot, holding two bottles of water. "Thought you might be thirsty," he says, offering one to me.

"Thanks," I say, taking it, the bottle cool against my skin.

He walks toward the kitchen island, sliding onto one of the barstools and gesturing to the empty space beside him. "Sit," he says, patting the seat.

I take a deep breath and slide in next to him, bracing for the conversation I know is coming. Argyros pads over immediately, like he senses the tension in the air, and settles between us. He circles once before curling into a tight ball beneath my chair, pressing his warm nose against my ankles and letting out a soft huff.

I gather my nerve.

"So about last night—"

"You don't have to explain anything to me."

"I know." I lift my chin. "But I want to."

His eyes sharpen, searching my face with that

quiet, careful intensity that always makes it hard to breathe. It's like he can see right into me—every thought, every crack.

"Just tell me, are you okay?"

"I'm fine."

"Are you sure?" His voice hardens, steel threading through it. "Because if he hurt you…" He pauses, something dark and dangerous flickering in his eyes. "I swear to God, I'll kill that piece of shit—"

"I said I'm fine!"

The words come out sharper than I intend. Hayes flinches, just barely, but I catch it. That quick flicker of hurt before he schools his expression back into calm.

"I'm sorry," I say, taking a careful sip of water to steady myself.

I don't know where the sudden anger came from. I'm not mad at Hayes. Of course I'm not. He wasn't the creep who cornered me in a frat house backyard. He wasn't the one who ignored my no.

And yet, a small part of me wonders.

What if Hayes hadn't pulled away and made me feel so disposable? If I hadn't spent the past few weeks feeling like I'd been quietly erased from his life? Maybe I wouldn't have gone looking for proof that I still mattered, or needed someone else to make me feel like I belonged.

But then I shake my head, the anger collapsing as quickly as it flared.

I'm not a child. I know the difference between responsibility and blame. I can own the fact that I put myself in a risky situation. That was my choice, not Hayes's.

And what happened after my terrible judgment wasn't Hayes's fault, either. Or mine. The only person responsible for that line being crossed is Dylan.

"I didn't mean for any of that to happen last night," I say. "And I'm sorry you got in a fistfight with your teammate."

"Don't apologize for that." His lips press into a thin line. "Dylan's a fucking asshole. He had it coming."

I set the water bottle down on the counter, my throat tightening.

"Yeah, probably." I swallow. "I just wanted to have fun for once. I never should've kissed him. I know that. But he was being so nice. He was paying attention to me, and it felt really good to have someone pay attention to me for once. And I—"

I trail off.

Saying it out loud makes it sound even worse, more pathetic. Needier somehow. Shame coils tight in my chest, and I feel stupid for admitting that part to him.

"Don't do that." His whole body goes taut, like a wire pulled too tight. "You have *nothing* to feel bad about," he says, voice edged with something quietly furious and protective. "That bastard is the only one to blame."

There's a rawness in him now, something wild flickering behind his eyes. The same fury I saw last night, barely restrained, and somehow just as ferocious even in daylight. It's not aimed at me. I know that Hayes would never hurt me. But it still rattles something deep inside me.

"This wasn't your fault. You did nothing wrong," he says, softer now, like he's anchoring the words in place for me. "Not one fucking thing."

"Yeah, I know that." I nod, slowly. "But I wasn't thinking straight either. I just… I wasn't myself."

"You don't have to be perfect to not get assaulted, Al." His voice breaks a little on my name. "God, I hate that I wasn't there sooner." He drags a hand through his hair, the motion rough with frustration. "Are you sure you're okay? Really okay? Just say the word and I'll gladly break his other arm for you."

I try for a smile, but it doesn't quite land.

"You don't need to worry about me," I say. "And definitely no need to maim Dylan in my honor or anything."

Though, truth be told, I didn't exactly hate seeing Dylan's smug, sleazy little face get flattened last night. Wouldn't cry if it happened again, either.

But I'm not about to tell Hayes that and pour gasoline on his already fiery temper. He could get in serious trouble with the school and the team. No matter how good it felt to see Dylan get what he deserved last night, I would never risk Hayes blowing up his future because of me.

"You sure?" he asks.

"Positive."

He gives me a long, hard look. "You're a terrible liar."

"I'm not—"

"If you say you're fine, I'll let it go." He cuts me off with a raised hand. "But, Al… you've got to be more careful. I saw you doing shots with him, and I get it, you were just trying to have fun. But Dylan isn't a guy to play games with. You know what he's like."

"Yeah, I know—"

"And he won't be the last asshole who tries something like that, either," he says, and something heavier settles behind his words. "You've got to be smarter than that. I won't always be around to save you. I need to know you'll make better choices, ones that'll keep you safe."

I stiffen, my spine going rigid.

"I don't need a lecture, Hay," I snap, fists curling in my lap. I know he means well, but I don't need anyone—not even Hayes—treating me like I'm some helpless damsel in need of rescuing. "I can take care of myself. I earned that green belt in karate, remember?"

He snorts, unimpressed.

"We were fourteen. You haven't been to a class in years."

"Okay, maybe I'm not a black belt like you, but I box now, too."

That almost earns a grudging smile.

"Look, I know you're a badass," he says. "But there are things out there you can't fight your way out of."

"Oh yeah? Like what?"

"That's not the point." He leans in, hands gripping my shoulders, firm and grounding. "You just have to be more careful, okay? I need you to promise me."

"God, you sound like my mother," I joke, trying to deflect and lighten the weight pressing down on the moment. "You going to warn me the Underworld's coming after me next?"

He doesn't laugh.

"Promise me," he repeats, his voice so serious it stills me completely.

The lump in my throat stops me from joking again, because beneath all the frustration, what I hear is concern.

Fear.

Love.

Even if he won't say those words.

More than anything, this conversation shows me how much he really does care. His protectiveness—it means something. You don't get that upset over someone unless they really matter.

"Okay," I say. "I promise."

"Thank you."

He leans back, exhaling hard. For a second, he looks… tired. Worn down in a way that makes him seem far older than his eighteen years.

"I just… I worry about you, alright? Probably more than I should," he confesses.

I shift closer, my hand finding his knee, resting there lightly.

"That's really sweet," I say, "but I don't need you playing hero. I just need my best friend back." My voice trembles, full of everything I've been holding in. "I really miss you, Hay. And I—I've been a mess. You've been so distant, and I've felt completely alone, like I don't even matter to you. And it sucks." I don't pull my hand away, even as I steel myself for what comes next. "So what is it? What's going on with you?"

He stills. Not just quiet—completely, unnervingly still.

"If it's Amber, I can handle it," I say, pushing past the thud in my chest when he doesn't answer right away. "Whatever it is… I can deal. As long as you and I are okay. Just, please, stop shutting me out."

Silence stretches between us, long enough that it starts to feel dangerous. Like if one more second passes, the ground between us might crack in two.

"It's not Amber," he finally says.

"It's not?"

He exhales, a slow, weighted breath, and shakes his head once, deliberate. "I never meant to push you away. Al, I…"

I lean forward, hope blooming painfully in my chest.

"Yes?" I breathe.

This is it.

This is the moment he says what I've been aching to hear. That he misses me. That I matter. That I'm still his best friend and always will be.

"I'm leaving Laguna Hills."

The words hit like a punch.

I jerk back.

"You're… *what?*"

His eyes meet mine, full of sadness. Regret. And something else, something raw and fragile that looks an awful lot like dread.

"Turns out my dad's business is worse than my parents let on. There's a hostile takeover, legal fall-out… it's bad." He swallows hard. "They don't think they'll be able to come back. Not for a long time. And they need me. When the semester ends… I'm moving to Athens."

"No." I shake my head furiously. "You can't."

"Al—"

"NO!" I repeat, louder, sharper. Like if I say it with enough force, I can undo what he's telling me. "This is college. You can't just… leave in the middle of it."

Cold spreads through me, fast and numbing, ice pouring straight into my veins.

This can't be happening.

My best friend—my only friend—is *leaving?*

The thought lands heavy and terrifying. How am I going to survive without him?

"I can finish school over there," he explains. "I'll get my degree in Greece."

"And football?"

He shrugs, but there's defeat in it. "It sucks. But Dad says it's just a game. Family comes first."

"And Argy?" My voice splinters. "Where will he live if you're gone?"

There's no way my mom will let me keep a hundred-pound dog in the apartment. I can already hear her reaction. I could try hiding him in my closet, but he'd bust out in five seconds flat.

"I'll take him with me. He'll be okay."

"Well, I won't!" The last word breaks in my mouth like glass. "What about me? I'm just supposed to lose you both?"

Argyros lifts his head and rests his chin on my knee. His warm eyes blink up at me, steady and achingly aware, like he understands exactly what's happening and is grieving it too.

I cradle his face between my palms, trying to keep control of myself, but it's no use. I lose it. The tears come, sharp and hot and blinding. Sadness hits me, so powerful it almost knocks me over.

"Please understand," Hayes says, his voice hoarse now. "I don't *want* to go, Al."

"Then don't."

"I don't have a choice." He looks down, blinking like it's taking all his strength to hold himself together. "If there were any other option, believe me, I'd take it. The thought of leaving everything I know… of leaving you—" His voice falters, the words getting stuck in his throat. "I guess that's why I've been distant. Why I've been pushing you away. I don't know how to say goodbye."

"Please," I beg. "Isn't there anything you can do?"

He shakes his head, looking broken.

"What about my mom?" Panic rises fast, choking and relentless. "She's slipping, Hayes. She's not okay. I don't know what I'm doing." I stand, grabbing on to his arm like a lifeline. "I can't do this without you."

Cold, gnawing fear slithers through me, sinking its teeth into the deepest parts of my brain. And then a thought slips in, so dark, so terrifying, I barely let myself think it—

What if I'm just like her?

Another memory stirs. Last night, something impossible. Hayes appearing out of nowhere. Dylan's body lifted and thrown as if it weighed nothing. I saw Hayes do something no human being is capable of. It was like something out of a superhero comic book— or a nightmare.

Maybe it was the alcohol.

Or maybe… it wasn't.

What if I'm already starting to unravel?

And if I am—if I'm truly losing my grip on reality —how am I supposed to survive without Hayes here to pull me back? To ground me. To remind me what's real.

Hayes rises slowly, the light shifting as his shadow falls across me. His hand comes to rest on the back of my head, fingers threading softly through my hair.

"You're stronger than you think," he says, his voice filled with sadness. "You don't need me. You'll be okay, I promise."

Maybe he believes that.

Maybe he even wants it to be true.

But then I catch something in his expression, something cracked and unguarded, and for one reckless, aching second, I know.

Hayes needs me just as much as I need him.

Maybe even more.

Each day runs into the next, like one big, horrible blur, ever since Hayes dropped the news that he's moving to Greece. It's as if the ground beneath my feet has been cracked open, and I've been free-falling without a net.

And yet, despite his impending departure—or maybe because of it—the last few weeks have been better between us. Hayes has really been making an effort. He's been calling. Texting. Showing up to French class again.

We've even been hanging out in the evenings and on the weekends, like we used to, though it's never just the two of us anymore. Amber's always around now too, glued to his side like a barnacle.

Still, I do my best to ignore her. I'm trying to make the most of what time Hayes and I have left. I know the clock's ticking. Every minute matters now.

Even Argy seems to sense it.

He's been extra clingy lately, shadowing me everywhere I go, pressing up against my legs when I stand and wedging himself into my side when I lie on the couch. It's like he's afraid I might vanish if he blinks. Even he seems to feel the countdown running out.

My mom still needs help. The weight of that hasn't gone anywhere, but I've learned how to set it down for a little while. To stop carrying it so tightly in my chest. There'll be time to deal with it soon enough. Right now, I just want to breathe. To feel something close to normal, while I still can.

I've also started thinking beyond NYU, just in case. Belmont in Nashville, maybe, or some tiny art school in LA no one's ever heard of. Without Hayes here next year, there's no reason to stay. I've spent my whole life dreaming of leaving this place. Now there's nothing holding me back.

LHU is pretty much a flop anyway, other than Hayes. I haven't really spoken to Rebecca since the Heaven & Hell party. We finished our project, turned it in, and that was it.

She's been pretending like I don't exist ever since. Even though I still don't know what I did wrong, I've accepted that I'm not going to have friends here. Maybe not anywhere.

Maybe I'm just the kind of person destined to go through life alone. Always on the outside looking in. Someone who never really fits in anywhere.

Time seems to fly by as I prepare for the inevitable—saying goodbye to my only friend, the only person in the world who's ever truly understood me. And my dog, too. My entire life is shifting beneath my feet in ways I can't stop or fully comprehend yet.

And then, somehow, it's already Halloween.

It also happens to be my eighteenth birthday— and the anniversary of the day my father disappeared.

Halloween's always been hard for obvious reasons. Hayes knows that, and every year, he's done his best to distract me.

We have a tradition.

We always spend the day together, just the two of us. When we were little, we'd go trick-or-treating, then end up at Hayes's house, gorging on candy since my mom never allowed sugar in the house. Afterward, we'd curl up on the couch and spend the rest of the night watching our favorite scary movies.

Once we hit high school, we ditched the costumes and going door to door, but everything else stayed the same.

The ritual never changes: first, we start with a classic slasher like *Friday the 13th* or *Halloween*, and then we wind down with a lighter horror-comedy. It's usually a toss-up between *Gremlins*, *Hocus Pocus*, and *Beetlejuice*, though *Beetlejuice* typically wins. Hayes and I share a long-standing obsession with Lydia Deetz.

I was worried he'd forget this year with everything going on, but he texted me yesterday to confirm, telling me to let myself into his parents' house and head to the movie room. He'd meet me there after football practice.

Best of all, no Amber.

The fact he's still showing up for this makes me think maybe we really are okay.

At least… until he leaves town for good.

After my last class of the day ends, I put on my coziest black velour sweatsuit—the one with tiny silver rhinestone skulls embroidered on the cuffs—and drive over to Hayes's to wait for him. I fire up the popcorn machine, the thick, buttery scent filling the air, and then curl up in one of the oversized movie room recliners.

Argyros is in full Velcro-dog mode. His massive body is tucked into a warm ball at my feet, pressed up against my legs like he's trying to fuse us together.

As I flip through the channels, I text Hayes to get an ETA. He doesn't respond, even though practice let out fifteen minutes ago.

I sigh, sinking deeper into the plush leather and pulling my favorite cashmere blanket up to my chin.

Why can't Hayes ever be on time for anything?

He knows how important today is.

For one thing, it's my birthday. I'm officially eighteen. I can vote, get a tattoo, buy tobacco—not that I'd ever want to—and even open a bank account, if I had any money to put in it. I'm an adult in every way one can be.

Except… nothing actually feels different.

I always imagined adulthood would arrive with some kind of magical shift. Like something big would happen the moment I turned eighteen. At least, that's how it goes in the fairytales.

You come of age, transform from ugly duckling to princess, and your long-lost prince appears to whisk you away to a glittering kingdom where you rule together, happily ever after. Or… something like that.

But nothing's changed for me.

Well, except that Hayes is leaving. And Argy too. Both of them headed somewhere thousands of miles away, across an entire ocean I can't cross.

I swallow past the tightness in my throat and scroll

through the streaming options until I finally land on the original *A Nightmare on Elm Street* movie. My stomach flips with a familiar thrill. I've always had a thing for Wes Craven. As far as I'm concerned, he was the undisputed master of horror. *Nightmare* is one of his best—second only to *Scream*—and Freddy Krueger, with his burned face and bladed glove, is pure nightmare fuel even all these years later.

Of course, the sequels were trash, except for *Dream Warriors* and *New Nightmare*, obviously. Those still hold up.

The movie starts, and I turn off the lights. The screen's eerie glow spills across the room, stretching shadows along the walls. I watch eagerly as doomed teens are hunted down and hacked to pieces, punished for a crime their parents committed long ago by killing Freddy. It's a timeless theme: sins of the parents, visited upon the innocent children and passed down like an inheritance.

Today of all days, the lesson about paying for your parents' mistakes isn't lost on me—even if my father's mistake is more abandonment than murder.

It's hard not to think about him every now and then, but especially on Halloween. The night he disappeared. The night everything fractured. I still have so many questions about my father, even after all these years.

Where is he now?

Does he ever think about us?

I shift in my seat, tugging the blanket tighter around me.

These are dangerous questions. The kind of thoughts that can drive a person crazy, if you let them.

Crazy—just like my mother.

My throat tightens and I crank the volume higher, trying to drown out the intrusive thoughts with a soundtrack of eerie music and cinematic violence.

How much like my mother am I?

Is my brain a ticking time bomb too, just waiting to explode?

And if so, how long until something—or someone—pulls the trigger?

I clutch the armrests, willing the spiral in my head to stop.

Where the hell is Hayes?

On-screen, a pretty blonde girl shrieks as Freddy tears her apart with his knife-tipped fingers. My stomach grumbles, hungry as blood splatters across the walls in pulsing bursts. I should probably be disturbed by all the death and gore, but I'm starving.

I pause the movie and head upstairs to raid the Vassilios' freezer, pushing aside endless stacks of frozen orzo and spanakopita Kora has Dimitra stock in bulk. I make a face when I spot a big container of Greek pagoto kaimaki.

Hard pass.

I've never gotten used to the piney flavor. Hayes loves pagoto, but to me it's too chewy, like eating a pine tree wrapped in rubber bands.

Reaching deeper, I finally find my old, reliable friend: Double Fudge Brownie ice cream.

Jackpot!

Spoon in hand and bowl loaded up, I march back toward the theater. As I pass the family gallery wall, my gaze snags on the familiar photographs lining the hallway. I've walked past these portraits thousands of times, but they still make me smile.

There's Hayes's father, grinning beside one of his treasured horses, the big dapple-gray, Phaethon.

A pang tightens in my chest.

God, I miss Phaethon. And the other horses, too. I wonder if I'll ever see them again.

Farther down the wall is what I like to call the Shrine of Hayes: toddler Hayes, wild dark curls and baby teeth. Little kid Hayes, grinning with a missing front tooth. Preteen Hayes, all long limbs and awkward angles in too-big jeans. And, of course, high school Hayes—breathtakingly, impossibly handsome.

Then come the family photos: Hayes and his parents. Always polished, always gorgeous and glowing. His parents look eerily the same in every shot, no matter the year. It's as if they don't age. Like vampires. It's a little unsettling when you really think about it, but there's no denying Hayes won the genetic lottery—either that or his parents have excellent plastic surgeons.

I even make a few appearances on the wall. Candid, goofy photos from birthday parties and school dances Hayes dragged me to. Senior prom. High school graduation. I grin when I spot my favorite: the picture of us at the Wizarding World of

Harry Potter, waving the overpriced magic wands Kora bought for us.

But tonight, something bizarre tugs at me as I study the wall, something I've never noticed before. There are no photos of Hayes's parents before he was born.

No wedding pictures. No engagement shots. No childhood photos. No extended family. Not even a glimpse of their own parents.

Nothing.

It's as if they didn't exist until Hayes did. Like they just... materialized from somewhere else, fully formed, the day he was born.

My phone buzzes in my pocket, snapping me out of my thoughts. My heart leaps as I check the screen, certain it's finally Hayes texting me back. But it's just Amber sending a GIF of a cat blowing out birthday candles and asking when I'll be home to open presents.

Apparently, my sister actually got me a birthday gift.

I'm weirdly touched.

Of course, I'm still annoyed with her for the way she acted at the Heaven & Hell party, and for constantly hovering around Hayes, always trying to pull him away. And then there's the whole *Hercules* play thing. I should probably be over that by now, but I'm not.

Still, her text chips away at my irritation just a little. It makes me feel kind of guilty, too, because I didn't get her anything for her birthday. She turned seventeen just forty-eight hours before me.

It's always been strange, how close in age we are. Barely a year apart. Technically possible, but still… weird.

Thankfully, the joint birthday parties Mom used to force on us stopped once Amber hit high school and decided I was suddenly beneath her.

Now we do our own thing.

She's got big plans this weekend, going out with her friends, ordering sushi and sake bombs with their fake IDs. Unlike my sister, I don't have a group of girlfriends to party with, but that's okay. I'd rather spend my birthday with Hayes and Argy anyway. Just the three of us and our movie marathon.

I'm not always a completely horrible older sister, though. I usually do get Amber a present for her birthday. I even thought about picking up something pink or sparkly—her two favorite things—but after everything that's happened lately, I didn't think she deserved it.

Now, I almost feel bad.

If her gift turns out to be even halfway decent, I'll have to return the favor. Maybe Hayes can help me pick something out this weekend.

I call him again. The phone just rings and rings.

Still no answer.

I blow out a breath, irritated and anxious all at once. It's already past eight. Hayes is never exactly punctual, but this is ridiculous. Practice ended over an hour ago.

I trudge back into the movie room, restart the movie, and drop into the recliner with a heavy sigh.

"What do you think, boy?" I ask Argyros, scratching behind his ears. "We'll give him a little longer, but if his inconsiderate ass doesn't show in the next thirty minutes, he's going to be in serious trouble."

Argyros yawns loudly, as if uninterested in my drama. Then he flops his head across my feet and promptly starts snoring like a chainsaw. I laugh, cuddling into him, and stack pillows around us like a mini fort.

I only meant to rest my eyes for a second, but the next thing I know, the film credits are rolling. I blink at the darkened screen, disoriented. Somehow, I managed to fall asleep even through all the blood-curdling screams and teens being butchered.

I grab my phone, a fresh spike of irritation rising as I check the call log.

Are you fucking kidding me?

It's almost eleven and still no Hayes. Not a single call. Not even a text.

I sit there, stunned, disbelief twisting into some-thing sharper. Angrier.

I can't believe this. My best friend stood me up. On my birthday. On the anniversary of the worst thing that's ever happened to my family.

Fury rises, sharp and fast in my chest. I know the smart move would be to go home, sleep it off, and call Hayes in the morning after I've had a chance to cool down. But I've never been all that smart when it comes to Hayes.

I stab at his name on the screen and hit call. As the phone rings, I rehearse the lecture in my head that I'll give him once he inevitably starts groveling, begging for my forgiveness.

Well—after I scream and curse him out, obviously. Then comes the lecture. A good one, too.

I'll tell him how disappointed I am. How he ruined my eighteenth birthday. That I might never forgive him.

Of course I will—eventually.

But he doesn't need to know that.

I want him to sweat and squirm and feel really shitty for a while before I even think about letting him off the hook. He needs to understand how badly he screwed up.

Finally, on the fifth try, he answers.

"Jesus, Alysander!" His voice is sharp. Unfamiliar. Cold. "What is it?"

I freeze.

Did he seriously just snap at me, like *I'm* the one in the wrong?

My mouth opens, but nothing comes out. I'm too blindsided to even form words.

"Well? Are you going to say something or not?" he barks.

"Are you serious?" I finally manage, voice cracking. "You're mad at *me*?"

This isn't how this was supposed to go.

I thought maybe something came up. Football

practice ran late. A school meeting. An emergency. Anything reasonable. But this version of him—angry, clipped, distant—I don't understand it.

"I'm not mad at you," he says tightly. "I just—I have to go. I don't have time for this right now."

I stare at the screen, my heart slamming against my ribs.

"You don't have *time*?" I explode. "I've been waiting for you for hours, Hayes. Where the hell are you?"

"What are you talking about?"

"We had plans!" Rage floods through me like hot lava. "Movie night. Your house. Halloween. You told me to come over."

There's a pause. Then, a scoff.

"I missed a movie, Alysander. It's not the end of the world."

That's it.

That's the moment the knife slips between my ribs and twists, cleaving my heart from my chest. Something inside me dies because I know, suddenly and with awful clarity, that whatever's been happening between us is worse than I thought. Maybe past the point of fixing.

He didn't just blow me off.

He forgot about me entirely.

"Not just a movie…" I whisper.

There's another pause as static crackles through the line. And then I hear it, the shift, like something clicking into place.

"Oh, shit. Your birthday," he mutters. "Al, listen—"

"Let me guess," I cut in. "Another frat party? Or wait—are you out with my sister again?"

"It's not like that—"

"You forgot," I say, the pain crashing through me, deep and merciless as tears burn behind my eyes. "You knew I needed you tonight, Hay. And you didn't show."

My hurt is laced through every syllable. I don't even bother hiding it anymore. I'm too tired. Too raw. Because it's not just tonight. This has been building for weeks, slow and quiet, like rot.

I can't pretend any longer. I have to face the truth.

Hayes doesn't care about me.

At least not the way he used to.

"I gotta go," I say, barely getting the words out. "Mom and Amber are waiting for me. They have... presents... and cake—"

"Al," he interrupts. "I'm in Athens."

I blink.

"You're... where?"

"I left last night."

"To Greece?" I ask, stupidly. "Is everything okay?"

The only logical explanation I can think of is that something's happened with his father's business, that something went wrong. Why else would Hayes board a transatlantic flight overnight, at the last minute, without telling anyone?

The silence on the line stretches, heavy and

unbroken. A strange, tight panic slowly claws up my spine, scraping against my ribs.

Then his voice comes through at last, low and fractured.

"It's my father."

There's a sound on the other end of the line. Soft. Jagged. Almost swallowed by the static. It's so unfamiliar, so alien to me, that it takes a moment for my brain to catch up.

Hayes is *crying*.

Hayes doesn't cry. Not since we were kids. And even then, he usually tried to hide it.

I sit upright, ice flooding my veins.

"What is it? What's wrong?"

Something inside me already knows this is one of those moments that splits a life cleanly in two. Before and after. I can feel the certainty settling deep in my gut, heavy and inevitable, like the world has tilted off its axis. Whatever comes next will change everything.

And… I'm not ready.

I want to hit pause. Stop. Rewind. Go back in time.

But I know we can't.

"He's *dead*," Hayes says, voice splintering into a million pieces. "My father is dead."

CHAPTER 18

I can't stop thinking about Hayes's father in the days that follow.

I know the world is vast and unpredictable and that people die every day, but until now, death has always felt abstract. Something that only existed in news headlines or on movie screens. Distant. Impersonal. The kind of thing that happened to other people, in other lives. Never like this.

This wasn't supposed to happen to *us*.

Death is supposed to come later. After college. After marriage. After kids. When we're older and worn down by time. When we're parents ourselves. It's not supposed to arrive when we're barely stepping into adulthood.

It feels like I've lost something forever, something I didn't even realize I had. Some quiet piece of innocence I'll never get back. The world seems tilted sideways, like one of those carnival fun houses lined with warped mirrors, everything bent and unfamiliar. Nothing looks quite right anymore, and I don't know how to move through life the way I used to.

Most nights, I end up crying into my pillow. Small, muffled sounds, like a private confession. Which is strange, because I wasn't even all that close to Hayes's father.

The man was always busy, always on the move. Important. Out of reach.

I saw him mostly at family dinners or big events, like Hayes's birthday parties and holiday gatherings. Even when he let me ride his horses or joined me in the ring, he was quiet, often somewhere else in his mind.

Still, he was the only father figure I've ever really known.

Perhaps that's why the grief hits deeper than I expected. Maybe it's not just the man himself I'm mourning, but the idea of him. The permanence he seemed to represent. Stability and power.

Aidan Vassilios was larger than life. He felt untouchable. If someone like that can disappear in the blink of an eye, then it's proof the world can change at any minute, without any warning.

No one—not even the strongest of us—is safe.

Apparently, it was a freak car accident. A truck veered into oncoming traffic and hit his luxury sedan head-on. Both Hayes's father and his driver were killed on impact.

I had to hear all of this secondhand from Amber.

According to my sister, the funeral was held in Athens, where Hayes's father was buried alongside generations of relatives in their ancestral cemetery. Hayes and Kora flew back to California shortly after to settle his father's estate, though no one knows how long they'll stay here. With his father gone, the family business needs Hayes more than ever. Another trip to Greece—a final, permanent one—feels inevitable.

It's hard not to be upset that Amber is the only one Hayes is confiding in. More than anything, I want to be the person Hayes leans on right now. Except he won't let me. He's shut me out completely.

He won't answer any of my calls or texts. Mom says his behavior is normal and that I should give him space. That people grieve in different ways and I shouldn't take it personally, because death can make people act strangely, even pull away. Especially when it's this sudden and shocking.

Fine, okay. I get that.

I just don't understand why he's sharing everything with *her*—his grief, his plans—while I'm left in the dark.

Still, it feels petty to bring this up to anyone. Now isn't the time to be dramatic or clingy. Not when Hayes is going through so much. So I try to ignore the ache in my chest and pretend not to hear Amber's late-night calls with him echoing down the hallway. Even when it breaks my heart a little more each time it happens.

"Yes, of course I'll go with you," I hear her whisper into the phone one night while I'm cramming for midterms in the kitchen, hunched over a big pot of coffee. Her bedroom door is open down the hall, and she's even louder than usual.

"Yeah, I get that. But you need me," she says, then pauses, like she's listening closely to whatever he's saying on the other end. "We'll figure it out."

Then I hear her annoying, tinkling laughter.

"Duh, yes, of course. I know it's *far*, Hayes." I can practically hear her rolling her eyes at the phone. "But I want this to work, too."

My stomach knots.

I have a sickening hunch they're talking about her traveling with him to Greece when he goes back. I don't know if Hayes plans to finish the semester at LHU or take a leave of absence now, but with his father gone, a move to Greece feels like a foregone conclusion.

It's not if.

It's when.

But is he really bringing Amber with him?

How would that even work? She's a senior. She still has to finish high school. Mom may be a pushover for Amber, but I can't imagine her signing off on something that drastic. Not before graduation, at least.

Unless they're just talking about a short trip during winter break. That would make more sense, though it's hard to believe Mom would let Amber fly off to Europe, even with Hayes. Our family has never even left California. And I have no idea where she'd get the money for an international flight.

Amber laughs loudly again into the phone.

"No, I suppose the whole princess part doesn't hurt either."

I don't even want to know what they're talking about now.

I slam my textbook closed and storm down the hallway, shutting myself in my room and curling up in bed. I have to remind myself not to overreact and remember my mother's advice. Hayes is hurting; he's not thinking clearly. I need to be patient. Cut him some slack. So even though what I really want to do is wring his neck, I bottle it up and keep it all inside.

The next day, I drive over with Mom to help her deliver the grief sachets she made for him and Kora. They're filled with herbs like lavender and tiny chips of rose-red rhodonite that she says are supposed to "calm the spirit," whatever that means.

I tell myself I'm doing this to be kind. To offer support. The truth is, I just want to see him and remind him I'm still here, even if he doesn't seem to want me anymore.

But when we arrive, no one answers the door. We quietly leave the sachets on the porch, tucking them beneath the welcome mat, and that's that.

When we get back home, I immediately head for my room and climb back into bed, where I've been wasting away for days.

Mom trails after me, her long, floral peasant skirt sweeping the floor. Her ponytail is tied back with a matching silken scarf covered in tiny butterflies. I catch her watching me with that firm, no-nonsense expression, the one she wears whenever she senses I'm slipping into that quiet, shadowy place inside myself.

"That's it. Enough moping around, Alysander," she says, planting herself in the doorway.

"I'm not moping."

I quickly shove my song journal beneath my pillow before she can catch a glimpse. Heat prickles at my neck just thinking about what's inside. In between studying for exams, I've been working out a new song

—a messy, heartsick ballad about painful unrequited love. One that even I know is way too on the nose.

"Your sister says you haven't gotten out of bed all week except for class," Mom says, crossing her arms. "She's worried about you. I am too."

I groan. "Ambrosia needs to learn how to keep her mouth shut."

Of course Amber told her.

I bet she couldn't wait. I can practically see Amber's smug little smirk as she told Mom how I've been holed up in my room, blasting sad-girl indie rock and plowing through an alarming amount of pizza and ice cream.

"This isn't healthy. Your aura's all black and blocked." Mom sits beside me, tucking a greasy strand of hair behind my ear. "Come on, you've got to get out of this funk. Shake it off, sweetie."

I snort.

"Okay, Taylor Swift."

"I'm serious. It's time to stop sulking—and start cleansing." Her gold bangles clink as she pulls a thick bundle of sage from her pocket and waves it like a magical weapon.

I duck away.

"Mom, no. You know I hate the smell of that stuff."

"Now don't be negative," she says, striking a match and setting the smudge stick ablaze. She gently blows until the tips glow red and smoke curls into the air. "A little sage will do wonders to clear out all this bad energy."

She stands and begins circling me with the smoking bundle like she's cleaning the air. Then the chanting begins. She starts speaking in another language—maybe Latin, maybe something else—as if she's performing an ancient ritual to chase away demons.

"What is this, *The Exorcist*?"

Sadly, my joke doesn't earn a reaction. She's in full healer mode now, impervious to my wit, as she smudges over my head and then moves to each corner of the room.

She smudges my bed. My desk. Even my closet gets the full spiritual cleanse.

"Here, now you try," she says, pressing the sage into my hand, wrapping her fingers around mine. "Like this, remember?"

She guides my hand through the motions, starting at the base and then moving up and around, circling the corners and rising toward the ceiling. I half-heartedly follow her lead, waving the sage in one hand while pinching my nose with the other.

"This is really unnecessary. I'm just sad, okay?" I mutter. "It's not like I'm about to start levitating or crab-walk down the stairs like Regan MacNeil."

I let out a dry laugh as I remember the first time Hayes and I watched *The Exorcist*. Me, half-hiding, half-giggling behind a throw pillow during the scariest parts, while he narrated every jump scare in a ridiculous, over-the-top Greek accent, mimicking the voice the demon used to torment the characters.

"That's not funny!" Mom snaps, her face pale with alarm. "Possessions are nothing to joke about. Spirits can slip through cracks in your soul if you're not careful, and believe me, grief leaves cracks everywhere."

"See, this is why I need Hayes. *He* would've laughed," I say, flopping back down onto my bed. "No one else gets me like he does."

"Oh, honey…"

Her expression softens as she wraps an arm around my shoulders, pulling me close. Her scent—rose perfume and a faint trace of her coconut-vanilla hairspray—settles over me like a blanket. Comforting and familiar. Like childhood and lullabies.

"I know it's awful about Hayden's father. And that you're upset about his move," she says gently. "But maybe this is just the push you need to branch out a little. To start figuring out who you are outside of him." She sighs, smoothing my hair like I'm a little girl again. "Maybe it's time to try something new. Make new friends."

"I don't want new friends—I want Hayes."

A single tear slides down my cheek. I swipe it away, frustrated.

"You never know. I bet there are lots of wonderful people at LHU," she says. "You just have to put yourself out there. Give it a real shot."

"You don't get it." I shake my head, my voice turning hoarse. "Hayes isn't some scarf from Free People. I can't just go out and replace him."

A sad little smile touches her mouth.

"I know this is hard, sweetie. But it's like I've always told you, this is what men do. Even the good ones." Her voice flattens then, taking on that bitter edge I know all too well. The one that only ever comes out when she's thinking about him—my father. "They all leave eventually."

"Mother." I pull away from her. "Not everything is about *him*."

But I can see it in her eyes. She doesn't agree.

And that's what hurts the most.

She really believes Hayes, the one person who's always been there for me, is just another version of the man who walked out on us like a coward before I was old enough to remember his face.

"Hayes and that—that *lowlife*—are nothing alike. And they never will be."

She folds her arms, giving me an almost pitying look. "I know Hayden's young, and not everything is in his control here, but the result's the same. He's still leaving you."

I bite my lip, resisting the urge to push back. To list every way she's wrong.

Because she *is* wrong.

Hayes isn't one of her deluded fantasies. He's not some vanished myth, like her half-baked theories about ancient gods and secret worlds. Hayes is real.

What we have, however pathetically platonic, is grounded in something solid. A lifetime of shared moments. It isn't make-believe or one of her fairy tales. And it sure as hell isn't tangled up in the strange make-believe mythology she's built around my father.

One day soon, we're going to have to have a serious talk about all this, but not today. Not when I'm barely holding it together.

"Please. Can I just have some space?" I press the still-burning sage bundle back into her hand and burrow under the covers.

"Sure, honey." She nods, reaching across my nightstand to snuff out the sage in the little ceramic bowl I use for hair ties. "You know, I was afraid this would happen one day. You act so strong, but you never properly grieved your father. When we don't heal those wounds, the pattern just repeats." Her voice softens as she pats my shoulder. "Abandonment doesn't go away. It just shape-shifts. Until you do the soul work, it'll keep finding you. Different face, same pain."

I press my lips together, blinking back fresh tears that threaten to overtake me.

"My only friend in the world is leaving the country. And he's taking my dog, too," I say. "So, please, forgive me for not being emotionally enlightened about it."

She exhales, a long, theatrical sigh perfected through years of maternal disappointment.

"Bad things happen to all of us, Alysander," she says. "If you can look back years from now and this turns out to be the worst pain you've ever felt, then you'll be one of the lucky ones. Believe me."

"Nice, Mom. You should write sympathy cards."

I grab a cold slice of pizza from the grease-stained, dented box on my bed and take a savage bite, tearing the crust with my teeth. Mom eyes the pizza with a judgy look, but to her credit doesn't say anything about it—for once.

"Well, if you don't want my advice, don't ask for it," she says.

"I didn't ask! You barged in!"

"Listen, honey." Her tone remains maddeningly even. "I think this is an important life lesson. It's time you understand that the only person you can truly count on is yourself." She leans in again, smoothing back the baby hairs on my forehead. "Well... and your mother and sister, of course."

"Men are trash. Got it," I deadpan, giving her a sarcastic salute. I finish the slice of pizza and shove the empty box off my bed. One more bite of junk food and I'll probably implode. "What about my dog? Am I allowed to be upset about Argy, or are dogs on your hit list too?" I snort. "I mean, he *is* male..."

She pauses, fixing me with a long, thoughtful look.

"Actually, dogs are worse," she says. "Your father told me that's how they tracked him here. It was the damn hellhounds. He said that's why he had to leave."

"Oh my God." I groan, burying my face in my hands. "Argy is not a hellhound, Mom."

She shrugs, entirely unfazed, as if she has no idea how utterly insane she sounds.

"Well, you never really know these things, do you?"

"Yes, I do. Because hellhounds DO NOT EXIST," I insist.

But for some reason, I picture Argy's teeth flashing in the light that day in the woods—so savage I was almost afraid of my own dog for a moment.

"Okay, baby. Whatever you say." Mom climbs into bed beside me, wrapping an arm around my shoulders, and the creepy image of Argy vanishes as quickly as it came. Her head rests against mine, warm and steady. "I just hate seeing you like this. I know losing something you love hurts like hell. But little by little, the sharp edges soften. Eventually, you'll get through it. And one day, you'll wake up and barely notice the ache at all."

I exhale, sinking into the quiet comfort of her embrace.

"You promise?"

"With all my heart."

"I don't know if I can live without him, Mom," I whisper, the sadness threatening to drag me under.

She brushes her fingers through my hair and kisses the top of my head. "Take it from me, honey," she says. "You never know how strong you are until you lose something you thought you couldn't live without… and survive anyway. I did, and you will too. Sometimes the heart has to break to grow stronger."

I glance over at my desk, my eyes locking on the bulletin board covered with photos of Hayes and me. Snapshots of us through time—birthday parties, bonfires, camping trips, prom. Each one hurts to look at, but I can't turn away.

My throat tightens as I smile at all the good memories… and then it hits me. In a few more weeks—or maybe even days—there might not be any more memories for Hayes and me.

These pictures might be all we ever have.

CHAPTER 19

I sit in bed after Mom leaves, anxious and unsettled. Everything feels out of control, like my entire world is crashing down around me and there's nothing I can do to stop it. Inside, I feel hollow. Numb.

I tell myself to breathe. To cool down. To give it time.

But I can't.

Fuck it.

I can't keep lying here, paralyzed and powerless. I have to see Hayes. I need to know he's okay. If anyone can pull him out of this, it's not Amber—it's me. He just needs to remember that.

I rip off my pizza-stained pajamas and throw on a pair of leggings and an old fleece-lined pullover to brace against the November chill. My hair goes into a low ponytail, and then I grab my keys and head to my car.

I pause for a breath in the driver's seat, debating as I look at my cell phone. I should probably text my mom and let her know where I'm going so she doesn't worry.

But I don't.

She'd only try to stop me, and my mind is already made up.

Just as I start the engine, my phone buzzes with a new message.

Come over. I need you.

My heart leaps as I stare at the screen.

It's from Hayes.

This is the first text he's sent since the night his father died. It can't be a coincidence. It feels like fate. Like somehow, he felt me reaching for him, and now he's reaching back.

Ten minutes later, I pull through the security gate at Laguna Hills Bluffs and wind my way up the long drive to the Vassilios home. The sky has already slipped into twilight, the last scraps of daylight bleeding out over the hills.

One by one, security lights flicker on, casting cold white beams across the trees and driveway. Shadows stretch long and low as I pull up to the front steps. Before I can even knock, the door swings open, and two people I've never seen before stand in the doorway.

Two jaw-droppingly gorgeous people.

Staring back at me are a man and a woman, a few years older than me, with the kind of striking looks that don't seem entirely real.

The man is aggressively tall, broad-shouldered and olive-toned, with a mouth made for trouble. Full lips, straight teeth, and the faintest grin playing at the corners. His hair is white-blond, bright as winter frost, cut clean and sharp, and he's got eyes the most intense shade of green I've ever seen, like polished emeralds. A thin scar cuts from his brow to the edge of his cheekbone, stopping just short of his jaw. It should ruin the symmetry of his perfect face, but somehow, it only makes him more handsome.

And judging by the smirk on his face, he looks like he knows it, too.

The woman beside him is just as breathtaking, but in a colder, almost reptilian way. Her eyes are like onyx, so deep and dark they barely reflect light. Thick curls spill down her back in a cascade of red, streaked with radioactive green at the tips. She's unnaturally still, her presence coiled and watchful, like a venomous snake lying in tall grass. Beautiful but lethal.

"Oh… hi," I say. "I wasn't expecting Hayes to have company."

There's a spark of interest in the man's eyes, intense and unsettling. Like he's been expecting me but isn't sure whether to be amused by my arrival—or annoyed.

"Alysander, right?" he asks, his voice low and smooth, like smoke curling through the air.

"Y-yes," I stammer. "I'm sorry… who are you?"

"Nikolas," he says, then gestures to the woman beside him. "And this is Selene. We've heard a lot about you." His lips twitch, like he's in on some joke I'm not.

"Nice to meet you," I reply, though the words come out a little stiff.

Truthfully, I'm not sure it is nice. Every instinct is telling me something is off. Hayes has never mentioned these people to me. Not once. And I know everything there is to know about Hayden Basileus Vassilios.

So who the hell are they?

And what are they doing in his house?

"Are you… Hayes's family?" I ask, eyeing them.

Am I finally meeting some elusive relatives? I wasn't sure they even existed.

The woman, Selene, doesn't answer. She just stares, stone-faced and unreadable.

"Something like that," Nikolas says. The two of them trade a glance, quick and quiet, like they're used to communicating without speaking.

I notice Nikolas still hasn't moved from the doorway, like he's blocking me from entry.

"Can I come in? Hayes told me to come over."

After a brief, measuring pause, Nikolas steps aside and opens the door wider.

"Did he?" he says, more observation than question. "Well then. We wouldn't want to keep Hayden waiting."

There's a trace of something in his tone. Not mocking exactly, but not totally neutral either. He almost seems… irritated by me. Though I can't think of any reason why. I've known the guy for all of two seconds.

Either way, I find it odd the way he says Hayes's name, like it means something different to him than it does to me.

I hesitate for half a second, then step inside. The moment I'm in the foyer, the light hits, and I get a full look at their outfits.

And… wow.

Nikolas wears a long black trench coat that hugs his broad, muscular frame like it was tailored just for him. His dark pants are sleek, tucked into heavy, steel-toed boots. He's like a cross between a sexy biker and a contract killer.

Selene's dressed similarly. A black latex catsuit clings to her like a second skin, glinting under the lights like oiled leather. Matching boots rise all the way up her thighs.

Other than the fact they're both in black, it's not exactly what you'd call proper mourning attire. They look like they just walked straight off the set of *The Matrix*.

"Uh, are you guys going somewhere?" I ask.

"No," Selene says, blinking slow and blank. "Why do you ask?"

I let out a quick, forced laugh. "No reason."

Okay. This is officially weird.

I head toward the kitchen, hoping they'll go back to doing whatever they were doing before I arrived, but instead, they fall into step behind me. Nikolas on my right. Selene on my left. They're like twin shadows, flanking me in perfect sync, close enough to make the hairs on the back of my neck rise.

Something about it feels… deliberate.

As if I'm being herded.

Like prey.

"Oh, you don't have to come with me. I'll just hang in the kitchen until Hayes comes down," I say, turning to pause. They stop, too—at the exact same time.

"We don't mind," Nikolas replies, his voice velvet-smooth, a sly, almost-smile flickering at the corner of his mouth. "Do we, Selene?"

"Not at all," she says.

I perch on one of the stools at the kitchen island, trying not to fidget under their scrutiny. I can already tell Selene clearly doesn't like me for some reason. Can't say I'm a fan either.

But Nikolas…

He's hot.

That much is undeniable, though he's a bit rigid, bordering on smug. And the way he looks at me? It's unsettling, like how Argy stares at his food right before he lunges. There's something almost predatory in it.

Still, under different circumstances—and with a drastically improved personality—I could probably be into a guy like him. Those eyes, those lips, the stupidly cool coat.

Definitely my type, unfortunately.

He leans forward, elbows on the counter, his gaze sweeping over me like I'm some strange abstract painting in a gallery he can't quite understand. And isn't sure he wants to.

"Can't believe I'm finally meeting *Hayes's Alysander*," he says.

I blink. "Excuse me?"

"You know he talks about you constantly."

Heat blooms in my cheeks. I don't know how to respond to that.

"Well… I hope I live up to the hype," I joke.

Nikolas's eyes move over me in a measured sweep. The air tightens between us.

"I doubt that's possible."

Okay then…

It's not just what he says, which I'm fairly sure is some kind of jab. It's the way his gaze locks onto me, cool and assessing, like he's already made up his mind. Like I'm being measured against some invisible standard—and coming up short.

Also—where the hell is Hayes? As usual, he seems to be taking his sweet time.

"So, um, how long are you two in town?" I ask, mostly to break the tension.

"Not long," Nikolas says. "If all goes as planned."

Selene lets out a soft, knowing laugh, and they trade another look I'm clearly not meant to understand.

I have no idea what's going on, or why they're being so cryptic about a harmless question. But apparently, these are Hayes's long-lost, sort-of-asshole relatives I've never heard of, so I push for normal.

"Are you guys from around here?"

Nikolas's gaze sharpens, just a fraction.

"No."

That's it. No explanation. No follow-up.

The silence stretches, awkward and heavy. I resist the urge to sigh. Granted, I'm not the most social person on the planet, but these two make conversation feel like an endurance test.

"Then where are you from?" I try again. "Greece? Like Hayes's family?"

I lean forward a little, genuinely curious. Hayes has always been cagey about his summers overseas, about Athens and the life he disappears into every summer. Maybe they'll finally fill in some blanks.

Selene laughs, dry and humorless.

"You ask a lot of questions."

"And you don't answer any," I snap back, my patience officially worn thin. "I'd just like to know who's hanging out in my best friend's house, that's all."

Another glance between them. Another secret I'm not in on.

"Well," Nikolas says, his voice velvety and faintly mocking, "if you stay patient, like a good girl, I suspect you'll get all your answers soon enough."

This guy is seriously something else. I honestly can't tell if he's flirting with me or threatening me.

Maybe both.

Selene cocks her head, eyes narrowing as she drags her gaze down my body in a way that makes my skin crawl.

"You're not what I was expecting," she says, tongue clicking against teeth. "You're different from your sister."

That throws me for a second.

"You know Amber?" I ask.

"Unfortunately," Selene mutters, wrinkling her nose. "All that pink. Who does she think she is— Princess Barbie?"

"Pink looks good on her," I say coolly, my spine stiffening.

Amber and I may have our issues, but I'm not going to let some Trinity-cosplaying wannabe in a latex catsuit trash-talk my sister to my face. I don't care even if she is Hayes's family.

I really, *really* don't like this woman.

Just then, Argyros comes charging down the stairs and launches himself into my lap with so much force, I nearly topple off the stool. I wrap my arms around his warm, wriggling body as he whines, nosing into my neck and licking my cheeks like it's been years since we last saw each other, even though it's only been a few days. It's obvious he missed me just as much as I missed him.

"There you are, Al."

Hayes appears at the foot of the stairs.

Our eyes lock, and for a moment, the world almost clicks back into place. He looks—God, he actually looks happy to see me.

Then his gaze flicks to the kitchen, and I watch his expression shift. He takes in the odd little scene: me, stiff and ill at ease at the island, while his supposed "relatives" hover around.

"Everything okay in here?" he asks, brow tightening.

That's when I realize Nikolas and Selene have moved. They're no longer on either side of me like looming shadows but have drifted several feet back, distancing themselves without a word. Their eyes are fixed on Argyros in my lap, watchful and wary. Almost like they're… afraid of him.

Which makes zero sense.

Sure, Argy looks like a half-rabid wolf on a bad day, but right now he's just a big fluffball melting in my arms, tongue lolling, tail thumping lazily. He's not exactly exuding killer animal energy.

So why are they watching him like he's about to rip them to shreds?

Or… maybe it's not Argy they're worried about at all. Maybe it's the person standing behind me.

Are they afraid of *Hayes*?

"C'mon, Selene," Nikolas says smoothly, already moving. He reaches for her elbow, confident and controlled, like someone who expects to be obeyed. "Looks like it's time for us to go."

Selene drags her eyes from Argy and casts a slow, syrupy glance at Hayes through heavy lashes. "Oh, but can't we stay a bit longer, Hayden?" she purrs, her voice suddenly turning breathy and flirtatious. "We were just getting to know your little friend."

My jaw tightens.

I don't like the way she's looking at Hayes. It's too familiar. Too hungry. Too… interested. Definitely not how you look at your family. Unless your family is on *Game of Thrones*.

"Selene. Now." Nikolas's voice sharpens, low but firm. She pouts but doesn't argue as he steers her from the room.

As they walk away, Nikolas glances back over his shoulder. "Pleasure chatting, Alysander. I'm sure we'll meet again soon," he says with that cold half-grin, more a warning than a goodbye. Then they disappear around the corner, their footsteps soft against the tile.

After they're gone, Hayes's eyes flick briefly to mine, uncertain, shoulders tense. "Sorry about that," he says. "They were supposed to leave before you got here."

"So… who are they, exactly?" I raise a brow. "They said they were family?"

He hesitates, then crosses to the fridge, opening it like he's looking for something before closing it again without taking anything. Then he drops onto the stool beside mine.

"They're, uh, cousins."

I nod, scratching behind Argy's ears as I search for the right words now that we're alone. I'd rehearsed a dozen things in the car on the ride over. I had all these big, grand speeches that felt right at the time, but now that Hayes is in front of me, all I can do is look at him.

His presence hits me all at once, like a wave I can never fully brace for. The familiar scent of his skin. The heat of his body just inches from mine. His face, his voice, the way the whole room sharpens and softens at once because he's in it. Even if everything's changed, he's still Hayes.

My Hayes.

He looks at me, those fire-blue eyes fading to ash. "Thanks for coming, Alligator," he says. "I missed you."

I swallow, my throat thick.

"I'm really sorry about your dad."

His gaze drops. And only then do I see it fully—the exhaustion carved deep beneath his eyes, the way his face is thinner, hollowed out like something's been scraped from the inside. He looks completely wrecked in a way I've never seen before.

"I still can't believe he's gone."

His voice cracks on the words and I scoot closer, reaching for his hand. The moment I touch him, I feel it. How fragile he is under all that armor. How close he is to shattering completely.

It scares me.

Hayes has always been the strong one. Quiet. Stoic. Unshakeable. The kind of guy who carries his pain without ever showing it, no matter how hard it hurts.

"Did you get the sachets we made?" I ask. "Mom said they're supposed to help with... you know." I shrug awkwardly. "Grief."

"Yeah. We got them." He nods. "Thanks. That was really thoughtful."

"How's your mom doing?"

"Not good."

"And the funeral?" I falter. "Was it... okay?"

He pauses.

"It was awful."

I wince, feeling like an idiot. I'm saying all the wrong things.

Of course, Kora isn't doing well, and obviously the funeral was horrible. What's next? Should I ask what kind of coffin they picked out? Which designer suit his dad was buried in?

"I'm sorry," I say again, hating how small and useless the words sound. As if they could ever be enough to fix all he's lost.

He sighs deeply, like he's trying to breathe through the weight of it all.

"You don't have to keep apologizing. That's not why I asked you over."

"I know." I squeeze his hand. "I just don't know what else to say."

He looks at me and something desperate and urgent shifts behind his eyes. "I need you to do something for me, Alysander—"

"Of course. Anything."

"You haven't heard it yet." He swallows. "It's going to sound… strange."

"It doesn't matter. Whatever it is, I'm here for you. Always." I offer a soft smile. "You know that, right?"

"I think I do… yeah."

He shifts toward me, slow and deliberate. His gaze locks onto mine like he's searching for something in my face—permission, maybe. A reason not to pull away.

"It's not just losing my dad. Everything's changed now," he says, voice low and rough. "There's no going back… even if part of me still wishes things were different. That I could… that *we* could—"

He stops himself and looks down, like he's said too much.

"We could what, Hay? What are you saying?"

My pulse jumps, breath stuttering, as his hand lifts, tentative at first, fingertips brushing my cheek. Slow, tender. His thumb drags a slow line from cheekbone to chin, sending a spark straight down my spine. It's like he's waking something up inside me.

Then his gaze drops to my mouth.

Not quick. Not subtle. Not by accident.

Intentional.

His lips part slightly.

And just like that, I *know*.

It's not a guess. Not a hope. Not wishful thinking or a daydream or delusion, but a certainty rooted somewhere deep inside. I feel it in my chest, in my bones, in the thrum of the air sparking between us. In the way time itself seems to pause.

This is real. He wants this.

He wants *me*.

The space between us disappears in a breath. My eyes flutter shut, my lips parting on instinct as I lean in further.

And then… I kiss him.

Soft. Hesitant.

I don't know what has come over me, what stupid, reckless impulse finally wins. I can't believe I'm doing this. I'm about to ruin *everything*. But just as doubt threatens to overwhelm me, and I start to pull away, he kisses me back.

His mouth is urgent. Unrelenting. Desperate for me. Like he's starving and has been waiting for this his entire life and can't hold back any longer.

And God—I feel it, too.

All of it.

He groans into me, hands sliding behind my neck, fingers threading through my hair. His body presses into mine like he can't get close enough. It's heat and gravity and need colliding in one impossibly perfect moment. The world spins and cracks wide open. His arms are the only thing anchoring me as the floor slips out from under my feet.

It's not just a kiss. It's a goddamn reckoning.

The kind of thing that ruins you and makes you forget there was ever a before. Something that rewrites fate itself.

But then, too fast, too damn fast, he pulls away.

"Oh fuck. I'm sorry," he says, stumbling back like he's been shocked.

"Hay?"

I'm still reeling. Breathless, tingling. My heart crashing like waves in my chest.

"We shouldn't have done that." His voice is rough, regret bleeding through every word. "That was a mistake."

"A mistake?"

Something inside me crumbles.

I know things are complicated between us. I know there are reasons. But hearing him call *that* a mistake? It guts me. With that one word, everything I've held onto for years—every secret hope, every hidden feeling—goes up in flames.

"We can't," he says, not meeting my eyes. "Amber—"

Shame rushes in then, hot as it floods my cheeks.

Shit.

Amber.

God—how did I forget about Amber? Even for a second.

Even if she's impossible. Self-absorbed, selfish, inconsiderate. Even if we haven't felt like real sisters in a very long time—she still *is* my sister. And Hayes is… what, exactly?

Her ex? Her almost boyfriend again?

Either way, even if they're not officially anything right now, it's still a shitty thing to do without talking to her first. It doesn't matter if her feelings for him are mostly for show, if maybe she only loves the way he looks standing beside her. It doesn't matter that my feelings for him go deep enough to undo me. That I know him better than anyone else and love him anyway. That he's the only person I've ever loved like this. The only one I could. It doesn't even matter that he sees me in ways no one else ever has and probably ever will.

None of that excuses what just happened.

A line was crossed.

Holy hell. What did I just do?

"Right. Of course." I take a step back, my neck burning. "You and me—we can't. Because you and Amber are—"

"No. That's not it." He cuts in. "You don't understand."

Suddenly, the air between us feels all wrong. What was electric only seconds ago is now jagged and torn.

"I should go."

"No, you can't." He grabs my hand and the urgency in his voice returns, stopping me cold. "Amber needs you. That's why I asked you over."

I freeze.

"Amber's *here?*"

My gaze sweeps the room, heart pounding.

"Not exactly," he says. "But she's close. I'll take you to her."

"I… I don't understand."

"I could try to explain, but you wouldn't believe me anyway. Not unless you see it for yourself." His grip tightens, voice softening. "I need you to trust me. Can you do that?"

I stare at him.

Despite everything—the confusion, the hurt, the mess—he's still *him*. Still the boy I've loved my whole life. My best friend in the world since we were five. My everything.

"I trust you."

A shadow crosses his face. "You'll come with me? No matter what happens next?"

"Hayes, you're acting really weird."

"Al, please. This is important."

Something in his eyes makes my stomach drop.

I swallow.

"If you go, I go. Right?"

He holds my gaze a second longer, like he's sealing an invisible oath between us.

"Good." He exhales, relieved, and laces our fingers together. "Then follow me."

CHAPTER 20

Hayes leads me out the front door of his parents' house while Argyros trots behind us, silent and alert, ears pricked. We descend the stone steps and emerge into the thick night air, passing beneath the flickering porch lights and down the illuminated drive until we reach the edge of the estate. That's where the pristine landscaping ends and the wild begins. A forest of fir trees rises ahead, dense and looming, their branches tangling in the night sky.

Hayes stops and switches on the flashlight on his phone, casting a narrow beam into the woods.

"Uh… what are we doing?" I ask, glancing around skeptically. "You sure Amber's out *here*?"

My sister is many things, but outdoorsy isn't one of them. The idea of her voluntarily wandering through trees in the dark? Not exactly on brand.

"Just keep going," Hayes says, placing a steady hand on the small of my back, nudging me forward.

My nerves hum as we cross the final pool of light on the property and step into the shadows. Behind us, the glow of the gas lamps fades, swallowed by the trees. It's nearly pitch-black now. Still, Hayes walks on like he knows exactly where he's going, like he's done this a hundred times before.

The air shifts as we enter the forest. Colder. Heavier. Laced with moss, loam, and something sharper, almost metallic, like ozone before a storm. Gravel crunches beneath my shoes, twigs snapping underfoot.

"It's not much further. We're almost there."

"Okay…" I carefully pick my way over jutting roots and slick stones, staying close to his side. "But, uh, where is *there*, exactly?"

"Relax, Al. Just trust me."

He pushes forward, and I have no choice but to follow.

We go a few more yards, and then he stops so suddenly, I nearly collide with him.

"Hayes?"

No answer.

He just stands there, perfectly still, like he's waiting for something. Beside us, Argyros freezes too. I glance down at the dog, puzzled. His ears are up. Tail rigid. Not a twitch of movement.

"Argy?"

The dog doesn't blink. Doesn't even breathe.

"He'll be fine," Hayes says, but his voice isn't exactly steady as he watches Argyros. "He knows what to do."

I let out a short, disbelieving laugh. "What does that even mean? He's a dog, Hayes. What exactly is he supposed to do?"

He swallows, hard, muscles tightening like he's bracing for impact.

"Al…" My name comes out rough. Almost guilty. "There's something I should've told you. About Argyros." A flicker of regret crosses his face. "He's not what you think," he says. "He's—"

Click.

The sound slices through the trees. A low mechanical whir rises from beneath us, like some ancient engine grinding awake after centuries of sleep. It starts deep and slow, but builds fast. Louder. Sharper. Like it's waking from the dead.

Hayes spins and pulls me into his arms. I feel the tension snap through his body, every muscle coiled tight beneath his skin.

"What's that noise? What's going on?" I ask.

This doesn't feel romantic—at least, I don't think it is—but my body didn't get the memo. Every inch he touches sparks like flint on steel, pulse flaring as his arms tighten around me.

"Don't worry," he murmurs in my ear. "This part doesn't last long."

The whirring deepens into a deafening roar, like a tornado. Then the ground beneath us starts to tremble, subtle at first, then violently.

"What's happening?"

"Just hold on," he says. "Whatever you do—*don't let go.*"

My mouth opens, but I don't get a chance to respond because the earth suddenly shudders beneath us—and then splits wide open.

An enormous black hole yawns at our feet.

I blink. Rub my eyes.

It's still there.

"Oh my God… what is that?" My voice shakes as I stare down into the hole.

Dark.

Endless.

Impossible.

"It's a portal," Hayes says, inexplicably calm. "And you and I are going inside."

"You're joking, right?"

Panic spikes through me as the air around us slowly begins drifting toward the hole. I try to imagine what falling inside would feel like.

Would it hurt?

Would my atoms come apart?

Would I be ripped into tiny little pieces?

"Don't be scared," Hayes whispers against my cheek as the whirring grows louder, hungrier. "I've got you."

Argyros barks a sharp warning and then, without hesitation, *leaps*—as in voluntarily, gleefully jumps— into the black nothingness beneath us. He disappears from view almost instantly.

I don't even have time to scream before a violent force yanks Hayes and me downward, like the pull of two magnets snapping together, only a hundred times stronger. Not gentle. Not slow. Like the ground itself has woken up and is swallowing us whole.

And then we *fall*.

Nothing but darkness surrounds us as we plummet through the cavernous hole, my body being pulled in a million different directions at once.

Deeper and deeper we go into an endless abyss.

The air warps around us, shrieking past like we've been swallowed by something ancient. Something massive and unrelenting.

Amid all the terror, my brain coughs up the strangest memory, and I think of those *Alien* movies. Not about Hayes and his reenacting the chestburster scene, but the part in the sequel when Ripley expels the queen xenomorph through an airlock and into space. For the first time, I actually feel bad for the alien. Because this? This feeling of being hurled through endless nothing?

It's absolutely horrifying.

We fall forever.

Or maybe for a second. A minute. An hour. Days. Months. I don't know. Time doesn't exist anymore.

And then—

Impact.

My feet hit solid ground and immediately give out, sending me sprawling into Hayes. I crash against him, fingers clawing at his back, the breath punched from my lungs.

"You okay?" he asks, untangling us and rising to his feet. He reaches down, hand outstretched, and helps me up.

"I—I think so?"

"Careful," he warns. "It takes a few minutes to adjust."

My legs wobble beneath me like cooked spaghetti as I try to stand. I feel like I've just stumbled off a roller coaster that's been spinning at triple speed and moving in reverse. Even leaning against his solid frame, I can barely stay upright. A wave of nausea surges, sharp and sudden, and I clap a hand over my mouth.

Oh God.

I'm going to throw up.

Or I would, if I had anything left in my stomach, but I'm pretty sure the portal wrung me dry. Food, air, my dignity. Possibly my sanity, too.

Something cold and wet streaks across my cheek in the most vile way. I flinch, shivering, wiping it away without thinking. Sweat, I assume, or maybe rain or mist, but then I realize with a start it's not that at all.

My brain scrambles to catch up with what I'm seeing.

No… not sweat. Not even close.

I blink, mesmerized, at the scene unfolding in front of me. Hundreds—no, thousands—of ghosts. Pale, translucent figures, half-formed and twitching, rising from the earth like steam. Some whisper. Some wail. Others scream with soundless agony, their mouths stretched wide as they swirl and twist like smoke on a breeze before vanishing into the sky above.

The *red* sky.

Not a romantic sunset red or a pretty, cloudy dusk red. Red like blood, like something torn open, raw and gaping and bleeding.

But even ghosts in the air and a sky like something from a nightmare don't compare to the monstrosity looming directly in front of us.

Just yards away, a vast sludge-black river churns,

towering waves crashing against a jagged shoreline littered with bones, bleached white and splintered like wreckage after a shipwreck. Docked at the water's edge is a ferry unlike anything I've ever seen.

It's massive, titanic in scale. Weathered and brutal, with tiered decks that rise from old, chipped wood and corroded steel. It looks like something dredged from the bottom of time itself. Something that should've been sent to a junkyard eons ago.

And the ghosts are *drawn* to it.

They surge forward in a silent flood, phasing through one another as they rush the dock, cries layered in grief as they vanish onto the broken decks by the thousands.

But the worst part isn't the river. Or the bones. Or even the ship.

It's the terrifying skeletal figure standing at the head of the dock.

He has to be at least ten feet tall, draped in a billowing black robe that sways though there's no wind. His back is to us, spine unnaturally straight. One bony hand clutches a long wooden staff, which he thumps rhythmically against the planks. Each strike sends more ghosts forward, herding them like cattle.

Then he turns to face us.

I gasp, stumbling back on instinct. *Nothing* should have a face like that.

Bone-white. Hollow. A perfect skull, stripped of flesh. No skin. No features. Just the raw, leering mask of death itself. It's like something straight out of one of my horror movies, except this time, there's no screen between me and it.

"What the *actual fuck* is going on?"

Hayes grabs my elbow and pulls me forward. "Come on. We have to get on the ferry before it leaves."

I dig my heels into the dirt.

"Are you out of your ever-loving mind? I'm not getting anywhere near that… that *thing*."

Hayes—the absolute bastard—has the nerve to laugh.

"Don't be dramatic. Charon's not that bad."

"Not that bad?" I stare at him. "He has no face, Hayes. NO. FACE."

I slap both hands over my eyes like that'll somehow make this all go away. A thin, humiliating whimper slips out before I can stop it.

I always thought I was brave and strong. The kind of person who stays calm under pressure. Who beats up punching bags and sparring partners for exercise. Who leans into the dark. Who laughs while reading horror books and can make it through any scary movie, no matter how bloody or grotesque. And yet, here I am, turning into a puddle of pure panic when faced with real-life terror.

I admit it's a little pathetic. Under normal circumstances, I'd be mortified. Me, a so-called badass who can't handle a skeleton with a boat.

But not right now. In this very moment, my pride doesn't even make the top ten list of things I'm concerned about.

"I know this is a lot," Hayes says, crouching beside me. "Just hold on a little longer. I'll explain everything soon. I promise."

Gently, he pulls my hands away from my face, his forehead brushing against mine. Steady and grounding. A quiet anchor in the middle of the chaos.

"Do I really have to?"

I can't stop my hands from trembling, my brain a muddled blend of fear and disbelief.

"I'm sorry, Alligator."

"But I don't know where it's going." I shake my head frantically, using the first excuse that comes to mind, no matter how lame. "And I have class tomorrow. I can't just skip it." I'm rambling now, but unable to stop. "What about my academic record? What about NYU?"

Hayes stares at me like I've lost it. And honestly? I probably have.

"Your academic record?" he repeats, flatly. "Are you serious?"

"If I miss too many lectures, my GPA tanks, and NYU goes up in smoke. And my YouTube is finally gaining traction." My voice cracks. "I have momentum, Hayes."

I know I'm not making any sense. I just fell through a literal hole in the earth, and I'm clinging to college credits and my social media stats. But it's like if I just keep talking about something normal, something rational, maybe I'll stay tethered to the world I understand.

Hayes exhales, sadness softening the edges of his face. "You're not going back, Al."

My breath stills.

"What?"

"Not right now, at least," he says. "Maybe not ever."

"Not *ever*?"

A tidal wave of emotion crashes over me as I picture my mother, pacing the house, checking her phone obsessively, unraveling with worry. She would be inconsolable if I just… disappeared. She would never stop looking for me. Never stop believing I was out there somewhere.

"Enough talking. We have to move—now." Hayes grabs my hand, urgency snapping tight in his grip. "If we don't get on that ferry soon, we're in serious trouble."

The fight drains out of me, and I let him pull me forward like a broken marionette, my limbs heavy and reluctant. Because what's the point? I don't know anything anymore. Don't know what's happening. Don't know what's real and what isn't.

As we near the shoreline, bones crack and splinter beneath my shoes like brittle twigs. My lip curls with disgust. I've always liked bones when they're cute little graphics on my clothes or glittering enamel pins. But stepping on them? Crushing skulls underfoot like seashells? That's something else entirely.

Finally, we reach the dock. Black, brackish water lashes against the ferry's hull, spraying a foul mist into the air. I gag and swipe it from my cheeks, grateful none of it got in my eyes, or worse, my mouth. It smells like sulfur and rot, like a thousand years of death trying to claw its way free.

God only knows what's actually inside it.

Hayes tightens his grip on me just as a monstrous wave crashes into the side of the ship. The rickety boat groans and lurches like it's seconds from splintering apart. Mr. Skeleton Face—Charon—raises one bony hand and waves, welcoming us aboard.

"Do we *really* have to get on that?" I ask, hating how pathetic I sound.

"Just follow my lead," Hayes says. "And whatever you do—don't look Charon directly in the eyes."

"Yeah, wasn't planning on it."

I keep my gaze down as we approach the ferry, watching each step carefully. The ground beneath glows scorched red-orange, like a Martian wasteland or one of my mom's more unhinged oil paintings. Bizarrely beautiful, but in a way that makes your insides twist.

Eventually, the cracked, alien earth gives way to splintered planks as we step onto a creaky gangway. Dark water below slaps hungrily against the belly of the ferry. Thick, restless, alive. My feet hit a pale, weather-worn deck, and then, finally, we're onboard.

The engine roars to life as the ferry lumbers forward. Another wave crashes, and I lose my footing, my feet skidding dangerously close to the edge. My heart lurches as Hayes grabs me, one arm snapping around my waist and locking me against his chest.

"You okay?" he asks, steadying me.

"Not even remotely."

I exhale a shaky breath as he guides me toward the back of the boat, and we collapse onto a cold, rusted bench.

As the ferry pulls away from the shore, I grip his arm, my eyes squeezed shut like that will somehow protect me from whatever's coming next.

The vessel creeps down the black river, and I try not to think about the ghosts swarming around us. Try not to feel the cold, pulsing shapes brushing past. But even with my eyes closed, I can sense them pressing in close. Thick and wet and pulsing with energy. Unrelenting.

This can't be real…

Red sky.

Black river.

Ghost ship, steered by a skeleton man in a realm of shadows.

And then it hits me like a punch to the gut.

Oh God.

This is it.

I've finally snapped, just like my mother. Seeing things that aren't there. Blurring the line between real and not. Falling into made-up worlds no one else can see.

Is this what it was like for her?

Is this how it feels to lose your mind?

Or worse—what if—

"Wait—are we in *Hell*?" I jolt upright, dread coiling in my throat. "Did that fall actually kill us? Is this… it?" I let out a weak, humorless laugh. "I mean,

I always thought I'd end up in Heaven. But sure. Plot twist."

Hayes snorts.

"You're not dead."

"How do you know?" I shoot back. "Dead people probably say that all the time. Remember the movie *The Sixth Sense*?"

"Trust me. You're very much alive," he says. "And this isn't Hell."

I crack one eye open and glance around. Yep, sky's still red. Ghosts are still swarming. And creepy-ass Charon is still manning the ship like some judgment-day crypt keeper.

"Sure looks like Hell..."

"It's Hades."

"And there's a difference?"

"Yeah. A big one." He huffs a quiet laugh. "Hell's just one realm inside Hades. Right now, we're at the border. This is the River Acheron, where souls cross over." He nods toward the churning black water. "Charon ferries them to the gates to be judged and sorted: Elysium, Tartarus, or the Fields of Asphodel." He gives me a wry, lopsided grin. "But don't worry. You're not here for that."

"Oh goodie. Then why am I here?"

He hesitates.

"I'm taking you to the Royal Palace."

I stare at him. "I'm sorry—the what now?"

"I'll explain more when we get there," he says, gently brushing a strand of hair from my face. "Just try to relax. Enjoy the ride."

I cross my arms and shut my eyes again.

Enjoy the ride? Sure. Just a casual river cruise through the land of the dead on a barge run by a literal skeleton. Totally normal.

After what feels like forever, the ferry finally slows. The sound of the gangplank lowering cuts through the silence like a drawn-out sigh. Hayes nudges my shoulder.

"We're here."

I open my eyes—and gasp.

Rising up before us is a castle that looks like it was conjured from some Gothic-soaked fever dream. A fortress carved from obsidian-black stone, its walls shot through with veins of molten copper and liquid platinum that seem to shift and ripple beneath the surface. Towering spires pierce the sky, crowned with sculpted flames of hammered gold. Facets of ruby, emerald, sapphire, and even diamond are set directly into the stone, catching the firelight, making the entire structure glitter like a treasure hoard dragged up from the earth's core. The place seems to breathe with shadow and fire, an eerie light pulsing from deep within the walls like it's alive—and watching. Encircling the castle are groves of pomegranate trees, their branches heavy with luminous crimson fruit, each orb faintly pulsing like a heartbeat, casting ghostly light.

It's all so breathtaking. Opulent and overwhelming. So beautiful it almost hurts to look at, like something taken too far, pushed just past the line of reason into something unreal.

And then there are the Palace gates. They're

colossal in scale, forged from interlocked iron etched with unfamiliar markings like runes. Set into the center above the entrance is a sculpted figure of a three-headed dog, each snarling muzzle bared, ruby eyes glowing as if they're tracking us. Coiled around the dog's base is a black serpent, its sleek body wrapped tight, tongue flicking like it's tasting the air. The image is like a nightmare version of a "Bad Dog, Keep Out" sign, but a thousand times more terrifying.

The formidable gates alone feel like a sufficient warning. Like something terrible might happen if you tried to breach those walls uninvited. Guards should be unnecessary. And yet, they're here anyway.

Dozens of them stand silent and unyielding before the entrance. They're clad head-to-toe in black leather armor, each one carrying a spear trimmed with glinting gold. Broad-shouldered. Intimidating. Their faces are expressionless, their stances rigid. They look more like statues than men.

Several guards near the front nod at Hayes as the ferry pulls into the landing square. The vessel shudders to a final stop, chains clanking into place.

Hayes rises and offers me his hand.

"Welcome to the Underworld," he says. "My home."

CHAPTER 21

I wake in the softest bed imaginable, stretching my arms and legs beneath cool, satiny sheets that glide like water over my skin. It feels like I've surfaced from a long, strange dream. Disoriented, but not in a bad way.

Somewhere overhead, psychedelic rock drifts in from hidden speakers. The vocals are low and dreamy, the guitar thrumming like a heartbeat.

Wish You Were Here. Pink Floyd.

One of my favorites.

I sit up and glance around. The lighting is dim and hazy; I can't see much. The fact that I don't immediately know where I am doesn't bother me as much as it probably should. I feel safe. Cocooned. Somehow, I know there's no danger here—unless it's the danger of getting too comfortable in a bed the size of a small country, listening to one of the best rock bands of all time.

"Mmmm." I sigh, burrowing deeper into the sheets. They smell incredible, like my mother's home-made lavender soap blended with something sweeter I can't quite place.

A deep, almost unnatural drowsiness settles over me, my eyelids growing heavy as sleep begins to drag me back under again.

"You're finally awake. Took you long enough."

My eyes snap back open and I turn. A massive figure towers against the far wall, arms crossed, watching me from the shadows like he's been there a while. Bright green eyes flick toward mine, cool, amused, and vaguely bored.

It's him.

Nikolas.

The impossibly gorgeous guy from Hayes's house. The one with the shock of white hair, the wicked scar, and the attitude. He's still in the head-to-toe black leather ensemble from Hayes's house, but now there's a sword strapped to his side.

A literal fucking sword.

He looks like some dark knight or ancient assassin. It's objectively alarming. But also… not *not* hot?

"Where… where am I?" I ask, my voice scratchy, like it hasn't been used in days. "What are you doing here? Where's Hayes?" I yawn, my jaw popping. "And why am I so freaking tired?"

"It's the atmosphere down here," he says. "It can take a toll on the body. You'll adjust."

Oh, right.

Down here.

As in, the Underworld.

A shiver ripples through me as everything comes rushing back. The ghosts, the black river, the skeleton ferryman, docking at the Palace gates and then… nothing. The rest blurs.

"So that was all real? I'm really in… Hades?" I ask. "I didn't dream it?"

"Afraid not."

"So, uh, what happens now?"

"Not my job to explain. That's for Hayden and the royals," he says coolly. "I was just here to make sure you didn't wander off or choke in your sleep. Now that you're conscious, I'm off babysitting duty."

He turns toward the door, then pauses. The corner of his mouth lifts in quiet, mocking amusement.

"Glad you survived the journey. Next time, try not to pass out," he says. "See you around, Alysander."

Pass out? What's that supposed to mean?

But he's gone before I can ask.

A beat later, Hayes appears.

"Hey, sleepyhead. How are you feeling?" he asks, his voice low and threaded with concern as he rushes over to me.

He's changed since I last saw him. He now wears a tailored black velvet suit, sharp and effortless. Shimmering gold trim runs along the lapels and cuffs, like fire flickering at the seams. Cufflinks glint at his wrists, and a gold pin rests on his lapel, ancient and ornate. The pin bears a snarling three-headed dog—ruby eyes glowing, a serpent coiled around its body, just like the one carved into the Palace gates.

The effect of it all is startling. Commanding. Powerful.

"Uh, why are you dressed like that?"

His eyes glint with a hint of teasing.

"You don't like it?"

"No, I—" I rub at my temples, trying to push back the strange fatigue. "You look good. Really good. It's just… what's with the whole Gothic CEO vibe?"

He chuckles, pulling the soft duvet up and tucking it gently around my shoulders, then leans in. His fingers brush a strand of hair from my cheek.

He's so close, I can feel his breath, cool and steady, ghosting across my skin.

"You really scared me for a minute there, Alligator."

"I did?"

"Yeah, you fainted the second we crossed the Palace threshold. Dropped like a stone."

I groan, dropping my face into my hands. That must've been what Nikolas was talking about.

"Oh my God. That's mortifying."

"Yeah, you kind of said that already—a few dozen times—while I was carrying you upstairs."

Wait—

"You… *carried* me?"

"What else was I supposed to do?" He raises a brow. "Drag you by the ankles?"

I burrow deeper into the sheets, heat creeping up my neck. "Please tell me I didn't drool."

"Just a little," he teases.

The chandelier overhead blinks to life as someone bursts through the door and flips a switch.

"So how's the little patient doing?"

My sister saunters into the room, and Hayes jolts back like he's been electrocuted, quickly retreating from the bed and taking a seat on the chaise lounge across from me.

I gape at Amber. Gone are the frilly pink dresses and ruffled miniskirts. Instead, she's clad in a stunning black gown I'd kill for, all taffeta and lace. A boned corset cinches her waist, the tiered skirt pooling like smoke around her heels. Her hair is twisted into a sleek French knot, the bangs pinned with sparkling diamond skull clips.

"What in the actual hell is going on?" I turn back to Hayes. "And why do you both look like you're headed to a party at the Haunted Mansion?"

"I know, right? It's horrid. Black is so not my color." Amber flops dramatically onto the edge of my bed, careful not to wrinkle her floor-length gown. "So," she says, gesturing grandly around the room, "what do you think of the digs? I made sure they gave you the best suite in the guest wing." She winks. "Well—second best."

I forget to be confused, or even annoyed, as I take in the room properly for the first time in the light.

The bed alone is a fantasy.

Massive and romantic, carved from dark wood with black silk drapes that spill down from a towering canopy. A whole family could sleep in it with room to spare. Beside me, sleek black-lacquered nightstands hold glowing candelabras and stacks of leather-bound books, their titles embossed in gold—but not English words. Greek, maybe?

At the other end of the room is a matching desk and more books, packed into shelves that stretch toward the vaulted ceiling. A large mirror framed in glinting obsidian crystals hangs on the wall, and next to it, a vanity table crowded with more makeup brushes and tools than even Amber owns back home, which is really saying something.

Damn.

If this is just a guest bedroom, I can't imagine what the rest of the Palace looks like.

"Minus all the black, yuck, it's to die for, right?" Amber chirps. "I mean, literally. Underworld, death —get it?"

"This isn't a joke," Hayes says, a muscle ticking in his jaw. "You know what's at stake."

"You're right." Amber's tone flips from playful to regretful in an instant. "I'm sorry. I was just trying to keep things upbeat."

She rises from the bed and drapes herself beside him on the chaise. Their legs brush, her arm sliding across his knee, fingers trailing like she owns him.

A wave of something hot and ugly spikes in my chest. I claw my fingers into the sheets, twisting them into angry knots. She's touching him like he's hers again. Like he didn't give me the best, most life-altering kiss of my life just hours ago.

The memory flares—his mouth on mine, the way he held me as if I was the only thing keeping him upright. Like he'd been dying to do that his entire life.

And now he's just sitting there, letting her press against him like none of it ever happened?

Before I can spin out further, I force myself to breathe. To focus on the situation at hand. Now isn't the time to fixate on my sister's hand placement. Bigger questions first.

"Okay, what am I missing?" I sit up straighter, my gaze flicking between them. "What *stakes*?"

"It's a long story," Hayes says, rising to his feet and pulling Amber up with him. "And you need to rest."

I kick the covers off with a huff, the silky fabric slipping to the floor like a fallen curtain. "I'm not going back to sleep until you start talking."

"Tomorrow," Hayes calls over his shoulder, already halfway to the door, Amber at his side. "Ambs and I have dinner with my mother. And we're already late."

I shoot him a sharp look. "Kora's here too?"

"I told you. Long story."

"Then give me the short version!" I snap. "Starting with your *cousins*. Like the guy who was in here five minutes ago, watching me sleep, with a sword at his side and major ruthless assassin energy. Call me crazy, but something tells me they're not actually your family."

I picture bitchy Selene and the flirty little looks she gave Hayes. Definitely not cousin behavior.

Then Nikolas flashes through my mind: that sexy smirk, those cold eyes like bottled forest fire. He might be good looking enough to pass for a Vassilios, but he's no blood relative. Of that, I'm certain.

Hayes stops in the doorway, his shoulders sinking like someone who's just realized they've lost the fight.

"They're Watchers." He turns back and exhales slowly. "They protect what matters here. Territory.

Gates. High-ranking houses," he says. "And the strongest serve my family."

"They're, like, our bodyguards," Amber chimes in.

I'm pretty sure she's trying to be helpful, but it only grates. I hate that she clearly knows more about whatever's going on than I do.

And why is she so damn zen about everything?

If anything, she should be the one freaking out about being trapped in the Underworld. She's supposed to be the sunshine-and-glitter sister. The one who screams at spiders and cries over chipped nails.

I'm the one who loves the darkness and weirdness —the moody horror junkie who doesn't flinch at blood and dreams in shadows. Yet here I am, feeling like I'm losing my mind, while she struts around in a couture funeral gown like she's at the Met Gala.

"But your dad was just a businessman," I say. "What did he need bodyguards for?"

He gives me a tight, humorless smile. "I think we both know my family's not actually in the shipping industry."

Oh. Right.

"Try to keep up, Ally." Amber snorts. "Hayes's father was the King of Hades, obviously."

I cough. "I'm sorry, the *what*?"

"Mr. Vassilios was Hades." She stares at me like I'm the slowest person alive. "You know. The Greek god?"

I look from her to Hayes, studying their faces, searching for the tell. The smirk. The punchline. But there's only silence and something sad and heavy in

Hayes's eyes, like a truth he's been carrying for too long.

"No… that can't be true…" I say.

It's impossible. Hades isn't real. He's a myth. A story.

And even if he was real, he's evil. The dark lord of the Underworld. He releases monsters, curses souls, and eats babies for breakfast—probably. Not a man I've known almost my entire life who wore polished, tassel shoes and Armani suits and made dad jokes at family barbecues.

"Look around, Ally. Is it really that hard to believe?" Amber says, then lights up like a Christmas tree. "And Hayes, he's the Crown Prince. That means he's next in line for the throne."

I recoil against the headboard.

"No. That's—no."

Crown Prince? What is she even saying?

This is *Hayes.*

The boy who once glued my fingers together in art class and stayed on the phone with me all night playing Truth or Dare when we both had chicken pox in fifth grade. The one who held my hand through heartbreaks, karate competitions, and scary movie marathons.

Yeah, okay, so he's always been a little… secretive.

No extended family. Vanishing every summer. But I always chalked that up to rich-people weirdness. Eccentricity.

And sure, there were weird moments I didn't want to think too hard about. The accident in the treehouse. The fight with Dylan. And okay, yes, I am currently sitting in a bed in a palace in another world.

There are things, obviously, I can't explain. But *this*? Full-blown Greek god royalty? If this is true—if this is real—then Hayes has been lying to me our whole lives. Everything I thought I knew about him was all a cover. A double life.

My hands grab a pillow, clutching it tight as the betrayal slices clean through me.

"I wanted to tell you so many times," Hayes says, regret etched into every line of his face. "But I wasn't allowed. There are rules. My father and his brothers made a pact. They agreed to hide their true identities from the human world. To avoid panic. Chaos."

"It was necessary to keep Hayes safe," Amber adds in a smug, know-it-all way. "Their family has a lot of enemies."

That flicker of jealousy returns, sharp and unwelcome. I hate how calm she sounds. Despite whatever rules Hayes had to follow, he clearly broke them for her first. She's not just finding out today, like I am.

"How long has she known?" The words scrape at my throat like sandpaper as I glare at him. "How long have you both been lying to me?"

"It's not like that," he says. "You have to understand, after my dad died, everything changed. Everything… sped up. I needed her help."

"But not mine?" The hurt spills out before I can stop it.

"Al, please—"

"So what, you just pretend to be human when it's

convenient?" I cut him off, struggling to keep my voice level. "Because I've seen you get hurt. Break bones. Bleed. You've grown up, Hayes. How is all that possible?"

"I'm not Edward Cullen, if that's what you're asking." A flicker of dark humor tugs at the corner of his mouth. "I was born eighteen years ago—same as you. The difference is, I'm immortal. I get to stop aging when I choose." He shoves his hands into his pockets, shifting his weight. "My mother was raised on Earth. She wanted me to have a normal child-hood, like she did. She thought it would make me a better ruler. As long as I spent summers here, I could live the rest of the year above."

"And your dad was here mostly," I say, putting it together. "That's why he was gone so much?"

"It was part of the deal," he says, nodding. "Mom wanted me to understand both worlds. But Dad had duties that couldn't wait."

More pieces slide into place. All those arguments about the family business. Hayes's future. The pressure.

This is why.

"Okay," I say, sagging back against the headboard, pressing fingers to my temples. A migraine brews behind my eyes, sharp and steady. "So you're the Greek god prince of... whatever this place is. That still doesn't explain what *she's* doing here." I jab a finger at my sister. "Or me. We're nobodies."

"Oh, let's just tell her already," Amber trills, prac-tically bouncing on her toes.

"Amber, no. Not yet." Hayes's jaw tightens. "We already discussed—"

"I'm going to be a princess, Ally!" she blurts, talking right over him, her eyes sparkling. "Like an actual fairy-tale princess. Isn't it amazing?"

"I'm sorry—a what now?"

Hayes's shoulders go stiff, and he looks away, like he's suddenly very interested in the walls.

"See, there's this prophecy…" he begins.

As soon as he says the word, a twisted thought slams into me. Maybe I've read one too many chosen-one fantasy novels, but if he tells me I'm his long-lost Olympian sister—if this turns into some sick *Star Wars* twist—I swear I will march myself straight back to that black river of death and jump in willingly.

But then I glance at Amber still draped all over him and feel a flicker of relief. No way she'd be acting like that if they were actually related.

"The prophecy is about me," she cuts in again, beaming. "I'm going to marry Hayes and become Princess of the Underworld. Can you believe it, Ally?"

A laugh escapes me, loud and sharp, and maybe a little manic. Of everything I've seen in the last twenty-four hours—hellmouths, skeletal ferrymen, black rivers, and screaming souls—the idea that Hayes and Amber are somehow destined to be married is hands-down the most absurd.

"What's so funny?" she snaps, one hand flying to her hip.

"Oh, come on." I shake my head. "You may *act*

like a princess, Amber, but that doesn't magically make you one."

I glance at Hayes, waiting for him to join my laughter and tell her to knock it off.

"She's telling the truth," Hayes says, his voice low and flat. "We have seers here. The gods have always relied on them." He goes quiet for a moment. "When I was born, Tiresias—one of the oldest and most respected—gave my parents a prophecy."

His tone shifts. His voice is mechanical now, like something he's memorized long ago:

> *"In the decade of the Prince,*
>> *a girl—part Earth, part Under—will be born*
>> *in the northwestern hemisphere during Samhain.*
>> *She will marry the Prince,*
>> *and by her will, the immortal races will be united,*
>> *and balance restored."*

I stare at him.

"You're telling me that vague-ass riddle is why you think my sister is your fated bride?"

Hayes has the audacity to just shrug.

"She fits the criteria," he says, then starts ticking things off on his fingers. "Same decade. October birthday. Western U.S. And she's a halfbreed—half mortal, half immortal." He meets my eyes. "Want to venture a guess how many girls check all those boxes?"

"But that doesn't make sense. Amber's not a half-anything. She's normal," I say. "Just like me."

Hayes shoots Amber a look, tense and tight. "I told you this was too much for today."

"She'll be fine." Amber waves him off. "She's tough. She can handle it."

"Handle what?" I bite out. "Just say it already."

There's a beat. Then Hayes exhales slowly, carefully.

"Your father wasn't mortal, Al. He was a Titan."

My chest locks up, my lungs straining as if all the air's been vacuumed out of the room.

A Titan?

Not a deadbeat. Not some coward who abandoned us. A literal Titan god. Just like Mom always said.

All those times I thought she'd lost it, spinning stories about gods and magic and bloodlines. I chalked it up to grief. Delusion. But she was telling the truth this whole time. And Hayes—

He let me believe she was crazy.

"How could you?" I whisper. "You let me think my mom was sick. That there was something wrong with her—"

"I'm so sorry," he says, his voice thick with guilt.

"You knew how scared I was. And you said *nothing*?"

His hands fall uselessly to his sides. He doesn't deny it.

"I couldn't tell you until you were here, in the Underworld—safe. There were rules…"

He uses that fucking word again—*rules*—like it

somehow excuses everything he's done. It makes me want to explode.

"That's bullshit! You care more about your precious rules than you care about me!"

His head snaps up, eyes dark with something primal and brutal.

"They would've killed you!" he roars. "Zeus. Poseidon. If they found out you knew, they'd have wiped you off the planet without blinking!"

I freeze, the force of his words hitting like a slap. But Hayes isn't done.

"That's why I didn't tell you," he continues, his voice trembling with emotion. "I'm sorry you're mad. I'm sorry even if you hate me now. But I wasn't going to gamble with your life." He takes a step forward, energy crackling off him. "I know you don't like how things are. I don't like them much either," he says. "But don't you ever fucking say I don't care."

My breath catches as the anger in me dies, doused by his confession like water on flame. As much as I want to hold onto the rage, to keep railing against all the ways I've been wronged, I can't. Because his words—the raw fear in his voice, the look on his face—I can tell he means it.

Every single word.

I still don't know why he told her first, but I believe him when he says it wasn't out of distrust. It's painfully clear he was terrified for me.

Another thought slams into me then, this one softer, more disorienting. I press a hand to my ribs, trying to ease the ache tightening in my chest.

My father.

He didn't abandon us like I'd always thought. He left to protect us, just like Mom said.

"Is he… is he here?" I ask. "My dad?"

"No one knows where Sonar is." Hayes shakes his head. "He was one of the Ten Forsworn—the Titan generals who defied Zeus during the war. After their defeat, they were sentenced to the Tartarus prisons for eternity. Decades ago, Sonar escaped. My father sent Watchers and hellhounds after him, and they tracked him to California, to your mother. But after Amber was born, he vanished again. No one's seen him since."

"Oh, who cares about him anyway?" Amber shrugs. "It's not like he was ever around."

Her words barely register as a new idea takes root. Wild, but not impossible: Northwestern hemisphere. October birthday. Halfbreed. Those aren't just Amber's markers. And if someone's going to rule the Underworld by Hayes's side, shouldn't it be someone who can actually watch a scary movie without covering her eyes the entire time?

Someone like… well, me.

"What if it's not her?" I ask Hayes.

"It's not you," he says too fast. Too firmly. Like it's a thought he's had before and been forced to dismiss and bury deep.

"How do you know?"

"There were other signs. Extraordinary ones," he says. "Amber was born during a Blood Supermoon.

It's a rare celestial event sacred to the Olympians and always marks a shift in power."

I scoff. "So a creepy moon shows up, and suddenly she's the Chosen One?"

"There's more," he continues. "The night she was born, every gate in Tartarus burst wide open. Every cell. Every seal. It took my father, Zeus, and Poseidon weeks to track down and contain the prisoners. But it wasn't just random chaos." His jaw flexes. "The escapees weren't running. They were searching. Heading topside. All of them. Moving with purpose."

"You're saying they broke out because of Amber?" My words are thin, uncertain. "To what? Find her?"

He nods. "If the prophecy is real, then she's the key to uniting the immortal races—Olympians, Underworlders, and the last of the Titans. The prophecy doesn't just promise a new queen. It promises a shift. For some, that's a good thing. But others will lose everything. Power. Position. Influence."

I sink deeper into the bed, suddenly ice cold despite the warmth of the luxurious bed.

I can't believe it.

We're back at *Star Wars*, but somehow, it's even worse than the long-lost Olympian sister twist. Turns out, I'm Hayes's long-lost Olympian sister-in-law.

"How long have you known it was her?"

Hayes won't meet my eyes.

"My father figured it out around my fifth birthday," he says. "That's why we moved to Laguna Hills. To protect her without raising suspicion."

The words gut me.

Every shared memory. Every secret. Every late-night call—was it just proximity to my sister? A job? Had I only ever been his way of keeping tabs on her?

Was any of it real?

"Why bring us here now, then?" I ask, barely holding myself together. "What's changed?"

Hayes's expression darkens.

"There was supposed to be more time," he says. "Time for us to live some life, explore the world first. Time for me to stay hidden until I was ready to take the throne. But someone made their move—they killed my father." His hands curl into fists at his sides, knuckles white with restrained fury. "As you can imagine, killing an immortal god isn't easy. We still don't know who did it or how, but with my father gone, everything's unraveling faster than expected. Power vacuums don't last long down here, and if they kill me or Amber before I'm crowned and married, it all falls apart. Earth isn't safe anymore."

"The important part is we're here now, Ally," Amber says, looking shockingly unbothered by all the talk of murder plots. "Mortals can't enter Hades—so, no Mom, no Brooke, no Tiff. But you? You're a half-breed too. That's why I begged Hayes to bring you here. There's going to be a big royal wedding when I turn eighteen, and you'll be in it, obviously."

"It's her decision, Amber. We talked about this," Hayes says, cutting her a look. He turns to me, something taut and unreadable in his expression. "Now that you know everything, it's your choice. You can stay. Or you can leave."

My heart stutters. "I can go back?"

"If that's what you want," he says. "But you need to understand what that means. You'll be alone there and if my uncles—or the wrong immortals—find out what you know, they won't hesitate. You're a threat now, Al. And they don't leave threats alive."

A chill races through me.

"But I'll be safe here?"

"Safer… maybe. But not safe." He hesitates. "The Palace protects us for now, but it won't hold forever. The throne is empty, and the balance is tipping. Whoever killed my father isn't done. They'll come after us down here, too." His voice drops lower, and something unreadable flickers in his eyes. "There's something else you need to know. If you stay, you'll have to participate in the Secular Games. It can be… dangerous."

"The what now?"

"It's tradition here," he says. "An ancient rite held to mark the crowning of a new ruler of the Underworld. It's a competition meant to cement the Crown's power. Everyone will be watching. Every house sending champions." His gaze locks on mine. "And thanks to your bloodline, you'll compete for the House of Hades."

A dangerous competition between immortals in the literal Underworld? That doesn't exactly scream warm welcome. I'm not entirely sure staying here is any better than going back home.

"You'll be fine, Ally. You can handle a little challenge," Amber says, brushing it all off with a wave. "Please say you'll stay. You can be my maid of honor!"

I stare at her, a sick twist curling in my gut. She says it like it's some kind of gift. Like me fighting in some deadly supernatural trial and possibly risking my life is some pesky minor detail—as long as she has her dutiful handmaiden smiling prettily at her wedding. She's so insanely self-absorbed she doesn't even realize she's asking me to stand beside her while she takes everything I've ever wanted.

Or worse—she does know and just doesn't care.

Amber has always underestimated me, and she's doing it again.

She has Hayes now. She probably thinks she's won. That I'll watch from the shadows like I always have and bleed quietly if the Games demand it. That I'll hold her hand and smile politely while she becomes royalty, marrying the one person I've loved in silence my whole life.

Stay quiet.

Stay small.

But I've spent eighteen years on the outside looking in. I'm done with that.

The Underworld isn't meant for people like Amber. It's meant for people like me. If this place wants a princess, it should have chosen more carefully.

Because I didn't come all this way to be anyone's maid of honor.

Want to know what really happened the day Alysander fell from Hayes's treehouse? Who actually saved her and how? Discover what Hayes was thinking in the moment everything changed—and just how long he's truly been protecting her and her family...

CLICK HERE to read this exclusive bonus story from Hayes's POV!

Don't miss **SALEM'S FALL,**
the bestselling, award-winning
thriller from Rektok Ross!
Available now!

CHAPTER 1
Boston, Massachusetts
October 1 (Four Weeks Until Halloween)

The whooshing of the heater kicks on, startling me as it echoes through the empty halls of Whitehall & Rowe. I'm all alone and still getting accustomed to the solitude. The law firm is usually bustling with the energy of a high-octane circus, but tonight, it feels more like a tomb. Almost everyone else is crammed into a hotel conference room downtown, across from the courthouse, prepping for Monday's big trial. Normally, I'd be right there with them, mainlining Starbucks and helping the partners prepare their openings, but instead, I'm here in my tiny office, working on a total snoozefest research memo. This is my punishment for failure.

I glance up at the glowing computer screen, my frustration simmering as I angrily peck away at the keyboard.

Top of my class at Harvard Law.

Summa cum laude.

Editor of the *Law Review*.

And yet, here I am, writing a ridiculous memo a first-year law student could handle, sidelined from the real work because I missed some stupid forensic report on my last case. There was no real harm done, but one misstep was all it took to go from rising star to the firm's black sheep. Now I'm stuck in junior associate purgatory while one of the biggest white-collar criminal trials of the year is about to start. Charles Brandt, CFO of juggernaut energy company Harborline Energy Corp., is accused of securities fraud. The case made all the papers. Brandt could go away for the rest of his life if he's found guilty—and my firm is defending him.

Of course we are.

Everyone knows we're the best criminal defense firm in Boston.

Woodsen is only here because of her looks.

I shake my head, shoving aside the memory of Mark Sharma's petty insults. Mark is such an asshole. He'd been a complete dick when I'd screwed up a few weeks ago, telling anyone who'd listen that I didn't belong here. Mark is just a bitter senior associate at the firm who's been gunning for my failure ever since I turned him down for drinks a few months ago.

I've dealt with guys like him my whole life. Because of the way I look, people are always quick to judge me. Underestimate me. I've heard it all before: The professors thought I was pretty—that must be why I got good grades. The faculty advisor had a crush on me—that must be why I got the best internships. I slept with hiring partners—that must be how I got my job at the most coveted criminal defense firm in the state.

Of course, none of it was accurate, and it all ignored the real truth: I was smart and worked my ass off. I kept my head down. I didn't party or drink or do drugs. And I was willing to do whatever it took to succeed, except sleep my way to the top.

Still, all they saw was blonde hair and big boobs.

Whatever. Screw 'em.

I pull my focus back to the computer screen, the lines of text blurring as my vision narrows. No, I refuse to be that girl, the one who fades into the background and accepts her fate. I have too much to prove. If they want a research memo, I'm going to write them the best goddamn research memo this firm has ever seen.

Lucky hops onto my work desk, his sleek black fur catching the fluorescent light. It's ironic, having a black cat and living just miles away from Salem's Fall, a town famous around the world for its witch trials. Growing up in New England, I'd always heard black cats were supposed to be bad luck, but Lucky's become family ever since I found him in an alley eight years ago. The only family I really have around anymore besides my little sister Madison and my Aunt Aggie.

My cat stretches out, yawning like he's had the hardest day of all, when he's pretty much done nothing but gotten two delicious meals, oodles of treats, and countless naps.

"Tough life, kiddo," I say, chuckling as I scratch behind his ears. "Don't know how you do it."

Lucky purrs in response, unfazed. Technically, we aren't supposed to have pets in the office, but since this is going to be another brutally late night for me—

and no one else is here anyway—I figure some rules are meant to be broken.

My phone buzzes on the table, and I groan as I see my little sister's name flashing on the screen.

"Hey, sis! Guess where I am?"

Madison's voice is too bright, too bubbly. Loud music pumping in the background tells me all I need to know.

She's drunk.

"Maddie, you better not be calling me from a bar."

"C'mon, James. It's Friday night!"

"And midterms are coming up." I pinch the bridge of my nose. "You should be in the library—studying!"

She giggles into the phone. "Well… I am with David, the hot guy from my study group I told you about. Doesn't that count?"

"No." I rub my temples, one finger poised over the red "End" button. "Mads, I gotta get this memo done. Go home—please!"

"Aww, don't be like that. This is your fault anyway." I can practically hear her pouting into the phone. "We were supposed to go to dinner tonight, remember? And you flaked. Again."

"Hey, someone's gotta pay rent and keep the pantry stocked with your organic gluten-free mac 'n' cheese and overpriced protein bars," I fire back.

"Ha ha, very funny." She huffs. "C'mon, Jamie. You always do this. You're always blowing me off for some stupid work thing—"

"Hanging up now—"

"Fine, whatever. Can you Venmo me drink money at least?" Her voice turns pleading, and I can picture her standing inside some too-crowded bar, swaying in her high heels and some cute new dress she probably charged to my credit card without asking. "We want to get another round."

"You promised you'd stay in and study tonight," I say, trying to sound stern, though a part of me wishes I could trade places with her.

God, I'd love to be out. Dancing. Drinking. Forgetting all about this damn job for a few hours. But unlike Maddie—a college junior with a decent fake ID and no real responsibilities—I don't have that luxury. I never have, not even when I was her age. I'd always been too busy working side jobs and hustling, taking care of her.

"Just one more drink, I promise! He's soooo cute. You'd really like him—"

"Madison—"

"Come on, help a sister out," she says. "Remember, you're the one that taught me not to let guys buy my drinks at the bar. So really, I'm just doing what you told me…"

I sigh. I'm supposed to be the hotshot lawyer, but, even wasted, my little sister can negotiate circles around me. If only she'd apply those skills to her studies.

"*Strangers,*" I correct. "I told you not to let strangers buy your drinks. Let this David idiot buy you all the drinks he wants. He can probably afford it—unlike me." I glance at the clock. It's almost midnight, and I'm too tired to keep arguing. "I'll send enough for one more round. Then straight home, okay?"

"Thanks! Love youuuuuu!"

Madison hangs up, and I quickly pull up the app, sending her money. I lean back in my chair, wondering for a moment what it must be like to be Madison. How would it feel to be free of all responsibility and worry? My constant and draining sense of duty. My fear of failure. Ever since our mother died— and Dad went to prison for her murder—it's been my job to take care of Madison. She doesn't know the half of what it costs me, but if I don't take care of her, who will?

Lucky nudges me impatiently with his cold nose, hungry for a treat. I give him a few catnip crunchies from my bag, and after eating them, he closes his eyes and drifts off to sleep. Off in the distance, the firm's main phone line starts to ring over and over. Even the late-night receptionist has gone home by now.

I settle back at my desk, staring angrily at my memo again. I'm supposed to be summarizing the current state of the law for expungement of criminal records for minors, listing out all the procedures. Some senior partner's spoiled teenage daughter got caught shoplifting, and I need to help clear her record so she can get into an Ivy League school her daddy probably bought her way into. Not exactly the thrilling work I dreamed of during my law school days.

I skim through a few Westlaw articles online, my eyes darting between the text on the screen and my own half-written sentences. The assigning partner is expecting this on his desk tomorrow at 7 a.m., sharp. My fingers hover over the keyboard as I glance at the clock again. My deadline is looming, and I can't afford another screwup, even on something as dumb as this.

I type into the search bar the address to a somewhat controversial legal website my best friend from law school, Katherine "Katie" Tang, told me about. They have old memos and briefs on there. It's not something any self-respecting attorney would ordinarily use—sometimes the research is outdated. And relying on it too heavily? That's plagiarism.

Still, this is stupid busy work, and I could use a few hours of sleep tonight. Plus, someone's gotta get home and make sure my rascal of a sister makes it back at a decent hour.

For a moment, I contemplate sleep and Maddie versus a teeny, tiny little ethics flub. My moral compass quickly loses, and it's not even close. Just this once, right? It's not like anyone's going to know. It's just a minor expungement, erasing a stupid shoplifting case for an entitled brat. This isn't exactly life-or-death.

"Whatever it takes," I murmur, taking a deep breath and copying and pasting.

After that, all that's left is a spell check. I'm almost done with the memo when my desk phone rings, the sound jarring in the otherwise silent building.

"James Woodsen," I say, putting the call on speaker so I can keep typing.

"Where the hell is everyone?"

The booming voice on the other end is Quinn Kensington, one of the firm's most powerful partners.

I straighten in my seat, a jolt of adrenaline coursing through my system. At only thirty-one, Quinn Kensington is the youngest senior partner at the firm. He was just named a "Top 40 Under 40 Attorney" in the entire metro area and is the only son of state Senator George Kensington. He's also movie-star handsome to boot.

Quinn is the partner responsible for hiring me, which is both a blessing and a curse. A blessing because being under Quinn's wing is the perfect place for any ambitious junior associate—unless said ambitious junior associate is also a pretty blonde, and then everyone assumes you were only hired because you must be sleeping with him. And I am very definitely not.

"They're all in prep for the Brandt trial," I answer. "Why? What's going on?"

"We've just been assigned a new high-profile murder case." He speaks fast, his words sharp.

"Okay… and?"

This is nothing new. We're Whitehall & Rowe. We get new high-profile murder cases every week.

"It's the Halloween Heiress Murder, Woodsen!" he snaps.

I suck in a deep breath.

"No way…"

The Halloween Heiress Murder is the murder case of the decade—maybe the century. It's been all over the news for the past year.

Vivienne Van Buren, a high-profile socialite, was found stabbed to death last Halloween. There was talk of dark cults and satanic panic. No one knew what was real and what wasn't. The murder itself was beyond bloody and gruesome, but that alone wasn't what made it so notorious. It was the fact that she was the fiancée of Damien Blackhollow—the gorgeous billionaire mogul whose family owns half of New England.

"Someone's finally been arrested?" I ask, trying to keep my voice steady. This is huge!

"Someone, yeah." Quinn makes a strange sound in the back of his throat. "You could definitely say that…"

<hr>

Want more?

***The Silence of the Lambs* meets *Labyrinth* in this dangerously addictive blend of twisty psychological thriller, legal suspense, and gothic dark romance, where nothing is as it seems. Don't miss this bestselling book in the**

Dark Seasons Thriller Series—perfect for fans of gothic settings, occult conspiracies, dangerous morally grey men, and books like *Verity*, *Haunting Adeline*, and *The Housemaid!*

GET SALEM'S FALL NOW!

CONNECT MORE
WITH REKTOK

I hope you loved *Realm of Shadows,* and if so, I would be very grateful if you could write a review. I'd love to hear what you think, and reviews online make such a big difference in helping new readers discover one of my books for the very first time.

If you'd like to keep up to date with me and be the first to know about any new releases, bookish news, and giveaways, please sign up at the link below. I'll never share your email address, and you can unsubscribe at any time.

Sign up here >>> www.RektokRoss.com

Please know I also adore hearing from readers. You can contact me anytime at my email at Rektok-Ross@gmail.com or through any of my social media channels (@RektokRoss, everywhere). And if you like readalongs and talking all things bookish, you can join my Facebook reader group *The Book Nook by Rektok Ross.*

Thanks so much for all your support, and I hope to hear from you soon!

Rektok Ross

AUTHOR'S NOTE
TO THE READER

Dear Reader,

First and foremost, thank you for reading *Realm of Shadows*. I know your time is precious, and there are a million other books you could be reading, so the fact that you chose mine means more than I can say. If you've been with me since my thriller days—*Ski Weekend, Summer Rental, Spring Harvest,* and *Salem's Fall*—you probably know this book is a bit of a departure. Moving from high-octane thrillers to a slow-burn supernatural romance/romantasy series was... absolutely terrifying, LOL. I wasn't sure if my readers would follow me, or if any new readers would find me. But now that it's finally here, I couldn't be more excited for where this series is headed. So however you found me—whether you came over from my thrillers or you're brand new to my world—welcome!

Realm of Shadows was born from my love of paranormal romance and romantasy books. I've always been a sucker for books like *A Court of Thorns and Roses, The Cruel Prince, The Forbidden Game, Darkfever, City of Bones, Twilight,* and *Vampire Academy* and have wanted to write my own series like this for so long. Greek mythology, especially, has held a special place in my heart since I was a little girl. Of all the myths, Hades's story has always been the one that fascinated me most. I mean... who doesn't love a dark, dangerous, and insanely powerful male main character? Amirite? Not to mention the gothic allure of the Underworld and its monsters, plus the epic love story of Hades and Persephone. But it wasn't until I was traveling across Europe with one of my best friends that the idea for this particular retelling—one centered around the progeny of Hades and Persephone in a modern college setting—hit me like Zeus's lightning bolt.

But *ROS* is more than just a Greek mythology retelling. It's a love letter to the dark, gothic fairy tales that shaped me—stories like *Labyrinth, Legend,* and *Edward Scissorhands*—where beauty lives in the shadows and in the monsters. What truly excited me about writing this book wasn't just the magic or mythology but exploring the quiet ache so many of us carry: the feeling of never quite fitting into the world you were born into, of being underestimated or misunderstood, of feeling like no matter how hard you try, you'll never be enough, never be chosen, and never get the life—or love—your heart longs for. I wanted this story to feel fantastical but also deeply, painfully human.

So light a few black candles, grab your favorite crystals, put on some moody goth music, and step into the Underworld with me. I hope this story gives you butterflies, maybe a few chills, and a romance that will have you kicking your feet under the covers. ;)

All my best,
Rektok Ross

ACKNOWLEDGEMENTS

As always, thank you first to my readers. You are everything, and I truly appreciate every single review, post, share, DM, TikTok/Reel, and email from you. Connecting with you and building my reader community is the greatest joy. Special thanks to my Street Team—you guys are amazing!—and also to all the "Book Nookers" in my Facebook book club and reader group, "The Book Nook by Rektok Ross." (We're always looking for new members! Come join us—I've got links to join on all my socials, and you can always email or DM me, too!)

Huge thanks to my talented editorial team: the fabulous Amy Tipton, Beth Lynne, Crystal Blanton, and Tandy Boese. Also, a big thank you to Kaitlyn Uglialoro, Becca Waldrop, Bryan Cohen, and Quinn Brooks-Ward, who have been pivotal to helping RRP grow.

Continued thanks go out to all my friends in the publishing and entertainment industries for your support of my work. Thank you always to the incredible booksellers, librarians, educators, and media who continue to champion my books. I see you and appreciate you. To all the incredible influencers and friends on social media, especially BookTok and Bookstagram, who have found my books and shared them—thank you! Special thank you to all the dear friends who are so supportive of me and this journey—you know who you are (because I've named most of you already in prior books, lol!).

Lastly, enormous thanks go to my family. To my mom, as always, the one who made me a reader. Dad, L, Lance, and Scarlett, for all the pep talks and love; and all the DeCesare/Howard clan—thank you for always cheering me on. Derek, Dani, and Ro—love you guys so much! To Michael, who makes this all possible; and last, but certainly not least, my furry writing buddies—Ghost and Blair.

ABOUT THE AUTHOR

Author photo © Agency Moanalani Jeffrey

Liani Kotcher (writing as Rektok Ross) is a trial attorney turned award-winning and bestselling author, screenwriter, and producer. An avid reader since childhood, Liani writes exactly the kind of books she loves to escape into herself: exciting thrillers with strong female leads, swoonworthy love interests, and life-changing moments. She graduated from the University of Florida and obtained her juris doctorate at the University of Miami School of Law. Originally from South Florida, she currently splits her time between San Francisco, Los Angeles, and Las Vegas with her husband and her dogs. She is the recipient of several awards, including the American Fiction Awards, IAN Book of the Year Awards, and the Chanticleer Dante Rossetti Book Awards. You can find her online at @RektokRoss and her website, www.RektokRoss.com. Join her Readers Group: www.facebook.com/groups/thebooknookbyrektokross/